TO THE MOON AND BACK

A HIDDEN WORLD

BOOK ONE

KATE HOLMGREN

CONTENTS

1. Locked Away   1
2. C A T Spells Cat   7
3. Cat   11
4. Dreaming   15
5. The World of the Loft   21
6. Get with the Program   25
7. Superheroes   31
8. Escape Plan   35
9. A Wish upon a Star   37
10. Astrophysics and Rocketry   43
11. Deception and Sour Milk   53
12. Back to the Drawing Board   55
13. Eyes in the Back of His Head   61
14. Tick Went the Clock   67
15. Missing   69
16. Applied Math   71
17. Ready or Not   75
18. A Friend on the Dock   81
19. The Grand Escape   83
20. Poe the Crow and His Deception   91
21. Lost   95
22. The Ruse   97
23. In the Deep of the Night   101
24. A Shoe Will Do the Trick   107
25. A Look Back into the Past   109
26. Moon Phases   121
27. Catch a Falling Star   127
28. Mischief, Short and Simple   129
29. Of Moonlight and Silver and Vapors of Light   133
30. Lift Off   135

31. Rooftop — 141
32. The Sound Of Sirens — 151
33. A Golden Maple Leaf — 153
34. A Change of Plans — 159
35. Twink—Or—What's in a Name? — 161
36. An Insanity Defense — 163
37. Trapped — 165
38. Rescue Plans Down Below — 179
39. Flood Gates — 185
40. She Knew — 189
41. Crying Wolf — 191
42. Does Poe Sell His Soul? — 195
43. A Leap of Faith — 207
44. Fight — 213
45. Conquer the Mountain — 215
46. Secrets in a Hidden Drawer — 219
47. Stranger than Strange — 221
48. The Stuff of Heroes — 227
49. A Battle in the Sky — 237
50. Habeas Corpus and Quid Pro Quo — 253
51. Beyond These Walls — 259
Bonus Section — 263
Backstories and Outtakes — 265
Did You Know? — 299
What Do You Think? — 301

Acknowledgments — 305
About the Author — 307

Book Production and Publishing Services by Miramare Ponte Press LLC
Moon Facts and Discussion Questions by Bethany Green
Cover design by 100Covers

It's a Lovely Day Tomorrow
Words and Music by Irving Berlin
© Copyright 1939 BERLIN IRVING MUSIC CORP.
Copyright Renewed
All Rights Administered by UNIVERSAL MUSIC CORP.
All Rights Reserved Used by Permission
Reprinted by Permission of Hal Leonard LLC

Hardback ISBN-13: 979-8-9881205-1-3
Paperback ISBN-13: 979-8-9881205-0-6
eBook ISBN-13: 979-8-9881205-2-0

Library of Congress Control Number: 2023906432

Holmgren, Kate
To the Moon and Back / Kate Holmgren
To the Moon and Back follows Sophie and her cat Justice on a hero's journey to unravel the mystery behind being locked away in an attic space filled with colorful artwork, clocks, and books.
ISBN-(hc) 13: 979-8-9881205-1-3

To those searching for the hero within.

1
LOCKED AWAY

SOPHIE

SOME EVENINGS, Sophie could hear her grandparents talking through the heating grate in the attic space above the living room. She eavesdropped every chance she got. Often Justice, her best and one and only friend, listened with her.

When is my dad coming back to get me? Has something happened? I need to know. Even if it's bad, she thought.

Theo's voice drifted up to them. She leaned down to catch every word. "I know you can't understand, Rosalie, but I'm thinking about caging that cat again. Remember? I did that before you gave him to Sophie. Whatever made you think she should have a pet?"

Sophie's eyes widened as her grandfather continued.

"That animal thinks he has the run of the house! How does he get out of the attic? We need to figure that out."

His voice rose higher. "I nearly tripped over him the other night. Would have woken you up, Rosey. We need to consider penning him up at night."

Sophie gasped. Justice reached out, held a paw over her mouth, and whispered, "Shush."

Her eyes grew wide. "Shush?" she mouthed, then hoisted him up in her arms and tiptoed away from the grate. She tilted his face up to hers. Nose to nose she asked, "Did you just talk? Did I just hear a cat talk?"

Justice clawed free, ignoring Sophie as he tore back to the floor grate. "Your grandfather's planning on putting me in a cage at night. Come on, we gotta hear this. Stay quiet." He crouched low, ears facing forward, his body tense and on high alert. "Great. Just great. We missed the rest of it and now they're walking back to the kitchen." Justice paced back and forth across the grate, ears flat.

"You're supposed to take care of me, right? I'm supposed to be your *pet*. I made a promise to myself I'd never again see the inside of a cage. Your grandfather locked me up before and now he's planning on doing it again—unless you stop him."

Sophie's mouth gaped, speechless, as her cat continued ranting.

"How long has it been since I last saw my wife? The front door's been locked, and all the windows are fastened shut; even with the attic door left unlatched, it's impossible to make my escape. Liza must be in a fright. Sophie, I'm going to need your help or I won't stand a chance."

Her mind exploded with questions about cats talking. *Can every cat talk or just mine? Why'd he wait so long to tell me? Is it a secret that cats can talk?*

Justice hissed. "Get your head in the game, Sophie," he said. "I can understand human, okay? You understand cat. Right now, that's the least of our worries. My family won't know what to do if I don't come back. We've gotta find some way out of this mess."

He strode back and forth. "What if I can't get word to

them? Liza seemed worried last time I was home... had something on her mind... something she said she had to tell me about.

"And Mantis needs me in his life. Needs me to show him so many things... " His voice trailed off as his eyes narrowed to slits.

"It's good I've been teaching my son how to kill. He must become a great predator, always alert, always ready to fight. Never caught and put into a trap like I was that night on the dock."

Again, Sophie found him right up in her face. "Truth be told, Sophie, you've become much too comfortable here and I don't think you're going to be much help."

A BEAM OF LIGHT FROM THE MOON CREATED A BRIGHT PATCH ON THE rug, while passing clouds made the light dance about. The rest of the attic was dark. Where was he? Under her bed? Curled up in her favorite reading chair? In the bathroom under the sink? He liked it there. Maybe it was cooler in that space on these nights when the air lay heavy, like now. She had so much she wanted to ask him.

It was miserable having her best friend angry and silent and who knows where.

Sophie tossed and turned for hours trying her best to fall asleep, but she couldn't. She went to her go-to—her memory game. The rules were simple—try to think of something that had happened, good or bad, and count how many details she could remember. But her mind kept going back to missing her cat.

Toward morning, her thoughts traveled back to the day Justice came into her world and into her arms. Oh! He was so soft. Hard to hold, too, and she clearly remembered the number of scratches he'd left on her arms that first week. She'd forced herself to get tough. She knew what would happen if she complained... *one less cat.*

She finally drifted off just as the morning light peeked through the curtains, her mind relishing the memories of those first days with Justice, her first pet.

Not too long after she was given her first pet, on a rather usual morning, Sophie noticed her spelling book lying out on the floor by her favorite chair, the one that was all cushiony and soft, perfect for cuddling up with a book. Uh oh. I was supposed to put my book back. All my books go back on the shelf every single night. *The schoolbook lay open to the word "JUSTICE." The definition followed: "fairness, righteousness, honesty, and integrity." The same thing happened the next day. The spelling book lay at the foot of her chair open to the exact same page.*

This is strange. I'm sure I put it back in its place on the bookshelf where Rosalie always tells me to. I'm sure I closed it and put it up on the shelf.

On the third morning, it happened again. Sophie stood a long moment lost in thought, then smiled broadly. That's the name I'll pick. I tried calling him Bart. Justice is a better name. A nice name. A nice name for my cat.

She was overjoyed when he answered to it.

It'd been a risk asking for a pet, but Sophie had had a strategy —she knew who to ask. Her grandfather would most likely have never said 'yes.' He always had a frown on his face or looked worried and he didn't say much.

Sophie rarely saw him, unless the faucet had a leak or he came up to recheck the window locks.

Her grandmother came up to the attic every day to bring a food tray, a new book, and sometimes clean sheets or another one of her clocks. She must have some sort of compulsion. That's what her grandfather called it—a compulsion about clocks. *Why in the world would she want another clock?* Sophie wondered each time one more found its way into her attic space.

Her grandmother also seemed obsessed with Sophie's education. Rosalie had equipped the attic with book after book, several computers, posters, maps, an artist's drafting desk, and paints and paper. The space was filled to overflowing with the bulk of it. Knowing her education was her grand-mother's soft spot, Sophie recognized the perfect opportunity to procure what she wanted most: a friend... albeit a furry one.

Sophie had begun with a few well-placed hints. "Rosalie, this chapter says taking care of a pet teaches responsibility, and you learn about animal behavior and science stuff like that. Did you ever have a pet?" *I won't tell her the real reason I want one. I'll never give her the satisfaction of knowing any of that.*

2

C A T SPELLS CAT

DAYLIGHT POURED through the window illuminating the wild sort of beauty of Sophie's attic home. Walls, plastered with Sophie's artwork, exploded with color layered upon color, competing with posters of every sea animal imaginable, pictures of puppies and cats, world maps, national parks maps, and a wild assortment of Rosalie's clocks.

Justice jumped onto her bed. Sophie's eyes flew open. He held up a paw before she could say a word. "I'm sorry, Sophie. I took everything out on you last night... all my worries about my family, all my anger about being held here against my will. Even my rage at your grandparents who keep you hidden away." He noticed the dark circles under her eyes.

"You didn't get much sleep last night, huh? Neither did I—after hearing your grandfather's plans to lock me up. I knew you were looking for me, but I needed some time to calm down and think about what to do next. Besides, it's hot in here. The bathroom's cooler. You could take a pillow, and some blankets to lie on, and sleep in the tub. Just a thought."

"You still mad at me?" Sophie asked. "I disappointed you. And you said you couldn't trust me to help." Her voice wobbled. "Then you ran off. You're always here by my side at night and I got scared. That's why I couldn't go to sleep."

Justice curled up on her lap, his eyes searching hers. "My friend, my life is at stake. Maybe my family's, too. It's finally come time to tell you my story. Please don't interrupt.

"I can't be caged. Sophie, I fly into a fury. My head feels like it'll explode, and I start to have wild ideas of how to fight back, but I'm trapped and can't do a thing.

"That's why, after a lot of thought, I named my son Mantis. *Preying* Mantis after Praying Mantis, you know—the Kung Fu martial arts." He saw her confused look. "Named after an insect. Ever seen one? One of the most aggressive insects on earth."

He got right up into Sophie's face. She crinkled her nose and backed up an inch. "But I spelled my son's name P-R-*E*-Y-I-N-G. My son will be the predator, not the prey, and he'll get some kind of payback for me. Even if I never can."

Justice peered deep into her eyes, begging her to understand. "Sophie, when trapped in that cage on the wharf, I soothed myself with thoughts of drawing blood. Anyone's. I must train my son to be a killer."

Sophie stuttered. "A k—k—killer? What are you talking about? I don't understand any of this."

"How long have I been in this house? I've lost track of the seasons." He glanced toward the window. "My son must be nearly grown by now. It's been far too long." He reached out and pawed her sleeve. "How many months, Sophie?"

"I—I—I don't know. Let me think... " she began to count back the months on her fingers.

He turned again to the window, hearing the faint sound of ocean waves in the distance. "Dear Liza... Mantis, my son. Wait for me. Please wait."

3
CAT

PREYING MANTIS

Preying Mantis rose from his sleeping place, arching his back in a satisfying stretch. The huge cat never felt rested. Even his dreams demanded much of him, and his thoughts, especially memories of his father, hounded him without mercy. The constant struggle to meet his father's expectations to restore the family's reputation, to exact the perfect revenge.

A beautiful moon bathed the farmstead in its light. He began his nightly reconnaissance, padding around the perimeter of the barn, moving with the fluid movements of his distant jungle relatives, crouching low and silent in the deep shadows. His stomach growled, the anticipation of his next meal making him salivate. *Maybe I can hunt up my favorite—a plump little mouse or two.*

Delicate branches swayed in the wind, creating moonlit shapes of diamonds and lace alongside ghostly forms of the night—a play of light and dark presenting the illusion of a fantasy world, all the while disguising the presence and purpose of this giant predator as he soundlessly crept among the shadows.

AND MOUSE — MURFEE

The smallest of ten kids in the Mouse family, Murfee felt invisible. Expendable, even. *Would they notice if I go missing?* she wondered. But after tonight her life would matter and everything would change. Never again would she be seen as a nobody. The littlest. Only an inch.

The tiny mouse waited in the dark barn loft, her heart pounding. She listened to the nighttime music created by her sleeping family. The combined sounds of deep, relaxed breathing, rhythmic snoring, and murmurings usually comforted her. Not tonight.

Are they all asleep? Maybe I need to get a count. She looked around the room and quickly dismissed the idea that one or more were still awake.

Time to make my way to my secret place, my special window, and my magic cape. No one must know of my plans. Someone's sure to stop me.

Number one priority, she needed to stay clear of the vicious farm cat. *I've got that handled. As soon as I have the magic, that cat won't stand a chance. Ha!*

Her scarlet cape held the magic, she just knew it. Dependable magic. And her plastic sword must be magic, too. The fact that their astounding powers showed up in her dreams almost every night was her proof. Murfee was in desperate need of these powers. Without them, she amounted to next to nothing.

Right now, her main worry was walking into a wall or tripping over something. *Come on, Murfee. You're not a klutz. You are NOT a klutz.*

4
DREAMING

JUSTICE

Sophie created a glorious mess. Large sheets of paper carpeted the floor with wild splashes of orange and shades of luscious purple, bold yellow, and vibrant green. Justice slow-walked a wide circle around his master's desk.

He climbed into his padded cat bed, circling to find the perfect resting spot. *My! Pure comfort. And at least for now, I can get some quiet. That kid could talk the leg off a chair. Sophie's quiet when she paints.*

His mind raced. Escape plans were going nowhere. He didn't know where to start. His thoughts jumped to his son, Mantis. *Is he doing okay? I can't wait to see how he's grown. How he's changed. Maybe he's a good mouser by now. I hope he's keeping his mother and himself nicely fed.*

Liza. He allowed a slow smile as memories carried him away. Unfolding something like a dream, he was no longer trapped in this small attic, but instead walking out on the pier in the moonlight, waves lapping, tantalizing smells of fish heavy in the air, a feline goddess by his side.

Bop! Sophie's chalkboard eraser slammed into the side of his face, chalk particles rising up to dance in the light. The large cat's body jerked, and he let out a throaty growl.

"Blimey, Sophie! Why in the world did you do that?" Justice demanded. He watched her hand fly up to her mouth as red blotches popped out on her face. Impatiently, without a smidgen of sympathy, he waited for her to explain.

"I—I wanted to know what you were smiling about. You went to some other place in your mind. I could see it. You left me." Tears pooled in the corner of her eyes, and Justice was angered further.

"Well, you don't need to cry about it. I'm the one that got bonked in the head. What were you thinking? Good grief, Sophie, I'm forced to be locked away with you and now you want my thoughts, too. It's not enough that I'm here by your side, your only friend in the world, and now you want my thoughts!" He stepped from his cat bed and strode over to her workspace as she began crying in earnest. "Brother," he muttered.

He watched as Sophie crumpled up her watercolor and dropped it in the wastebasket. "I didn't know I was going to throw my eraser. I don't even remember picking it up. Temporary insanity—that's what it was—I wasn't even thinking."

Justice was startled. He'd never witnessed Sophie throwing away even a scrap of her artwork—the attic walls were papered with every artistic attempt—and this was telling. Justice forced himself to control his anger, modulating his tone, "Okay, I'll make a deal with you—"

Sophie interrupted him with a hiccup, her voice shuddering, "I know you're my only, only friend and that I'm lost without you. I'm sorry. I'm being selfish." With a balled-up hand, she wiped her cheek. "Of course, you don't ever have to tell me what you're thinking. I don't let Rosalie know any of my thoughts."

"First thing, take a breath. This isn't the end of the world and friends fight sometimes. They do." He lowered himself onto his haunches for a talk.

"If you calm down, I'll tell you a bit of what I was smiling about." He was relieved to see her brushing off tears, then leaning closer to hear what he had to say. "It's a long story to put into words, but I'll try.

"Liza. The first time I met her… " His eyes closed at the thought, "Oh! She's beautiful, Sophie. Her coat is the palest, shimmery gray. Wait until you meet her. You'll see—and… " He drifted into the memory. "That night she seemed to be watching ships in the harbor. There was a peace about her. It's hard to explain. She really drew me in. Something like floating back to shore from a distant wave.

"I walked up to her, trying to act cool and calm. She giggled and told me her name. Liza. All I could do was stutter. You should have seen me, Sophie, I was all nerves."

"And then? This is way better than any book I've ever read."

Justice chuckled. "She was the one to start the conversation. Can you believe it? 'You must be a Wegie, or at least someone in your family was. My gosh! You're huge.' That's just what she said.

"I tried to answer. Not a single sound came out, but she continued talking to say that her grandfather on her mother's side was a Wegie. I didn't have the first clue—a Wegie? But she didn't seem to notice." Justice turned to the window a moment before turning back. "Sophie. I was struggling to say something—anything— but really, I couldn't. Lucky for me she kept right on going."

He could hear her words even now.

"She said that I looked like a Norwegian Forest cat… a water-loving cat. A Wegie. But that she took after her tiny grandmother, Georgette, a Cornish Rex." Once he began to reminisce, he couldn't stop. "She said she'd never liked to swim but asked me if I did, and that made me even more tongue-tied. I half nodded as she went on. She said she talked a lot when she got nervous. She giggled and I was lost. Simply lost." Justice grinned.

"And then what?" Sophie asked. "This is like the part in stories where the romance starts. I bet nothing like that will ever happen to me."

"Well, it won't if you never leave this place, that's for sure. And where did you hear the term 'temporary insanity?' One of your books?" He noted her agreement. "Somebody needs to tell you that life, *real* adventure, is found out there." He lightly jumped up onto the window ledge. He peered out at the ocean, barely discernible in the distance. "Now let's get our heads back in the game."

PREYING MANTIS

The warmth of the midmorning sun brought a stillness to the farm. An air of laziness and complacency. The milk cow rested in the shade of a giant cottonwood tree. A dozen laying hens quietly pecked about, searching out seeds and unlucky bugs. Collapsed behind the tree rested one extra-large cat, Preying Mantis, exhausted from a nighttime battle fought and won, his sated stomach a testament to the spoils of war.

Surely there's another way to live. I can't go on like this forever. He let his mind go blank, and at last, he slept.

Wisps of strange thoughts, feelings, and even the scents of ocean-side breezes filled his mind and his senses. Endless rolling waves of silver called his name, seemingly intent on drawing him down into its depths. He fought to bring himself awake. *It's kill or be killed. And I can't be found sleeping.*

5
THE WORLD OF THE LOFT

MURFEE

MURFEE MOUSE TIPTOED through the darkness of her home high in the ancient barn loft. Fingers of moonlight came in through the old, tattered roof, and small patches of light danced and shifted about as if they were coming along on her adventure. *Forget all the dreaming, Murfee. Now's when the real adventure starts.*

Murfee's dreams for weeks had been nothing short of magical. She had soared high above treetops, her super-powered cape billowing behind her. Some travels whisked her up into the stars, those flights were amazing but exhausting too. *Enough already!*

Random shadows played across the barn walls. Murfee wiped a cobweb from her face and winced. *Last night was a complete flop—nothing went the way I planned. Running into a wall didn't help. And my nose still hurts.* She sighed. *The light of the moon should help now that most of the clouds have drifted away. Walking around in the dark was tough.*

The tiny mouse groaned as she heard her parents' footsteps approaching. She scurried into the first hole she could find. *Unbelievable!* Her parents walked in and stopped a short distance away. *How'd I miss them in my count? Rats!*

Her breath came out in soft, soundless puffs. This knothole was making her claustrophobic.

Uh oh! Moe's out of bed. Probably looking for something more to eat. He better not mess up my plans. He'll live to regret it.

Murfee saw Moe squeeze into the deepest shadows, his purple tam askew on his head. Her youngest brother, colorful as his plaid cap, was trouble.

Murfee, secure in her hiding place, waited and watched.

Spellbound, she looked out at the magnificent beauty of light spilling through the cracks in the ancient barn. The dilapidated roof was an awning of stars made of moonlight and starlight breaking through the smallest fissures. Dust motes danced and the ordinary was swept away by the collective effect of each and every sparkle.

Mother and Father Mouse, locked in deep conversation, seemed unaffected by the splendor surrounding them.

Father took his wife's face in his hands and gently tipped her face towards his. "I haven't seen you smile this entire day." She met his gaze but didn't answer. "Tell me what's wrong."

"Are they all in bed? All safe? You checked on them, right?" Mother's question skirted around his own.

"All ten, Fay. Everything was quiet last time I checked. I hate to admit it, but I couldn't wait to put them down for the night. But you haven't told me why you look so worried. Tell me now."

Mother's sigh sent the sparkling dust motes flying, which made Murfee grin. She strained to hear.

"Cats can't fly. That's part of why we've stayed here, right? Cats can't fly." Mother paced a few steps away before turning back to Father. "Our food supply is dwindling. Every day the pile of grain grows smaller, and still we stay."

Father said nothing.

"Cats. It's been all about cats and our fear of them." She spat out the words. "Even now, we can't seem to decide what we need to do. All because of cats! We're safe here in this place —here high up in the loft. That's what you've always said. We'll be safe here."

She turned away again. "Nothing without wings can touch us here, that's what you told me. You said we'd be safe here, forever. But cats aren't the only danger, Quin." Her beautiful brown eyes, usually so soft, were hard as she pivoted to face him. "I'd be better off with a promise from the Man in the Moon—in a world made of cheese."

Cheese, how long since we've had cheese? Murfee wondered. She thought she saw Moe wipe a blob of drool from the corner of his ever-starving mouth. She watched him pat his middle and duck deeper into the shadows and disappear. He'd made a safe getaway—but where was he off to?

Faylena continued her rant. "Why did we have all these babies if we can't feed them? You said you'd keep us always safe. You promised." Her final two words landed flat and accusatory and left an uncomfortable silence in the loft.

Murfee had never heard her parents arguing before and she watched them with growing unease. Her stomach dropped and she waited to see what happened next.

Her father squared his shoulders and stood up straighter. Murfee relaxed. Father always knew what to do.

"I'll find a way. I'll find another food supply. I'll need to leave the loft to do it." He peered through the cracks at the bright moon. "Not until the moon is just a sliver of light in the sky. You'll have enough food for you and the kids until I get back."

He reached out and traced her face with a fingertip, a gesture full of love. "Faylena, look up. Look up," he said, his eyes shining. "Don't ever forget, we're under the very Canopy of the Presence. See the light finding its way into this old loft? See all the wonder, all the protection it promises? The Architect high above is keeping us safe, every one of us. You don't need to worry—there's nothing to fear."

Mother and Father Mouse stood gazing up at the star-studded roof. Murfee raised her eyes, too. "Can't you see it, Fay?" Father whispered.

She took a moment to answer. Her voice was flat. "I see holes in an old roof, Quin. Holes in a roof that leaks."

6

GET WITH THE PROGRAM

JUSTICE

"Sophie, we need a plan. If we're ever going to get out of here, there's stuff we need to figure out." Justice was growing impatient. *It's way past bedtime. How many books can that kid read? She needs to get some sleep, then get her head back in the game.*

Sophie sat under a halo of light with her nose buried deep in a book. She looked up. "What? Cat, what? You told me last night all the windows are locked; the doors are locked. I've listened at the grate every single time I hear them talking down below. But I haven't learned anything that could help. What more can I do?"

"Who's Bart?" he asked.

"Bart? I don't know anyone named Bart."

Justice strode over to the chair where she sat. He took a graceful leap, landing easily on her lap, but knocking the book out of her hands, sending it flying across the room.

"Gee, thanks. Now I've lost my place—just when it was getting good," Sophie said.

Justice started to purr as she stroked his fur. "Hey! Don't try to distract me. You know I'm right. We need a plan and a good one. When I first arrived, you kept calling me Bart. That's an unusual name. It must have some meaning."

Sophie thought for a moment. "I don't know. It just came to me. When I looked at you, that's the name that came out."

Justice resisted purring louder as Sophie returned to stroking him, deep in thought.

"Would you want to go with your father if we found him?" He peered up at her intently. "Would it help us to find him if we could find Bart? Do you know if he had a last name? That might come in handy..." He rubbed his head against her sleeve, at last satisfying an annoying itch.

"I have other questions, too. If I'm able to make my escape, and I find a safe place, how can I communicate with you to join me? How will I be able to tell you how to make a run for it or where we can go to get help?" He stopped the stream of questions, a bit out of breath.

"Give me a minute. I was in the middle of a 'who done it'— the lifeguard or the cook—and now you're asking me to think about our plan for escape. Can't you ever give it a rest?" she asked.

Justice rearranged himself on her lap. "Tell me what you can remember. Maybe you'll think of something that will help."

"I don't have a clue," Sophie said. "Why the sudden interest in getting out of here? Or do you like to solve mysteries, too?" She reached out to tickle him under his chin, but Justice twisted away.

He made a harrumphing sound as he flew off her lap. With defiance in his eyes, he turned back to glare at her.

"Sophie, this isn't funny. It's not often I'm scared but time's running out and I think we're getting jammed up. Your grandfather's conversation with Rosalie about caging me at night was a big wake-up call." Justice noticed her shocked expression and his look softened.

"My friend, I'm afraid I've become complacent which could come with a great cost." He saw puzzlement on her face but kept right on going.

"It used to be so easy when the house wasn't locked up like Fort Knox. I could slink through the entire house in the dead of night. Make my way to the maid's quarters of the old wing where unfinished repairs and construction left a window pane missing. I'd slip out, then slip back in just before dawn, with nobody the wiser. I saw my family often. You never knew I hadn't been curled up at the foot of your bed all night. Tell me, you didn't, did you?" He peered up at her, looking for a response. Sophie appeared unreadable.

"Liza and Mantis need me. You need me. I thought I'd found a balance going back and forth but I should have worked harder at getting out of this house while I had a chance. Getting us both out. Now we're trapped in this attic and there'll be no help if we don't help ourselves."

"Complacent, what do you mean?"

"Sheesh, Sophie, that was one of your spelling words last week along with the definition. It's not up to me to remember. You gotta keep up. You can start by learning to quiet your own thoughts for a minute and then listen." He sighed.

"Complacent just means I got comfortable. I dropped the ball... for both of us, I guess, and my family, too.

"At least now you know your pet cat can talk. Up until recently, it's been a one-way conversation and lordy, girl, you talk nonstop. Now there can be some real teamwork. You and me." Sophie scooted forward in her chair to catch every word.

Justice gave her a look of approval. "Your dad's name is Lane, near as I can tell. Rosalie often mutters the name as she walks up the stairs. It's kinda weird, she talks to him like he can hear her. Maybe she's going a little nuts.

"I'm looking for any clue, any thread of memory that can lead us further. I have an obligation to get you to a safe place. I won't have peace until I do. I need to get you back to your true family... people who have your best interests, people who surround you with love—out in the real world—not held captive in an attic like this. Who does that? Seriously?

"As for asking about Bart... if we can't find out something about your dad, maybe connecting with one of his friends could lead us somewhere. When we get out of here, there'll be a lot of ways to search. Libraries for a start."

"Rosalie picks up books for me at a library, right? Lots of mystery books." Sophie started to laugh. "Next thing I know you're going to tell me you know how to read." Justice grew quiet. At last, he nodded.

Sophie flew to her feet. "Wow! What else haven't you told me? Why did you wait so long to spill the beans? Why didn't you at least tell me you could talk?"

Justice strode back and forth. "Well... for starters, I'd have had to keep up with your constant jibber jabber and carry on a slice of the conversation, if you ever stopped to catch a breath. Instead, I've sauntered off, leaving you talking to yourself. Face it, Sophie, nobody can talk like you."

She plunked herself back in her chair and looked down at the bunny slippers on her feet. Justice walked up to her and tugged on the hem of her pajamas before leaping up onto the arm of her chair.

"Old man Francis taught me how to read, though he has no idea that he did. And always with the stupid pointer of his." Justice made a face.

Sophie fidgeted and Justice slid off. "Give me a little warning, wouldja?" He jumped back up and resettled himself.

"Francis, one of my friends out on the wharf, captained an old fishing boat, and early most mornings he'd launch out into the deep blue waters with tourists and fishing poles and all manner of gear. Sometimes he'd take me along.

"Before he let even one of those greenhorns, as he called them, step aboard, he'd take his faithful pointer, the length of a broken fishing pole, and point. Twenty rules. Word by word, slow and deliberate, read from a handmade sign, all his rules they'd better follow.

"Ad nauseam. No, you haven't had that term in spelling. It just means most annoying. There were mornings he lost most of his customers that way. They walked off, forgoing their ocean adventures, but Francis never seemed to mind.

"The remarkable thing was that I started putting letters and sounds together. It was the beginning of my learning to read." Justice sighed deeply. "I wonder if the old fellow is at it still, his craft riding out upon the waves, his face nothing but a smile. I'd like to think he is. A captain of his own destiny. A captain riding the high seas." A pensive expression played across his features but a moment before returning his focus to the looming problem at hand.

"Think. You've got a good head on your shoulders, whether you know it or not." Again, he hopped down to the floor and began to pace. An uneasy quiet settled in.

Finally, he watched on as eight-year-old Sophie turned to the window, her expression sober. Quietly, she began to speak in a listless monotone to the reflection staring back at her, of a girl with wild copper-colored hair, eyes—one a soft pale green, the other a light ocean blue with flecks of gold.

"I don't know much about my dad. I know, I know, he's my dad, but I don't remember much. We moved around a lot. I remember being hungry. And really scared a couple times. I've tried to remember and it's kinda weird, but I just don't."

Justice wanted to comfort her, go to her side and snuggle close, his deep-throated purr quieting her heart, but the greater need was to stay tough—for the moment at least.

He noticed her shifting her attention to the apple slices on a plate and buttered popcorn piled high in a bowl on the side table. Sophie spoke. "Maybe there's no place to go. No place to go if we do make our escape. Maybe there's nothing more than this. Then what we've got."

Justice's voice rose. "You don't have to come. Maybe you're settled here, but I'm not." He climbed up onto the windowsill and stared out at an orange moon floating in the nighttime sky.

7
SUPERHEROES

MURFEE

MURFEE MOUSE AVOIDED DISCOVERY, creeping along like a shifting shadow on her way to her secret hiding place. All without a hitch. Inside she was shouting and singing and jumping up and down with joy, but she made not a peep. *I haven't stumbled or run into anything either. And my nose is healing up.*

She lifted aside straw, handful by handful, to uncover magical treasures—a scrap of red velvet and a small toy sword. Both items, discarded and long hidden, were discovered wedged between the barn wall and the crumbling camel-back trunk. "Finders, keepers—and now they're mine!"

She gathered up the piece of scarlet fabric and wrapped it around her shoulders, tying it into a loose knot at her neck. The makeshift cape hung on her small frame and puddled at her feet. What if *she* could be a hero? What if everything she'd seen in her dreams was coming true and both her cape and her sword were full of magical powers? *Maybe I can be a hero.*

Five days before, in the early dawn, Murfee had been wandering alone through long-forgotten rooms in the loft when she stubbed her toe on the corner of a broken-down cardboard box partially buried in the hay. "Toes! Toes are the worst!" she muttered under her breath. "Ouch, ouch, ouch!" She sat down, examining her injury. "Don't think it's broken. Guess I'll live after all. But it still hurts."

Soon, though, she was drawn back to her discovery of the box and to a colorful picture of an apple orchard resting inside. Maybe the grove she could see from her special window? The illustration reminded Murfee of her own Crayola drawings, but this artwork was exceptional, and she found herself holding her breath. Here the orchard glowed as if it were the most magical place.

She stepped closer to get a better look in the watered-down early morning light. The name "Sarah" was written at the bottom right-hand corner. Just the one word. Sarah. Murfee scratched her head.

Sliding the picture aside she came across piles and piles of comic books. Here, on those pages, she met Superman. And Batman. And Robin. Mesmerized, she turned page after page.

All three of these heroes wore capes. Superman flew the highest, while both Batman and Robin seemed tethered to the earth, even in the midst of their own wild adventures. Superman wore the most magnificent ruby-colored cape, much like Murfee's beautiful scrap of velvet.

Now she beheld her own marvelous cape. What if it held magical powers meant for her and her alone? She, Murfee, had been the one to discover the velvet cloak and the pink plastic sword lying nearby. "Destiny—right?"

As if it had a life of its own, a slim comic slipped from the box, coming to rest at her feet. It was covered with artwork featuring birds and reminded Murfee of an important book in the Mouse family's small library, a book treasured for the many magnificent, realistic drawings of birds, and filled with knowledge and intrigue of a world outside the barn.

Murfee knew only one bird in her real life, an old crow, her friend Poe. He was always so nice to her whenever she'd discover his presence in the shadows. She'd call out to him, and he'd fly to her and make small talk for a while.

She chewed her lower lip as her mind drew her back to the Mouse classroom several days before. Father had asked each of them to spell out a word. "Audubon." That day he was teaching the science of flight and aerodynamics along with a spelling lesson—believing learning happened by creating connections in the brain. Father supposed things were connected every bit as much in the real world, too.

Murfee just wanted the school day to be over. Someday she'd be through with school.

The book, *Audubon's Birds of America 1950*, was handled with great care, as its pages were brittle. "Audubon." Father had them count the vowels and she had gotten it wrong. Math! Well, maybe it wasn't really math that was the problem that time—she'd been daydreaming and missed counting the "A" at the beginning of the word. A bad end to an otherwise pretty good day in class.

Murfee studied the comic she held in her hands. "*The Hawk and the Sparrow* by Terrance," was written in a banner at the top. Below it, the words "Winged Warriors" were drawn in large letters. Its pages exploded with bold, beautiful colors —colors resembling those in the stunning picture of the apple orchard that continued to hold Murfee enthralled.

It was as action-packed as the other comic books she'd been leafing through, but this time the heroes were birds! Captain Hawk, his sidekick Sami Sparrow and The Masked Deceiver, a barn owl using his actual mask-like face to conceal his own thoughts and feelings, making him invaluable for counterintelligence operations and intel gathering. At times, the trio worked in tandem, but each had their separate battles and victories, too. And each hero wore a cape!

Captain Hawk and The Deceiver both flaunted royal robes of purple lined with brilliant blue, but the tiny sparrow, Sami, sported a scarlet cape much like Murfee's. The one-inch mouse was mesmerized. "A superhero almost as tiny as me."

There were a number of these hand-drawn comics buried in the box. Murfee excitedly dug through the pile and brought each out into the light. *Did someone hand draw these images frame by frame?* She thought so. The renderings of each bird were magnificent, exacted by someone both observant and talented, and who clearly loved birds.

That smallest warrior, Sami Sparrow, was absolutely extraordinary. There were many rescue scenes in which Sami flew high above mountaintops, treetops, and towns. Once, she traveled so far above the earth, somewhere way up in the heavens, that the pictures themselves made Murfee dizzy.

Sami could spin and dive, all the while avoiding danger, to come away from each adventure unscathed. Sami Sparrow —the one to save the day.

Murfee had found her hero to emulate. Murfee would wear her own red cape and fly into her very own adventures. She vowed that she would. *And, hey, it's kind of neat... I have something not one of these amazing bird warriors has: a pink plastic sword. How can I lose?*

8

ESCAPE PLAN

JUSTICE

"Sophie, wake up. I'm leaving. I think I've found it—a way to escape and a way to return. Down through an old laundry chute which blasts me down into the basement under the old wing. Then on my return, I climb up a trellis with vines that've grown up onto the roof, then slide down the other side where I come in through a missing windowpane on the top level of the house—the window right next to the landing. That is, if I can still fit. Then all I'll need to do is unlatch the attic door. And that I can manage."

"You aren't disappointed in me, are you? I haven't been any help," Sophie said. "I don't know where I belong, maybe never will. At least you have a real family... I hope you find them, and everything's all right.

"Justice, do you think I could meet them someday? You could tell them I speak cat. Maybe they'd like me, then."

"They'll think you're great. Don't let yourself think otherwise." He turned to leave. "I'll tell them you're the best. Just the best."

"Justice! You're leaving tonight? This night?" she wailed.

"You don't need to get so dramatic. I'm coming back after I see how Liza and Mantis are doing. As soon as I take care of them, I'll be back and we can figure out our next moves. You'll do just fine without me." He looked over at her. "Stop your blubbering right now. Crying won't help, it'll just make your nose get stuffed up." He allowed her to give him a hug and a kiss on his cheek, but that was enough. "I'm not going across the sea. I'll be back before you even know it.

"You've got lots of books to read and plenty of art paper to paint with all the colors. The perfect opportunity to make a giant mess. Heck, maybe one of your detective books could give us some ideas for your escape and what we need to do to prepare. Work on that."

<hr>

SOPHIE

Sophie lost herself in thought. None of the stories she'd recently finished said anything about small girls trapped in attic spaces or how to make an escape with a cat.

When she came up for air, so to speak, Justice was gone as if he had never been a part of her world. It was then she cried, and cried hard. And just like he warned her, her nose got all stuffed up.

9

A WISH UPON A STAR

MURFEE

EVER SINCE THAT early morning discovery of the cardboard box and all its treasures, Murfee's nighttime dreams had been astonishing. Each time, she, Murfee Mouse, was the superhero of all superheroes—wearing her scarlet cape and brandishing her sword with unmatched panache. Full color—just like in the "Winged Warrior" comic books. Her dreams were action-packed, each time they had her heart racing, and *she* was the one to save the day.

For now, Murfee kept the comic books a secret. Maybe there would come a time to reveal all of it, but until then, she wasn't planning on sharing.

What if I could fly high up into the stratosphere? Go anywhere unafraid and fearless like Sami Sparrow, and have my own unbelievable adventures? Hey! Maybe then I'd be somebody. Be special, extraordinary, not just the littlest. And maybe meet up with the Winged Warriors superheroes someday. She held her hand over her heart and a contented sigh escaped.

Though none saw her as strong and heroic, she was brave on the inside. She would race to the rescue of her family if they were ever in trouble. Pluck them out of the jaws of death. Not that she wanted anything bad to happen, but she'd be ready.

It's past time to stop the daydreaming and to seek out the real adventure, Murfee thought as she peered through the triangular opening made by a weathered board swiveled out of place. Luckily, her secret window was on the southeast wall of the barn loft and downwind of prevailing winds; she lacked the strength to pivot the board back into place when that was needed.

On the opposite side of the barn, their classroom window operated much the same. It took several of her brothers to adjust the wooden board when the strong winds blew through.

Murfee's soft blue-gray eyes reflected the wonder of the night. "Fly me to the moon…" she sang beneath her breath.

One lone cloud drifted across the face of a glorious moon, casting strange shadows on the land. But it soon floated away, dissolving into tissue-paper wisps, and was gone. Pinpoints of light pierced the sky. A blazing star trailed across the heavens.

"I'd like to slide down a star. Or be way up there—looking way down here. That was a wishing star. Magic *and* a star! Now I can make a giant wish—and wish for anything I want. I could travel clear up to the moon and make a name for myself. Be more than 'Hey, Inch.'"

Murfee positioned herself at the tippy-toe edge of the makeshift window. She could see far past the tops of the apple trees.

Time to test the powers of the cape. Gathering its edges, she spread her arms wide, like a small colorful bat about to take flight. She glanced at the dirt below. In an instant, she got the shakes. Her stomach flip-flopped. A sick feeling traveled from her belly all the way up into her throat, and her arms went cold and clammy, even under the heavy velvet.

Closing her eyes to blot out the ground made her head spin, and she wobbled back and forth, struggling to steady herself on the ledge. She managed to grip the side of the makeshift window until she could stop trembling.

Murfee squinted one eye open, and then the other, taking great care not to look down—when something moved at the edge of her vision. Taking a careful peek off to the right she spied a small vole poised to leave the safety of the corn. *There's a brave little fellow*, she thought. *Out to have an adventure same as me.* Her confidence returned; her stomach stopped rolling.

Triumphantly she twirled her cape and attempted a small bow, but the queasy feeling rushed back, and she teetered precariously once again. The weight of the velvet fabric made her movements awkward and slow. Murfee struggled to find her balance. Her eyes became round saucers knowing she was about to tip over the edge.

A strange and wild gust of wind blew out of nowhere, filled the bulky fabric of her handmade superhero cape, billowed inward, and threw her entirely off balance. She fought to stay on her feet, but another powerful gust lifted her and sent her flying back into the loft.

Thump! She landed sprawled, spread-eagle on the floor, and moaned. Struggling to her feet, heart thudding in her chest, she fingered the sore spot on the back of her head and winced. *Still, the magic of the cape saved me. Tonight was proof of it! That fall would have been a long way down.*

Her brain spun. *Okay. How am I ever going to make this work? Maybe I can make the jump if I keep my eyes shut. Trust the powers of the cape. It might be tricky 'cause I'd have to look down first to land in the right place, and* that *might make me sick.*

I'd like to soar over that cornfield for starters. Maybe land in the middle of it. Or I could fly over to the giant maple tree. I'll fly off to somewhere when the wind is gone, she decided. *But first I need to get over this fear of heights.*

Flashes of lightning lit up the sky on the far horizon. A high cloud bank passed over the moon, then rumbled away, leaving the orb again free to flaunt its luminous beauty. A light wind rustled the leaves of the corn and lifted the hem of her beautiful cape. Oh! How she loved the feel of it. Soft and cozy. *And it's mine and mine alone.*

Murfee tugged and pulled her cape in around her. She crawled into a small knothole that held her snug and safe, then dangled her legs and gazed up at the stars, taking the utmost care *not* to look down.

She now knew for certain that her beautiful cape had magical powers. Tonight, she'd seen proof. It had saved her from falling. She just needed to get over her fear of heights.

Hmm... It was the perfect time to take stock of everything and figure stuff out. Did she really need her pink sword? It might be hard to carry her weapon while flying through the air.

But if her cape was powerful, maybe she could ask for even more magic, all a hero would ever need. She could leave the sword behind. Specific powers. Hmm... which ones? Murfee scratched her head. A power of invisibility—that would be great. Disappearing would be wonderful. Murfee could escape the near-constant teasing and harassment of her brothers and sisters. If she were feeling sad or just wanted to be off by herself, she could get away, too.

She could be an international spy with the power of invisibility. Hidden secrets would be secret no more. Becoming invisible would sure come in handy if she needed to elude danger—of any kind. And it'd be a lot of fun. Murfee's smile lit her entire face. She pictured scaring Moe out of his wits. *Just once.*

What about powers of the mind? Murfee's eyes stared off into space as she chewed her bottom lip. She'd like to be a lot brighter up on top. School was hard sometimes. Mathematical equations were the worst. Spelling was terrible, too. Smarts would make everything easier, and maybe she'd be the first to be asked on a team, instead of the last.

She let out a happy sigh. *Hey! Maybe Father would move me up to the front.* She'd be featured as the star pupil. She'd ace every test and never worry about looking like a fool. Not one more nightmare about that.

She cupped her face in her hands. Getting over a fear of heights—that had to be her first magical wish if she was gonna be practical. *That could be a superpower.*

Murfee continued to stare off into the distance. *I'll write a goodbye note so nobody worries when they find me missing. That's easy. Okay... what else?*

Her eyes grew wide, and her hand flew up to her mouth. *Rats! Cats! I forgot about my awful fear of cats. I'm afraid this might take more than a wish. How does any mouse get over that?*

10

ASTROPHYSICS AND ROCKETRY

MILO

MILO WATCHED as Moe Mouse slid sideways into the room, his brother's plaid tam now balanced perfectly atop his head. Moe thrust his arms wide. "Guys! Do I have news! Real news, not anything I dreamed up. I heard Mother say the moon is made of cheese. Now I get the importance of our lunar mission. We're going to the moon, and we'll bring back cheese! How come I'm the last to know these things? You never told me the real story. We're bringing back cheese, right? We'd better up the storage compartment on our rocket ship to the max." Moe's excitement had him nearly vibrating off the floor.

Milo soundlessly mouthed the word cheese and rolled his eyes. He sneered. "*We?* You haven't done one thing to actually help with this project. All you do is yammer and get in the way and make a mess. You're going to regret getting involved now." He got right up in Moe's face, then turned his head, "Dahson, we have our first volunteer! Moe's gonna put his money where his mouth is—for once."

Moe paled, gulped, and took a step back.

"Moe, what is it about you and food? Don't you ever get filled up?" Milo asked. Moe screwed up his face and shrugged.

Dahson, the recognized brainiac of the bunch, cleared his throat to get their attention. He began reading aloud from his notes. "Here's the definition of the word astrophysics: 'the branch of astronomy that deals with the interaction between matter and radiation, and studies the physical nature of stars, other celestial bodies, and the cosmic microwave background.' I found this definition included in the 'moon' section of our reference book. Perhaps that will somehow help." Looking off into space, Dahson pushed plastic doll glasses back up the bridge of his nose. Though they were missing both lenses he often said he was nearly blind without them.

The Mouse family, eleven of them at the time, as the youngest, Peep, wasn't born yet, had discovered Dahson's bright yellow specs and Moe's Scottish purple tam along with other doll clothing and accessories, crayons, and more in the dusty camel-back trunk not long after they moved into the loft. Moe had since worn out the matching Scottish kilt. A lone encyclopedia, the 'M,' discovered off to the side of the chest, was another surprise. Dahson repeatedly read it cover to cover.

Milo, Moe, and Dahson were in their "Boys Only Club," a large open area far away from their living spaces and the classroom. This was a space unknown to their parents, and at least for now, the girls, as far as Milo could reckon.

"Focus, Dahson. Space study has got to come later," Milo preached. "We only want to go to the moon and back. That's the place to start. I'll be the first to volunteer for a longer mission when we get some of the equipment figured out," he added.

Moe, pantomiming huge explosions, asked, "When do we

bring out more firepower?" Milo did his level best to ignore him.

The area looked like there'd already been a major blast. Off to the side, a homemade firecracker rocket rested on its launch pad. Three additional rocket ships were in various stages of completion. Small paper scraps covered with the most recent calculations carpeted the floor.

Milo's Tinker Toy tower dominated the room with its triple-decker height. Though a bit unstable toward the top it was remarkable. Hidden in the shadows, deep under the eaves, was a large wooden crate overflowing with small firecrackers 'by the thousands'—Moe always said. These were the ones the boys fastened to the Tinker Toy pieces to create their rocket ships. But the crate also contained quite a few long, thick fuses and good-sized blasting caps that could pack a real wallop. At the bottom of the crate were the novelties—spinners, Black Cats, a few Roman Candles, bottle rockets, and a handful of sparklers. Boxes of matches, too.

POE

Poe, the ancient crow, watched from rafters high above. He vaguely remembered listening in months earlier as all four mice spoke vows of secrecy. How he wished he was part of the club. It would be good to have a friend, even *one*. Poe let out a soft, drawn-out sigh as he tucked his crippled wing closer to his side.

Three. He only counted three of the Mouse brothers. Where was the fourth? *There should be four.* He now spied Lipton standing sentinel at the room's entrance, looking bored to pieces.

LIPTON

Lipton's mind began to wander, and as often happened as of late, his thoughts traveled back to the accident that had changed his world. He'd been nothing but shortsighted. He had always been uncoordinated, so whatever made him take the dare? He remembered feeling important to be chosen. Oh, what a fool he'd been.

Climb across the thin, high cable that spanned the width of the loft. That was the dare. *A fine idea*, he'd thought. He made it almost to the halfway point when he started to lose his balance. Then he was upside-down and hanging on for dear life, and moment by moment—oh, so agonizingly—losing his grip and horrifyingly falling to the ground. He thought at the time that maybe he'd died. But the explosion of pain in the days that followed told him he had not.

His mind sometimes took him back to those awful moments, just as if they were happening again. Sweat would drip down his forehead, his heart would almost beat out of his chest, his vision would blur, and his breath came in pants.

He could feel himself falling. Slow motion. Down and down and down as the floor rushed to meet him.

Lipton looked at his poor crooked tail. It ached some days. Especially when the weather changed. It made him cautious and quiet. The fall had changed his life, maybe forever.

His injury and the panic weren't the only consequences. Mother almost fainted when she heard about his accident. She made Lipton stay in bed for more than a week and for the first several days and nights checked on him every hour on the hour.

The kids reacted to her constant monitoring and worry by unanimously agreeing to keep Mother in the dark about all future accidents or even any near misses. They figured it was in her best interest, and most definitely in theirs. She seemed calmer now, but her frequent safety classes continued to require the participation of all ten of them.

Lipton Thomas remained on guard duty, and his mind continued to wander. Expressions of both sadness and vulnerability traveled across his broad face. With a slight grimace, he released his tail and sighed.

A towering giant of a mouse, sometimes his brothers called him Jumbo just to tease him. The moniker made him overly self-conscious about his size and his innate awkwardness. In his mind, Jumbo rhymed with Dumbo so it made him feel stupid, too.

If only his nickname could help him feel big and important, instead of feeling small and shrinking on the inside, the way he felt now.

Nobody ever, ever gets a do-over, he thought. Nope. You can never go back.

MURFEE

Lipton had dozed off at the entrance to the secret firecracker building site. His assignment of keeping out all trespassers had apparently bored him to sleep. It was easy for Murfee to move past his guard post and take a sneak peek. She had an idea the boys were hiding something as time after time her favorite brother Milo disappeared for hours. For much of the last week, every evening she had pummeled him with questions about his day. Where had he been? What were they all up to? Anything new?

And she never got a satisfactory answer. Instead, Milo simply kept changing the subject.

Murfee had to find Milo, tell him she was leaving, and say goodbye in person, and she couldn't wait any longer. Maybe she'd leave tonight.

Murfee looked back and saw her baby sister, Peep, trailing her. She motioned for her to stay back. *Good grief. What a pest! Does she need to be in on everything?*

Murfee tripped over a small blasting cap and several of Moe's spent matches and tumbled into the room. Her noisy entrance was noticed at once. "What are you doing here, you little inch of a mouse? Get her out. No! Tie her up. Oh. This could spell trouble." Moe seemed beside himself.

Milo hurried up to the two of them, apparently to rescue his sister. "Murfee, I wondered when you'd get here. You're just in time to help us review our most recent calculations of angle and trajectory. If we want our first lunar flight to be a perfect success, we're going to have to get this right." Moe's mouth fell open. Murfee's eyes grew huge.

Milo tapped Murfee on the shoulder and then motioned for her to follow. The two walked over to the Tinker Toy tower, then began to climb. "I had to get you out of there before Moe decides what we need to do with you. He has a pretty narrow focus sometimes. And to be serious, there is a lot at stake."

Murfee couldn't hold back a goofy grin. She did her best to keep up with her brother's rapid ascent. At last, they took a seat on the very top rung, the Tinker Toy tower swaying ever so slightly.

Milo said, "First you gotta promise to keep this all on the QT, 'cause there's no way Mother would let us keep the explosives. Father, maybe. Mother worries about everything, you know—lately she thinks one of us is going to be attacked by a bird or a cat. 'Nothing could be further from the truth,' Father says. We're safe. Nothing can reach us up here so high in this loft." Murfee's eyes widened.

"Can you imagine what she'd think of something that could explode into a gazillion little pieces? And those biggest firecrackers are really, really somethin'," he boasted.

Milo did a pantomime of a great explosion and a rocket's flight through the hole in the roof high overhead. Firepower! A rocket would need it to blast out of the old barn and continue up to the moon—so far above in the night sky. She finally understood. Murfee's eyes popped. "Wow!"

"Oh, I gotta tell you the latest news," Milo's eyes danced. "Moe told us something wild. He heard Mother say the moon is made of cheese so now he thinks our mission is a great idea. Unless it's up to him to step up to the plate and pilot the rocket. Which he won't, you know. He's chicken."

Cheese... a world made of cheese. In that instant, Murfee began picturing her parents as they talked about a food short-age, the Man in the Moon, and a world made out of cheese. *How could I have forgotten? Whoa. Maybe there's a way to help. A rocket ride to the moon to get cheese. I could be the first to volunteer.*

Her true destiny and the reason for her magic were finally revealed. A rocket ride straight to the moon. "Oh! Milo, I've wanted to talk to you, sometime when there's no one else around." Her eyes were shining. "I have a secret, too. And you can be sure I'll keep yours. Cross my heart and hope to die." Her words poured out in a rush, "See—I have a special magic, superpower cape. It's red and it's beautiful. Wearing it makes me strong and brave. I know this from my dreams. It's true!

"Maybe I can be your astronaut on your moon mission. I

could do it if I took my magic cape." Murfee was beside herself. She wouldn't even let her fear of cats stop her now.

Wearing her cape, with eyes closed and the rocket aimed at the moon, all she'd need to do was hold on with all her might. *If* she was careful and didn't look down. Right? *Right?* Supernatural magic would ensure a perfect moon lift-off. Dahson would've perfectly calculated the rocket's return trip, too. Wearing her superhero cape, all bases were covered.

Faith in the magic—that's all she needed—that and Dahson's spectacular brain. She could depend on him; he came through every time.

The next minute, Dahson called out for Milo's help. Milo gave a 'thumbs up' before nimbly scampering down to join him, leaving Murfee all alone with her thoughts.

Unbelievable. Here was the opportunity she'd been waiting for her entire life. A rocket standing at the ready to take her up into the stars. She'd be flying off into a grand adventure. A worthy one, too. She'd bring back food for her family.

All nine of her brothers and sisters were clueless. None of them realized the fix the family was in, or that they needed a superhero—instead, their father was making risky plans to keep them all fed.

Murfee had to convince the boys that she'd make the best mouse astronaut ever.

She was tiny—the perfect size for flight. She'd climb aboard their rocket ship, get a firm hold, one of them could light the fuse, and up she'd go.

The minute she started to call out to Milo to wait, her eyes were drawn to the lone rocket on a launch pad below. Within a hair's breadth, her fear of heights reared its ugly head. Her arms and legs began to quiver. Trembling, Murfee grabbed hold of the Tinker Toy top rail to stop from falling, taking great care to look anywhere but downward. Disgusted, she muttered to herself, "Really, Murfee, how are you gonna manage a trip to the moon and back? You can't even open your eyes and look down without getting the shakes." How much could she depend on the magic? That was the question. It looked again like her superhero adventures were off to a shaky start.

11

DECEPTION AND SOUR MILK

SOPHIE

SOPHIE'S GRANDMOTHER, Rosalie, was diligent about bringing cat food and filling Justice's special saucer, though Sophie felt the urge to keep her cat's absence a secret. Somehow it seemed important. So, for a couple of days, she dumped that day's milk down the bathroom sink and hid the dry cat food in the back of her closet and under her bed. Maybe this was her special part of carrying out the escape plan. She liked to think it was.

Where was her faithful friend? Was he safe? Had he found his wife and his son? Were they safe, too?

A life with Justice in it filled her dreams, she missed him so. And now her living space was starting to smell a bit of Kitty Kats-Kats Lunch and Snacks and her bathroom—ugh—of sour milk.

12

BACK TO THE DRAWING BOARD

POE

THAT EVENING, Poe, the shiny black crow, flew into the barn loft, and unseen, landed without a whisper. As was his habit, the ancient bird cowered in the shadows.

He looked down from his wooden perch, his beady eyes narrowing to slits. He watched as Murfee Mouse wrapped a scrap of deep red velvet around herself, securing it at her neck.

It reminded him of something. He tilted his head to the side. *Now, what was that?* Elusive memories moved through the confusion of his mind, shifting about. A cape, a purple cape. No, not a cape, a piece of clothing a prince would wear. Prince Poe. Dressed in royal robes. Prince Poe. He tilted his head, a puzzled look on his face. Why couldn't he remember? It seemed that his entire life had been lived in the world of the barn. But then why did his mind go to these thoughts? "Lily," he softly whispered. "Hmm. Who's Lily?" Gnats. His thoughts were nothing but gnats.

His head jerked and he came back to the present, to little

Murfee Mouse playing dress up. The name Lily, along with his memories, drifted away like the mist.

The fabric was pretty and Poe was drawn to it. Poe wanted it. Poe liked nice, pretty things and shiny things to steal and hide, to make his own. The world owed him for his misery.

A damaged left wing was a constant reminder of an accident when he was barely hatched, later making him the target of cruelty. The old bird was hypervigilant and often fearful, though he did his best to appear perfectly calm and collected to the Mouse family and anyone else he encountered.

The oily crow was devious, clever, and power-hungry as well. There was no other bird quite like Poe. At this moment, he was transfixed by the beautiful piece of scarlet. He couldn't tear his eyes away. At issue was the fabric's color. What he'd give for an ebony-colored cape! Powerful Poe. Powerful Poe!

Poe was the real-life Batman, the living, breathing Caped Crusader. For now, his shiny, blue-black feathers would have to do. But he'd show them. Somehow, he would, and he'd have all the power; they'd all answer to him.

Poe thought back to days before, watching as Murfee discovered that stash of comic books—which now rightfully belonged to him. What would a mouse want with a comic book?

As soon as Murfee had left, he'd torn out pages and carried them, one by one, to his special lair. His treasured portraits of Superman, Batman and Robin, and Two-Face now adorned its walls and fluttered in every little breeze. It was as if they were coming to life right before his eyes.

It was almost a shame he had no one to share the images with, most especially that of Batman, whom he emulated at every chance, and of Two-Face—the old crow was acutely drawn to him.

Oh! He better not forget what he was doing now—trailing

the littlest mouse. And what a stupid little mouse she was. Murfee thought Poe was her friend! Stupid, stupid little mouse.

A look of darkness transformed his features but a moment. *That beautiful scrap of red velvet—Murfee shouldn't have it. It belongs to Poe. It would look good on Poe.*

MURFEE

Murfee let out an audible sigh. With a troubling sense of urgency, she had left her sleeping family to make it to her secret place in the loft. There was so much to think about. Her family needed a superhero, and soon.

She took a seat on a nearby straw bale while she tried out superhero names for size. "The Red-Caped Crusader, Conqueror of the World, Guardian of the Galaxies. Marvelous Mouse. Murfee the Marvel, Mouse Wonder." None seemed to roll off the tongue. "Mouse Marvel. Hmm... that might be the ticket. With this magic cape I, Murfee Mouse, am now Mouse Marvel!" She took up her sword, then stood with wobbly legs on the top of the straw bundle. After steadying herself, she lunged forward, thrusting her weapon at an unseen foe.

She thought back to the small vole she'd seen the night before. Was he, like Murfee, getting ready to start a hero's adventure? She needed to practice her own hero skills before she took off into the world.

With a flying leap she attempted a gallant, flawless vault to the floor, but instead tripped over the scarlet puddle of her bulky cape. Trapped in layers of velvet, she tumbled and spun all the way down. Mouse Marvel looked more like a strange little sausage wrapped in a ketchup-colored bun.

Murfee shook her head in disgust, rolled her eyes, and struggled to remove herself from the fabric that held her tight. "Boy. This hero stuff might just take more than a little practice. Glad nobody saw that 'cause I feel a little foolish. I get made fun of already, I wonder what they would call me now. Sheesh!"

She furtively glanced around to reassure herself that she was indeed alone, failing to see one crazy crow. She stood, dusted pieces of straw off her treasured cape, and picked up her sandwich-pick sword. "But if there is one thing for certain, with this cape and my trusty sword, I am much more than an inch. When I have them with me, I have all their superpowers." A huge smile lit up her face.

Murfee held the sword at arm's length and studied the tip of it. "My having discovered the magic was destiny. My family needs me."

Murfee lowered her weapon, lost again in thought. The worrying words of her mother returned. Food shortage, cats, and anything with wings. "If I say yes to the assignment, I'll be taking on a double mission. One for food and another to keep us all safe from cats… Oh! And any danger that could fly in to reach us in the loft." Her eyes grew wide. "Serious stuff. Still, with my magic, I'd be the right hero for the job."

Poe let out a coarse laugh. A surprised and delighted Murfee turned and saw him hiding in the corner and quickly set all concerns aside. "Why! It's Poe. My good friend, Poe!"

Appearing startled at being discovered, the bird flew to her with his awkward and crippled flight. "Littlest Mouse, Poe is most delighted to see you," he said as he bowed low.

Murfee's father's voice thundered. "Nose count. Time for bed! And, yes, I mean all of you."

"Gotta go. See you soon, Poe." She laughed at herself. "I'm a poet and didn't know it." She tore off her cape and covered it and her plastic sword under layers of straw, then raced from the room.

POE

The demented crow shook his head and snickered in disgust. "Murfee *is* a fool, not Poe. Never Poe. He is the smartest of crows. Murfee, a hero, ha! Never ever. Poe will be the real hero, and everyone will love Poe.

"Poe will soon have it all. All the magic and all the power. Powerful Poe—Conqueror of the World, The real Batman, Poe the Crow." The old bird puffed out his chest and smoothed out his tail feathers. Moonlight bounced off them, making them gleam.

Sometimes he was afraid, but tonight everything seemed his for the taking.

FATHER

The Mouse children minus one stood in a line. Father counted as their names were called out. "Lipton Thomas, Dahson, Pip and Squeak, Maddy, Minree, Milo, Moe, Murfee... Murfee. Murfee? Oh! There you are. Murfee and Peep."

13
EYES IN THE BACK OF HIS HEAD

MOE

NOT ONE OF the ten kids seemed to be able to sleep. Was it possible their internal clocks were connected to an ever-enlarging moon floating in the night sky?

One thing for sure, it didn't take much persuasion for Moe to interest them in a ghost story. He grabbed his treasured purple tam and plopped it on his head as they scrambled to join him. So much for all ten snug and safe in their beds.

Theatrical, showboat Moe Mouse soon had all brothers and sisters lined up before him according to size. Murfee was the only one unhappy with the process. "Not again. I'm tired of being the last one in line. Peep is the baby—she should be on the end. And what does any of this have to do with your story, Moe? I just want to hear some kinda-scary stuff."

Dahson absentmindedly readjusted his yellow doll glasses. "Murfee, just humor him. It's neither a logical nor a necessary measure but remember we're talking about Moe."

Moe gave his brother an angry look before turning back to

face his sister. "Well, Murfee, you *are* the smallest. Even if you stretched. Just get in line and be ready to listen."

"Hey, Murf!" called Milo. "Before you or anyone else lodges another complaint, I have one. I'm missing my magnifier... I can't find it anywhere. Did you borrow it, Murfee, and then forget to bring it back? Better yet, did anybody borrow it without even asking me first?" Milo glared at each of them in turn.

The magnifier in question was a miniature magnifying glass Milo had found at the very bottom of an otherwise empty Cracker Jack box. It was the toy prize inside. "Nobody's seen it," someone spoke up. Milo's siblings, all but Moe, shook their heads in silent agreement.

Brother Moe stomped his feet in frustration. He couldn't have cared less about the missing item. "Come on, guys. Time's a-wastin'. This evening is all about entertainment—the kind that will keep you awake in the night—not about anything Milo's worried about." But Milo was not to be dissuaded.

Milo's voice rose higher. "Whoever took it, fess up. I never know when I'll need to examine something with magnification. Looking through it can change what a guy can see. I want it back!"

Murfee glared at Milo. "I would never take it without asking. Thanks a lot for the vote of confidence."

Moe, his cap at a crazy angle, jumped up and down in frustration. "What happened to the spooktacular evening I've planned? Get with the program, folks! Pip and Squeak, stop dancing around and get serious."

Pip and Squeak, identical twin girls who habitually finished each other's sentences, were inseparable and often obnoxious. They danced, they sang, and they occupied a self-sufficient world of two.

Minree, on the other hand, was the true dancer of the

family. She danced wherever she went. Yet when she was not pure movement and grace, she was shy beyond words. She was the first to quietly sit down and settle herself for the story.

Maddy, the bossiest of the bunch, plopped down beside her sister, then proceeded to take charge of the group. "Everybody, look at me and Minree. Listen up and sit down. Moe has his story to tell and you're all wasting his time."

Moe was in his glory and his element—he had an audience.

"Ever hear the story of Tyrus the Cat? He lives down in the lower regions of this very barn—he's a wild mouse-chaser." Moe leaned in closer as his voice took on a fever pitch. "Rumor has it that he's the size of a large dog—or maybe a cow."

He paused a moment to check every expression, then thrust two fingers in the air. "That cat has two sets of eyes—to see you better with—one set in the back of his head. You'd better each hope he doesn't come after you," he finished.

Peep began to cry. She was still very much the baby, spoiled and coddled. She had been born premature and struggled for weeks to live.

Her cradle was an ancient silver kitchen ladle, the rounded portion of the bowl resting in an indentation of the rough wooden floor, the handle of it resting in a crack in the wall. They had all taken turns rocking it through the long days and nights. Present day, this same spoon provided great fun used as a slide. Peep, the twins, and especially Maddy, spent hours racing down its handle, down, down into the rounded portion, then out into space, only to land without a scratch in a mountain of straw.

Peep's real name was Prasilla, but when the tiny mouse first roused and made a peep, she'd been called Peep, and has been ever since. How was it then that she had grown so big and so fast? Sometimes, because of her size, everyone in this bunch forgot how young she was and expected her to act much more grown up.

Lipton Thomas, nicknamed Jumbo by his brothers and sisters, was large and lumbering. He was kind and gentle-hearted, and without pause, he scooped up the baby of the family to console her. Moe was unfazed and continued with his tale. "All his eyes are golden slits, awful, evil. And he can see in the light or in the dark. He can always find you—anywhere. Any time, any place."

Lipton commenced rocking Peep back and forth as she began to sob in earnest.

That kid has a set of lungs! Moe thought, fearing all the racket would stop all his fun. Better tone things down before he got in a jam.

"Hey, guys. I could be wrong about all of this. Tyrus the Terrible may be that cat Father talks about that is so ancient he doesn't have a tooth in his head. The cat who chases a mouse just 'cause he likes to. Spits it out if he ever does catch one of us 'cause he doesn't even like the taste."

Peep's sobs became loud hiccups.

Murfee at this point looked beyond disgusted. "Which is it? A wild and terrible mouse-chaser with two sets of eyes—or an old toothless feline that couldn't catch his own tail? Give us something scary."

"It is at least illogical. It simply cannot be both," Dahson stated.

Moe racked his brain. How could he deal with the situation with Peep and at the same time maintain his captive audience? Oh! He had a revelation. Something to shut up Peep and keep everyone's attention. Something quiet. A shadow puppet show.

He created the illusion of a monster cat pursuing a tiny

mouse, the scene distorted even further by the rough barn wall. Somehow even Moe himself was frightened.

Then he watched on with trepidation as Father and Mother walked into the room. He was in trouble now; he could just feel it.

Mother turned to his father. "Quintin Cornelius Mouse, those boys need to quit with the ghost tales. They all need to get to sleep." She looked at them and frowned. Father Mouse nodded in agreement.

"Your mother's right. Settle down. Now. No talking," Father said as he looked straight at Moe. He raised his eyebrows. "This means you." Moe did his very best to look remorseful.

Ten little mice were soon again snug in their beds. The wind picked up with high-pitched moaning as it tore its way through cracks in the old barn walls.

Ten little bodies lay ramrod straight in their beds. Unmoving, breathing as quietly as possible, the whites of their eyes shining in the moonlight.

MURFEE

Would the magic in Murfee's cape protect her from mouse-killing cats? If she were wearing it right now, would the magic keep her both safe and unafraid? She was the last to drift off to sleep.

14

TICK WENT THE CLOCK

SOPHIE

Tᴛᴄᴋ. Tick. Tick. Tick, tick, tick. TICK. TICK. Tick, tick, tick-tick. Unrelenting. Louder and louder. Inescapable. Not even a pillow and bedcovers could shut out the incessant sounds of the dozens of her grandmother's clocks. Louder and louder went the ticking of the clocks.

Sophie couldn't get the sound out of her head. Dancing shadows played upon walls and desk and moved across the faces of the infuriating ticking clocks. Where was Justice? Was he really coming back or had he left her for good? Maybe he had. If only the clocks would stop.

An exhausted Sophie turned on a small night light and began quietly removing batteries from all the clocks she could easily reach, then carefully rehanging them each back in their rightful place on attic walls.

15
MISSING

JUSTICE

FOR TWO DAYS AND NIGHTS, Justice searched entire neighborhoods for his wife and son, poking around familiar places and questioning each and every cat he encountered along the way. It was surreal. Liza and Mantis were nowhere to be found. No one knew a thing. It was as if his family was nothing but a dream.

The night's darkness had settled in like a shroud, the night air heavy and salty on the tongue as it wafted in from the sea. Without warning, the huge cat's legs gave way and he fell flat to the ground.

I'll be no help to them at all if I collapse on this very spot. Better get up, find water, and something to eat. His legs, however, refused to obey. A night owl hooted. Fireflies began their nightly dance of light.

"They couldn't have just disappeared." He turned his head to search the sky as if the answers he sought could be found there. *Gone without a trace. They didn't just vanish. Someone's got to know something.*

Lying there, helpless as a newborn kitten, Justice felt his chest loosen as he stared up into the heavens. *What was it Liza was always saying, something about the Architect high above watching over us all? Something like that.* The huge feline let his thoughts go blank, his heartbeat slowed, and his entire body relaxed as if he was sinking down into the earth.

The face of his beautiful bride appeared in his mind's eye. He could almost touch her, and though he reached out, he could not reach her. "Justice, stay strong. Your son needs you. First search for your father. Find him and you'll find your son. And remember always, my love is with you still."

Her image faded and her voice floated away as if nothing but a passing cloud, disappearing silently into the dark of the night.

16

APPLIED MATH

MURFEE

THE NEXT DAY, Father gathered all his children around him to begin his homeschool lesson, "Mountains and Mountain Ranges." The huge *M* encyclopedia, the only letter they'd found near the camel-back trunk, was spread out before them. Murfee's eyes were drawn to the picture of a mountain climber scaling Mount McKinley, then to one of a red-suited skier flying down a snow-covered slope.

Murfee liked the snow, though she had seen little of it since the classroom window usually remained closed on snowy days. But sometimes the soft white stuff came unannounced, found them unprepared, and left a large white drift. And sometimes, if it were snowing just a bit, Father and Mother would leave the window open and let them watch.

Murfee liked to stick out her tongue to catch the snowflakes and to watch the snow melt in an instant on her outstretched hand. She loved its beauty and its whiteness.

Father cleared his throat, bringing her back to the present, and Murfee made a silent promise to concentrate on the lesson. "Let's see," Father hesitated a moment, then began to read. "The difference between a mountain and a hill is essentially one of size. The difference is not clearly defined. Hmm." Father paused. Then he continued, "Mount Everest is the highest mountain in the world, rising to twenty-nine thousand twenty-eight feet."

A thoughtful silence filled the loft. Finally, Murfee raised her hand and asked with wonder, "Father, how high is that mountain compared to me?"

Milo jumped up and down waving his hand wildly. "I know, I know!" Father nodded for him to continue. "Murfee, it's simple arithmetic. Just a matter of converting inches to feet," Milo said with his chest all puffed out.

"I would agree," said Dahson. "But first, as one would need to know, exactly how tall *is* Murfee?" Every eye turned toward the littlest mouse.

Murfee colored, then stammered, "I guess I'm around one inch."

Moe, sounding quite innocent, asked, "Father, could you bring that paper ruler? Do you know where we left it? 'Cause then we could really learn a lot about the math."

"A ruler? Well... okay. I'll be right back," Father scratched his head, then quickly left the room.

"She's not even an inch. Bet she's not even close. We really don't need a ruler, just grab her arms, I'll grab her feet," Moe said, puffed up with a great false sense of importance. "Stretch her out. We can get a rough idea how small she really is."

They all gathered around as Moe pushed Murfee to the floor and pointed to her to lie still.

As Murfee lay there, she knew she had never felt more humiliated. She was a joke, nothing more, and she'd only been kidding herself about being a real-life hero. Things would never change unless she did, and she'd better start right now by standing up to Moe.

Murfee struggled to get up off the floor the moment their father's footsteps were heard, which propelled Moe into action. He pulled her to her feet and motioned for everyone to return to their seats. Then he gave them a thumbs up, cautioned Murfee with his glare, and waved at Milo to continue. Father walked in.

Milo, at first clueless, had a confused look on his face. "Huh?" Then a dawning, "Oh! What do you think? I hate fractions... Let's just round her off to an even inch," Milo said. "Then we don't even have to measure her. Boy, I love math! Let's see, twelve inches in a foot. Twelve times twenty-nine thousand and twenty-eight feet equals sixteen carry the one, four-five, zero, eighteen carry the one, four-five.

"Move over one, eight, two, zero, nine, two. It all adds up to six, thirteen carry the one, two-three, eight, fourteen carry the one, two-three. Whew! Murfee, the mountain is three hundred, forty-eight thousand, three hundred, thirty-six times the size of you," Milo said proudly.

Pip and Squeak began to chant in a sing-song voice, "Murfee is an inch! Murfee is an inch! No bigger than an inch! Nah-nah-nah-nah-naaah-nah."

The little twerps. Will they ever be out of my hair? she thought. She scowled at the two of them. Pip and Squeak stared back, put their thumbs in their ears, and wiggled their fingers.

Father frowned, then chastised the twins before dismissing everyone for the day. Murfee decided to stay put. She needed to think. Were her feelings the least of it? The Mouse family was in trouble and needed a hero and magic could make all the difference. *She* could bring back all the food they'd ever need. Father wouldn't have to leave the safety of the barn.

She heard footsteps approaching. It was her father. He

reached out and gathered her up in his arms, holding her close for a long moment. "Do you know, my littlest one, I've had days just like this growing up?" he said. "Many of them. But I had someone special in my corner and she helped me get through all of it. She saved me from great discouragement." Murfee was all ears. "Would you like me to tell you about my auntie sometime, someone I wish you could have met?" His eyes took on a faraway expression. "Aunt Wilamena. She passed away long before you were born, but I know she would have loved you." Murfee looked down at her toes.

Father's face was full of concern. "Auntie's gone, but you have someone to champion you on. You have me. Don't you ever forget it."

MURFEE WALKED THROUGH THE BARN LOFT, TRAVELING A FAR distance to where surplus hay was stored, as she wrestled with feelings and the brand-new thoughts swirling through her mind. After a time, a sense of optimism floated up and settled.

It was almost unbelievable. Her family needed her. Well, not *her* exactly. They needed a superhero. Someone with daring. Someone with magic. Someone like Sami Sparrow or someone like Mouse Marvel!

Lost in thought, she stood frozen in place. *I wish there was an instruction book on magic powers. What if you have to hold your mouth just right?*

At last, she crawled up and onto a dusty old feed sack and made herself comfortable.

What *was* it like for Sami growing up? Or for Superman... was he even a hero in class? Did he ever get a bad grade or get made fun of for the wrong answer? Uh oh! What if you had to be smart to save the day?

17
READY OR NOT

MURFEE

Murfee wasn't hungry that evening, though she came when supper was called. She had a slight headache and worrying about the food shortage had tied her stomach in knots. Each of the ten children received their usual careful measure of oats, tonight piled high on Mother's small pearl button plates, a matched set she held dear. Both parents said they'd already eaten.

Murfee played with her food, then silently scooted her portion over to Moe. Frankly, she was tired of his complaints that there was never enough to eat. She'd bet he was born hungry. At least when he was filling his face, no one heard a word out of him. Her brother barely looked up from his food in acknowledgement.

After supper they washed their faces and went off to bed, but every one of them seemed unsettled. *Maybe the ghost story from last night is in the back of everybody's mind,* Murfee wondered. Moe's made-up cat-shaped shadows had most likely caused more than one heart to skip a beat.

Moe asked if they wanted to have a little fun, and the idea of a distraction suited them just fine. He pulled on his Scottish tam, held a finger up to his lips, and motioned for his siblings to follow. Murfee was as curious as the rest of them and didn't hesitate.

Undetected, they made their way through the darkened barn until they reached what had been dubbed the music room, which held the family treasure—an antique radio plugged into an electric outlet in the wall. Music spilled out of it. Snatches of news reached the Mouse family's ears and brought a bit of the outer world into the isolated world of the loft. It was here Moe found his target for the night. Their parents, wrapped in each other's embrace.

The massive, glass-fronted, brass-trimmed Philco radio poured out songs interspersed with static. Its lighted dial gave these two figures standing near a soft candlelit glow.

Mr. and Mrs. Mouse made quite a pair. Father, Quintin Cornelius, had a stocky build, was easygoing, and his face was often creased with a laugh or a smile. Mother, Faylena Annaletta, was slender, feminine, and a bit fragile in appearance. Beautiful soft-brown eyes dominated her features, and a single strand of doll-necklace pearls lay at her throat. When Quin moved to adjust the radio's dial, Fay stared off into space and absentmindedly fingered her precious pearls.

Quin returned to stand behind her just as the radio began to play clearly. "Fly me to the moon... " He gently placed his hands on her shoulders and whispered something in her ear. She smiled and leaned back into him.

The song broke off, replaced by annoying static. Quin turned off the radio before returning to take his wife in his arms. He began moving her about in a waltz, humming softly.

At first their children watched silently, and their presence remained unnoticed. Then Moe and Milo began comically dancing with one another. Maddy glared at them, and the twins did nothing but giggle. Murfee couldn't help but laugh. But what had she just witnessed—two people in love? *Someday maybe I'll fall in love, too. For sure this looks romantic.* She blushed at the thought of seeing this private moment between Mother and Father. Perhaps they all should have stayed put.

MOTHER

In pantomime, Mother counted noses, looked unsure, recounted, then shooed everyone off to bed. She turned back to her husband. "Quintin, it's just too much. Being an only child never prepared me for any of this." She wanted to cry. "Maybe if they weren't so busy and always on the move. And if I can't even get an accurate count, how can I know every one of them is safe?"

Father took a step closer. "Sweetheart, that was all ten of them—and they're all safe." He chuckled.

"It's not funny. They have me outnumbered—*and they know it*," she countered, holding back tears. Father looked at her and shook his head. He seemed to be struggling to suppress a grin.

But then his mouth tightened and he took a deep breath. "I've been putting something off but there won't be a better time than now." She put a hand over her mouth. He continued, "Fay, I hate to make you worry more—you do that too much already."

Mother Mouse's face paled as Father went on to explain that he needed to leave sooner than planned to search for food for the family. It was strange; the pile of grain was shrinking twice as fast as his earlier estimates. Now all twelve lives were at stake, and though the risk would be much greater traversing open stretches in the light of an increasingly full moon, waiting wasn't an option. He'd begun preparations. The minute they were completed, he would leave.

Questions tumbled through her mind. What if something terrible happened? What if he was killed and she never learned the how or why? Not knowing would be the worst. What would she do if he never came home? Could she carry on without him? How could any of them? Her entire body shuddered.

She willed him to listen. "You can't leave now. The moon's almost full. You told me you'd wait. You told me that." Her beautiful eyes pleaded. "There's too much moonlight and not enough shadow. I have some grain stashed in a hidden cupboard for emergencies like this. Any time the children leave their oats uneaten I gather them up and store them away. None of us will go hungry. You have to wait." She reached out and pulled him closer. "Tell me you'll wait." He gave a slight nod of his head. Tears wet her face. "Don't leave me. Don't leave. Not now."

***

MURFEE

The children were back in bed and sleeping soundly, all but Murfee, who was replaying the day in her head. She had tried and failed to stand up to Moe in class, then the twins made the situation even worse for her and she ended up looking like a wimp.

Every morning, come rain or shine, this very morning

included, she made plans to do better—to stand up tall and defend herself. Today she was a total embarrassment. Then, with a wry chuckle, she remembered Father often muttering something about the best-laid plans of mice and men. Best laid plans. He might as well have been talking about hers.

Quietly she crept out of bed. "What do Pip and Squeak know about anything? Why do I even listen? And Moe's an idiot," she said under her breath.

Stealthily she made her way to her special place in the loft. She had a ton of questions. She stood before her makeshift window and looked out at the stars as if they held the answers she sought.

Was she ready to be more powerful than any-sized mouse in the world could imagine—with superpowers like Sami Sparrow or Superman, the Man of Steel? She'd be responsible for a great deal, most especially for the safety of her family. She'd have to be ready for all possibilities. Hmm. *What would happen to Superman if he ever lost his cape? Would he fall from the sky?* she wondered. Did he ever become afraid when he wasn't wearing it? Surely, he took it off when he went to bed. What would he do if danger came in the middle of the night? Did he ever walk into a wall or have a really bad day?

She chewed a fingernail down to the quick. What did it take to be a hero? Did she have an actual right to the magic of the cape? And if just anybody could wear the beautiful cape without being something special on the inside, was it simply magic and nothing else?

If that were the case, baby Peep could wear the cape. Showboat Moe could be a superhero. Even Poe the crow.

Murfee was still afraid of the dark. She was afraid of cats— real ones—not the ones of Moe's ghost stories, but cats who in fact ate little mice, the ones Mother worried about. Her fear of heights hadn't left her, and no amount of wishing made it so.

Everything was at stake for her family, their safety *and* having enough to eat. Milo was brave. Maybe he could find a food supply and protect them from danger. Maybe he should wear the velvet cape.

She paced back and forth, then stopped abruptly. "Destiny. This has to be destiny. *Mine.* I'm the one who found it." She turned from her window view. "Quit overthinking everything, Murfee, and get back to work." Suppressing a yawn, she refastened the cape's knot at her neck. "First, I'm gonna need to start acting like a superhero—today I acted like a real pushover, and it was the worst! What if I wow 'em with my sword skills?"

She took in a lungful of air, then exhaled in a mighty puff before squaring her shoulders. "Guess I've got some practicing to do." She picked up her pink plastic sword and sliced it neatly through the air.

18

A FRIEND ON THE DOCK

JUSTICE

DEEPLY TROUBLED, Justice made his way down the pier to the water's edge. Without thinking, he found himself humming Liza's favorite song, *Catch a Falling Star*. Tears began to wet whiskers and face, but slowly and surely dried up as the gentle ocean waves quieted his heart.

Liza and Mantis would have loved this night. Smiling, he could picture his son bailing off the end of the pier, swimming out into the waters until his mother called him back. Mantis climbing back up onto the wooden pier and shaking himself off, laughing as he sprayed droplets of ocean water upon the both of them.

Startled, Justice heard footsteps a moment before he spied his friend, Joe, a dock worker who had long been known to speak cat. Joe crouched down and with a quiet, most-solemn voice, delivered the sad news about the death of Liza and the disappearance of Mantis, his beloved son.

"I buried her in the deep shade of that towering sycamore

tree, you know, the one the two of you loved. I thought you would have liked that.

"I'll never forget the picnic the three of us shared there in that special spot, the same day Liza and you told me she was expecting in the spring. It's a beautiful place, a peaceful place. And as to Mantis, I haven't seen him since he was small, a long time before you left, and I knew nothing about Liza getting sick." Justice saw what appeared to be sadness and regret travel across Joe's face. "Guess I just got busy with life, busy with work on the wharf. Justice, I didn't know. I'd have come and found you if I had."

As Justice felt hot tears blur his vision, he bent his head to the ground. Joe reached out and stroked his fur. "Let me know if I can do something for you—anything."

Joe stood to leave, then stopped to say, "Justice, you've got a lot of support here on the dock. I've told many your story—some of them can't believe I talked to a cat—but a bunch of them do. The nonbelievers, well, they seem to know this is really important to me. They saw my grief when Liza died so they'll help, too. We'll put our heads together to help if you ever need it—maybe as you go off to find your son." He reached down and ruffed up his fur.

Justice lifted his head to look up into the face of the kindest, most gentle human he'd ever met. The soft brown eyes of the tall and lanky redhead stared back at him. "Remember, you big lug of a cat, you're not alone," Joe said. "You'll know how and when to find me."

19
THE GRAND ESCAPE

POE

THE MIGHTY PREDATOR, a great horned owl, floated down out of the nighttime sky, alighting on the large branch of the giant maple tree. Blended into the shadows was Poe, the black crow, determined to control his trembling. Waiting and watching to see what might next unfold.

A small vole took a step out from the safety of the cornfield; a cat the size of a small bulldog padded soundlessly forward, staying hidden in the deep shadows, then froze mid-stride, Poe watching it all.

From the shelter of the towering corn, a heavy-set female vole exploded onto the scene, grabbed the tiny fellow, and jerked him back into the tall, crowded stalks. She waved a finger in his face, scolding him at length. All the while, the little vole hung his head and rubbed a toe in the dirt.

Then she wrapped her small one in her arms and sobbed. She released him at last, and after more finger wagging, with her son nodding his head, left him to move further back into the stalks.

The little guy stood motionless for a moment, looking thoughtful, then took a quick peek out from the shelter of the giant corn.

There was not a breath of wind. Lighted fireflies flitted about, and the scent of fallen leaves and corn tassels mingled in the soft air. The moon, a beautiful orange-gold orb, hung in the sky.

Poe remained hidden in the deep shadows of the night. His beady eyes darted about. He would survive it all—maybe he could even have it all. The old bird would find a way to use what he saw, what he learned, and the true power would be his. He was the smartest, smartest crow!

A gentle breeze began to rustle the corn and the leaves of the large maple tree.

MANTIS

The cat never took his eyes off the tiny vole at the cornfield's edge, the little morsel's protector now nowhere in sight. The feline's large golden eyes narrowed, and globs of saliva drooled down both sides of his mouth, sliding in a lump down the back of his throat. He swallowed twice. His eyes watered, but he never blinked. Hungry though he was, he would not give his position away. Supper was at stake as well as his reputation, which drove him more than any hunger could.

His father had named him Preying Mantis. And it was his father's wish that Mantis make a name for himself, and that his son's reputation would grow year by year until all who saw him saw only power and his cold, cold heart.

His sweet mother Liza had called him her little man, her Manny. Liza held a place in his heart that was both tender and full of pain—she had once been his entire world. These things he remembered.

The only way to stay focused now was to leave his memories of her a blur, and if truth be known, that was easy. She and her words to him once again became no more than a watery shadow.

He'd think instead about redemption. The redemption of his family and his family name. From what he'd heard about him, his grandfather Tyrus had brought shame to all who would follow. Mantis had never met Tyrus, but he'd heard the stories time and time again.

Tyrus was known in family legend as a harmless mouse-chaser. If he ever caught a mouse, which was always much to his surprise, he would immediately gag and spit it out. He simply enjoyed the chase.

My grandfather was an old fool, Mantis thought. *Why would any mouse-chaser worth his salt catch 'em then let 'em go? "Tyrus the Terrible" he was not. I'll make up for the family dishonor. I am a mouse-killer, an annihilator.*

And yet again, the tiny vole returned to stand at the very edge of the tall corn, his mother's warning seemingly unheeded. He stuck out a foot as if he were checking the temperature of the water before taking a plunge.

With one last quick backward glance, the small vole turned and ran without fear from the field and into the open.

At this, both the owl and Mantis sprang into motion. The huge bird of prey flew like a heat-seeking missile; the feline, a mass of moving muscle, was pure grace in motion. A bone-jarring crash accompanied blurred imagery of shape, color, and billows of dust. A terrible screech rang out through an otherwise quiet night.

MURFEE

High above, Murfee Mouse put down her plastic weapon and moved at once toward the loft window. *What was that? Something doesn't sound right. Hmm...*

A cricket began chirping and she turned to listen. She liked the soft nighttime noises of crickets, the horses down below, and the occasional swish of a bat flying through the barn. She dismissed any worry and returned to her sword practice, innocent and ignorant of the danger and violence right outside the walls. All at once the loft became eerily quiet and Murfee noticed. *Odd. Guess I didn't realize what downright silence feels like. There's not often much of that in the loft.*

She solemnly addressed the invisible and now silent cricket. "Dear Cricket, allow me to introduce myself. I am the renowned superhero Mouse Marvel, and I'm preparing for a most grand adventure. You can call me Murfee if you want. What's your name and why did you stop making your beautiful music?"

She waited a beat but heard no response. "Don't be afraid. You can talk to me. Cat got your tongue?" She took a couple steps forward but couldn't find him. "It's much too quiet now, and I don't know that I like it. Would you chirp a song or two for me? Please?"

MANTIS

Outside, the dust cleared, and tufts of hair and feathers large and small wafted to the ground. For one small moment, there was not the breath of a breeze or sound of an insect; the world was in silent witness to the life just lost. Then movement and sound came back in a roar as two powerful predators faced off in the darkness. Mantis the victor, swallowing his meal with a crunch and one good gulp, the owl hissing and spitting in rage. A pair of nighthawks swooped low, their eyes glowing ruby-red in the moonlight, then darted away. Frenzied movements and wails came from the cornfield.

What a night! Mantis, deeply satisfied with the night's outcome, felt unshakable, undefeatable. Pulsating power thrummed through his veins.

This win was sweet and he paused a moment to savor it. What a beautiful night—he would be hard-pressed to surpass it.

The owl pulled Mantis out of his musing, his voice labored. "Please bear with me until I catch my breath and find my voice." Mantis rolled his eyes. *Get over yourself. This victory is mine—better luck next time, chump!* And he prepared to move back into the shadows.

The owl got right up into his face. "Patience, patience!" the owl screeched. "And allow me to introduce myself. I am The Professor, The Winged Tiger. You *will* note my amazing five-foot wingspan." He stretched out his wings. "Truly, I am the most savage bird of prey." Folding them back to his side, he watched for the cat's reaction. Mantis offering none, the massive bird blinked his two huge and beautiful eyes before initiating a long and grisly stare-down. The face-off between the two warriors was heart-stopping, and tension vibrated in the air.

The owl spoke in quiet, rigid control. "Cat, my neck is capable of rotating a full two hundred and seventy degrees. I can see in all directions." He paused, perhaps for effect.

"My talons apply more than three hundred pounds per

square inch of deadly crushing power." The great horned owl demanded fear, demanded reverence. Dark energies radiated from him like lightning bolts. Still, Mantis never moved a muscle, never once blinked.

"Add all of those abilities with my most powerful intellect... but truly, I digress. Most incredible is what I offer you today: my services. For you see, your death—I promise to take care of it. Down to the most minute detail. Watch for it."

The owl then narrowed his eyes and fell silent for a time. When he again spoke, his words were dripping with sarcasm and infused with tight, pent-up rage. "'Oh, now, now, now, the only now, and above all now, and there is no other now, and now is thy prophet'... That was Hemingway, *For Whom the Bell Tolls.*"

Mantis remained unmoved. *I'm not giving this pompous blowhard the satisfaction of any reaction. This guy can just get lost.*

But the Professor was relentless. "It's no surprise that went right over your head. But here's something I am sure you *can* comprehend. I will be with you always. In the light of day. And in the darkest dark. Anywhere and everywhere on this round globe of Earth. Your 'now' will always be lived in fear. Of me."

He took a step closer. "But fortunate you are, too. I offer my special services, something few are ever given—a certainty about your death. You'll have no worry. I will take special care of it for you."

Mantis's heart fluttered; his chest felt funny. It was as if he was aging by the minute. *What is it about this bird that's starting to get to me? I've never been known to step away from a fight and I won't start now. But... it's like he's looking deep into my soul, seeing fear I've somehow hidden away—even to myself—and bringing it up to the surface. Crazy, I know, but that's how it feels.*

Mantis struggled to pull his eyes away. He watched as a wicked smile spread across the owl's face.

The large bird then lifted off with easy movement and was soon gone from view, but not from the mind of the huge cat. An involuntary shudder snaked down his spine, and he struggled to grasp what he had just seen and heard and felt. One thing was certain: Mantis had just made an enemy for the remainder of his life. However long that turned out to be.

POE

Poe, still crouching in the deep shadows, shrunk smaller still, as all his horrific plans of manipulation and domination evaporated like vapor. He covered his eyes with a contorted and crippled wing. "Stay quiet, Poe. Shhhh. No one sees you, Poe. They never saw Poe."

20

POE THE CROW AND HIS DECEPTION

POE

Poe let the terror of the previous night slip from his mind as if the violence had never happened. It was a brand-new day, and the crow was back in business.

Poe could not help himself. At least, that is what he often told himself the moment he was about to do some dastardly deed. Poe liked excuses. "Poe is Poe is Poe. And Poe likes shiny things. He does. He does. Always has. Poe is Poe is Poe."

The shiny black crow had been zany for as long as anyone could remember. The joke was that he'd fallen out of the nest and had landed on his head, which was in truth, the truth. Nearly the entire tree had blown down in the storm.

Injured badly and with no parents to be found, it had been natural for most to give him a free ride. But, if truth be told, Poe was much more capable than he ever let on, even to himself. His flight, though neither graceful nor strong, had great endurance and direction. His mind was cunning and capable, too. The thing was that he wanted an excuse for anything and everything. The world, to his way of thinking, owed him everything.

Perhaps things might have gone differently in his life if not for the abuse he had suffered at the hands of two boys—well, one boy, really. Carl. Carl Dunbee. Caging him was not enough, Carl taunted and teased and poked him hard with a stick. His brother Charlie did nothing to stop it.

Years had passed, yet at times Poe felt like he was right back in the rusty birdhouse, fighting for his life. His way of handling these moments was to take leave of most of his senses. Poe, the crazy crow. Night and day. Day and night. Delusions danced around him like a swarm of gnats.

Now he was thinking how he'd like to have Murfee's cape and her pink plastic sword. Then remembering his earlier plan, he thought, *Poe should have the fine reputation that goes with it, too. Poe is Batman, the superhero of all superheroes, and the sooner they all realize it, the better.* The cape itself could be a game-changer.

Hmm... Murfee thinks she's the greatest. Poe is the greatest, not the Littlest Mouse. No, Poe. And Poe is Poe is Poe. Hero is Poe. Batman is Poe. "Master of All, Poe will be. Oh! Trouble, Murfee Mouse. Poe brings you trouble in River City." Unrelenting power was what he now sought, and no one could ever imprison or make fun of him again.

Poe the Psychotic Crow now had a new and cunning low-down plan, one of deception, one steeped in troublemaking. A setup that would drive a wedge between the best of buddies. One that would bring him all he had ever wanted—all the treasure and all the power. Then he'd finally be content, this time he would. It would all be enough for him this time. Then he would be a good crow.

He waited until the Mouse family was busy in the class-room then flew silently through the barn as only he knew how to do. Stealthily, oh so quietly. Murfee believed he was her friend. Ha! Poe had no friends. Never had, never would.

And her brother, Milo—she treated him like he was so smart and so special. Poe had often seen the two of them with their heads together. Poe would get him, too. No one—no one was as smart as Poe!

On and on his twisted thoughts swirled.

The poor old crow had not a clue that what he might be feeling was jealousy, pure and simple. He could not remember ever having family or any friends he could trust, but for a time with a small girl named Lily. She had rescued him and made him her prince. Sadly, those memories were for the most part filed away in his mixed-up brain. Now, his wounded spirit sought retribution, while his ego deluded him with inflated ideas of grandeur.

Whenever he did feel loneliness or a truth he did not want to face, he gave his crazy thoughts free rein, but Poe never saw himself as anything but in full control of his faculties. Little did he know that he was gaining the reputation of being half a bubble off. He would have been offended, for sure.

It would not be long before he would have all the power he craved. Murfee's power. The power of the magical sword and the magical cape. Master of All—Poe the Smartest, Smartest Crow.

Hero is Poe. Soon all would be made right in his world. He'd never need nor ever want anything again.

"Hero Poe. Hero Poe! A handsome hero is Poe!"

The crazed bird flew to several parts of the loft where he had hidden stashes of stolen treasures, shiny, pretty things. All precious objects that caught the light, sparkled, glittered, glowed.

His loot consisted of an assortment of many lost objects belonging to the Mouse family, which he had transported in a threadbare but trusty tobacco pouch. A springy spring from a ballpoint pen, Moe was still looking high and low for it, one of Maddy's hair bows, Dahson's yellow pencil stub. How amazingly lucky it was that he'd stolen Milo's magnifier just for fun. Ha!

Poe was hungry for the chance to get his hands upon Mother Mouse's shiny string of pearls. He had wisely decided he needed to wait awhile, though. Too many things coming up missing too close together and the mice might get suspicious. Oh! He was the smartest of crows.

He angled his neck off-kilter as a memory floated to the surface, as from murky waters, of a reflection in a wavy mirror of a small crow, a brooch of diamonds with a large ruby fastened at his neck. Then he heard the voice of a young girl. "Birdie, look at my birdie. Don't you look pretty!" His eyes narrowed and he tried to focus on the beautiful sparkly, but the vision blurred and drifted away like a puff of smoke. Poe frowned, then rightened himself to concentrate on the task before him.

At last, he picked his spot, one soon to be revealed—his plan soon to unfold and bring Murfee and Milo down. He made a single trip to snatch Murfee's prized cape and sword (awkward and clumsy though his flight was) and another to transfer Milo's magnifier from the first hiding place to this one. Together cape, sword, and magnifier would be found!

Poe was so satisfied with himself that he snickered out loud, then quickly covered his beak with a contorted wing. *Oh! That Poe. He is a very devious crow.*

21
LOST

JUSTICE

Justice, mesmerized by endless waves lapping up onto the shore, lost himself in memory after memory, image after image. Courting beautiful Liza. Their midnight wedding on the courthouse steps. The birth of their son, so tiny then. Laughter and dancing. Teaching his son, Mantis, the proper ways of being a cat, a mighty predator. A killer.

Times of being away from the two of them. Times filled with worry.

Thoughts of his father began drifting in. He could do nothing but weep.

22

THE RUSE

THE CHILDREN ENTERED the music room each on tiptoe. A lone electric light bulb and the soft glow of the radio's dial illuminated the space.

Soot-covered Moe, a sight to behold, side-stepped—without a moment to spare—into the deep shadow of the radio just moments after his failed attempt to impress his siblings with a crazy firecracker trick. *Now his only chance is to hide*, Murfee thought.

Milo shimmied up the wall and flipped off the light switch, then scrambled back down. Only a faint glow of the bulb's filament and the radio remained as Mother came into the room.

She smiled at her brood, then clapped her hands together. "Come. Come, children. Time to get a head count. And a bedtime kiss." All but one of the ten gathered around her.

With forefinger and silent lip movements, she counted heads, but several of the children quietly and strategically shifted positions. Murfee found herself holding her breath.

We're not going to upset Mother. Not another safety lesson. Not again.

Mother looked at first puzzled and then concerned, her large eyes full of worry. A second time she counted. "Nine. I count nine. I'm one short. Even on my recount. All right, children, stand still while I count again." The kids stole silent glances at one another.

Murfee snuck a side-long glance at Moe, trembling in the shadows.

All at once, ever-perfect Maddy, her ever-present, perfect hair bow in place, walked over to her mother's side, looking sour, appearing ready to tattle. "Mother, I don't know how to tell you..."

Moe shifted from one foot to the other.

They all watched the agitation growing on their mother's face. Murfee was surprised to see Maddy walk up and pat her mother's arm. "Don't worry—everything's fine."

Maddy became a bit theatrical. "You know, it must have been one of those days. You'll be okay. We all have them now and then."

She seemed to stall by standing directly in front of Mother. "There's an easy explanation to all of this. Ah. Ah, you see—"

Mother looked frantic. "What, Maddy? What explanation? Tell me!"

"Well, now, Mother. You see, you counted only one twin, then you counted them twice, but forgot and subtracted times two. And Minree was dancing around with one of her ribbons, I think you counted her twice the first time, but then didn't on the recount."

Murfee looked on with amazement at her sister's performance as Maddy helped out brother Moe.

Looking sad, Maddy's voice began to warble. "I don't think, don't think you even counted me. You started to... It's okay,

Mother. And as for the math, I could explain it all much better if I could write it all out."

Mother appeared beyond confused and it worried Murfee. She watched on as her mother patted Maddy absentmindedly on the head and then pulled her close. "You're all precious to me. Every one of you. It's already been a long day; something seems a bit strange about it. Out of place." She shook her head.

"I heard this loud noise just a moment ago... and it didn't sound like a passing train. More of a boom than steel upon steel, the clank and clatter of a passing railway car... although those have been known to rattle your ears." She frowned as her eyes appeared to look off into the distance. "Your father tells me the empty coal cars make the thunderous noises that make my heart flutter and worry me in the night." Mother Mouse twisted her pearl necklace, her frown deepening. "Yes, tonight *was* strange.

Murfee watched on as her mother's expression turned again to one of puzzlement. Mother turned to her children. She spoke haltingly. "And I smelled maybe, maybe a whiff of... something. To bed. Off you go now that I know that you're all safe. And... sleep tight."

Father called out from an adjoining room, "Faylena, you only need to worry if you come up with an extra." She sighed, then squared her shoulders and forced a smile.

The kids scattered the minute she left, Murfee among them.

23
IN THE DEEP OF THE NIGHT

POE

A DROWSY POE, safe and hidden in the shadows, watched as the enormous bird barreled down out of the sky, alighting directly at Poe's feet. With impressive drama, The Professor spread his magnificent wings.

Poe became fully awake in an instant, all cylinders firing. He'd seen this deadly creature before and had hoped to never again lay eyes on him. *What does he want from Poe?* He felt himself beginning to sweat. *Poe stays safe. He does. Poe stays in the shadows. Go away, you big bird. Leave Poe alone.* He wanted to fly away but instead found himself glued to the spot, paralyzed with fear.

The owl's beautiful eyes held him spellbound—Poe could not seem to tear his eyes away—then began to speak to him in a false, sugary tone. "Dear, dear Poe. Please allow me to introduce myself as I do believe we have never formally met. I am The Professor. Don't be afraid, my new friend, my very near and dear friend. I am bringing you a gift. I will let you into my closest confidences, you lucky, lucky bird! I have the most wonderful plan, and I want you to play an important part."

Poe knew what danger lay before him. He wasn't buying any of this old spiel. He needed to stay in control, act quiet and cool. He reminded himself he was powerful Poe, a most amazing crow. Clouds scuttled away, revealing the large, round face of the moon. Diamonds of light glanced off the enormous eyes of the great horned owl. In that exact instant, memories flooded the ancient crow's neurons. Nurse Betty! The name came unbidden, and along with it the terror of the terrible dolly in some other time and place. Poe's days were numbered.

But no. He was safe. Lily would keep him safe. He was her little prince dressed in royal robes. Which was he—a powerful prince ready to rule, or a poor little baby bird alone in the world? Thoughts swirled around him as massive quantities of adrenaline pumped through his veins. Poe began to tremble and quake.

The Professor became enraged. The condescending sweetness of the great horned owl vanished in a flash. He shook with pent-up fury, his voice now tight and controlled. "Why are you afraid? I'm taking all the risk involved. There will be no blood on you. Nothing will happen to you if you do exactly as I ask."

"Blood?" Poe paled. His entire body began to spasm. At this The Professor seemed further infuriated, his eyes two pools of molten coal.

Poe spoke in a jerky sort of cadence. "Poe is Poe is Poe. Poe stays safe. Stays hidden all the time. How did you find Poe? Why do you need him?"

"You're the weak link in my scheme," the great horned owl said under his breath. He reached out lightning fast and with deadly talons grabbed him around his scrawny neck so that the two were eyeball to eyeball. Poe's eyes looked like they would pop out of his head.

"Listen to me. Listen as if your life depends upon it—which by the way, it does."

The Professor spat out his words slowly. "I have watchers everywhere and they all report to me. My scouts tell me there's a family of mice up in the loft of the barn. Twelve of them, to be exact. An even dozen. That very family of mice, along with you, are going to help me kill the cat."

"Kill the cat?" Poe sniveled. "The giant cat?"

The great horned owl screeched. "Here's how it's all going to work. Listen, silly bird!" Sighing dramatically, he released his deadly hold on Poe. "Your job is to enlist the mice, thereby drawing out the cat. You're lucky beyond your wildest dreams that you even have a job! Otherwise, you would be dispensable —worth nothing more than your poor, skinny self. I, on the other hand, am the indisputable ruler of the land. You, Poe, should always bow to me. Now. Do it now!"

The ancient crow attempted an awkward bow, gave up, and curtsied instead. The great horned owl's eyes narrowed. "You'll need to deceive them—they're your friends, right?" The Professor smirked, "Deceive them *just this once*." Poe became deathly quiet.

The Professor laughed like a maniac, his eyes gleaming in the moonlight. "Here's what you do. Start by telling them the truth—that huge cat is preparing to kill them—one by one. All of them. Get them worked up, get the entire family scared.

"I need the Mouse family for bait, you see. And I need them out in the open to draw out the cat. The night of the full moon, I expect to see all twelve of them walk out onto the old telephone wire and wait for me. This is how you sell it, Poe. Tell them it's important I meet them there out in the open. It's their show of faith, see? They put their trust in me, and I'll be their protector for the rest of their lives."

The owl's eyes narrowed to slits. "That predator cat is

always watching; he'll see the mice spread out across the wire. I've been tracking his movements. He'll climb up the old windmill tower, and while he's trying to figure out how to trap and kill that family of mice, he'll be totally distracted—that's when I'll destroy him. Then you'll all be safe. The Mouse family *and* you."

He leaned in closer yet. "Don't you dare tell them I'm using them for bait. I've gone to a great deal of trouble devising this magnificent plan—all for your benefit and your friends, the mice. Don't let me down."

The Professor's voice softened and slowed just a moment. He seemed to be considering Poe and his situation. "You know, that vicious cat eats small and medium-sized birds. Sparrows, robins, blackbirds. Crows. He'll always be on the hunt for you."

Poe gulped. Tears formed in the corner of his eyes as he fought both the need to escape and a stupefying fear that made it hard for him to move.

"Though I will be gone at times over the next several days, I am putting everything in motion," the owl said. "Give me your agreement to be ready. Comprendé, Bird?"

Poe remained silent, but The Professor again demanded an answer. His eyes steely and his tone terrifying, the owl continued, "Look at me! Listen! I have the intel—now I need the mole. Your very life depends on it, got it? You'll make sure I can find every one of them—or you'll answer to me. Which is it, Poe?" He leaned in closer.

"I'll need you to have that family of mice positioned in place when the time is right. Don't act suspicious in any way. Keep track of all twelve—don't let them scatter—it's important that they're all in one place. Vitally important."

Poe struggled to breathe. In and out. In and out. He tucked his head under a wing. His failsafe—he would hide.

And much to his delight and amazement, when he uncovered his eyes, the owl was no longer next to him. In fact, The Professor was nowhere in sight. "Oh! Poe is a lucky bird. Lucky bird is Poe! Prince is Poe?" He took a hasty swipe at the salty tears pooling in the corners of both eyes before awkwardly swooping out of sight, his destination undetermined, traveling blindly to anywhere. Anywhere to get away.

MANTIS

The farmstead again returned to the beautiful serenity of earlier in the night. Starlight and moonlight covered every bit of every surface with a silvery softness and looked like something out of a book.

The slightest of breezes arrived in waves, balmy, then with a slight coolness, the air seeming to drift and dance about as if it were finally invited to the party. Fireflies flitted through the tall grasses and locusts made their presence known. Nothing, no, not a thing, seemed out of place. All was right with the world. And nothing was not.

But in this—the deep of the night—someone else was present who saw and heard it all.

Someone who had remained perfectly hidden the entire time. An unseen predator. Mantis, the cat.

24

A SHOE WILL DO THE TRICK

SOPHIE

Rosalie came through the door carrying a food tray brimming with the day's meals and snacks. She set down her load with a piercing cry, instantly aware that many of her clocks had stopped ticking. "Sophie, do these need batteries? I forgot to bring some. Tell me next time when one stops!"

"Rosalie, I want—I *need* for the clocks to stop. I can't sleep. All I can hear is tick, tick, tick. I need them to stop!"

Rosalie's face turned florid. "Each and every tick of the clock tells me I'm one moment closer to my son, your father, coming back. Listen! You'll hear. He's coming. I thought he was coming last Tuesday for your birthday. But he didn't. Here's your card." She pulled an envelope out of her apron pocket, flopping it down on Sophie's desk, then began aggressively brushing Sophie's hair. Sophie winced and cried out. Rosalie set the hairbrush down and picked up a pair of scissors. She began to trim the ends of her granddaughter's hair.

"Rosalie! I want bangs. I keep telling you I want bangs," Sophie twisted away.

Her grandmother looked off into the distance. "I'll need to wait for Lane to come back and ask him what he thinks."

Sophie's voice grew strident. "He's never coming back. Your clocks are stupid and he's never coming back. Rosalie, I hate your stupid clocks, I hate the loft. I hate—"

A deep moan escaped unbidden from her. "Can't you call me 'Grandmother,' just once?" Holding her chest, Rosalie turned pale, threw the scissors down, and stumbled from the room.

<hr>

SOPHIE AIMED A SHOE AT THE NOISIEST CLOCK—ONE SHE HADN'T BEEN able to reach. The clock fell down, crash landing on her reading chair before bouncing up in the air, onto the floor, then rolling in tighter and tighter circles across the room before coming to a dead stop.

25
A LOOK BACK INTO THE PAST

JUSTICE

JUSTICE THE CAT lived for time spent with his young son Mantis, and Liza his beautiful wife, time that gave him something to hold onto and helped him get through many long, lonely days and nights of life now apart.

The best moments were those he'd shared with his small family, of the simple and indescribable joys of the freedom that he so cherished. The wonder of it was something Justice could never quite put into words. The frosting on the cake. For those very moments, he was in heaven.

Life on the edge of the wharf was as good as it could get. Oh, the choices that lay before him, the salty breezes that blew in from the sea and the soft and rhythmic sound of water lapping on the shore, the fresh catch of fish that flopped in nets, and the salvage of fish heads just waiting for a fine dinner by moonlight, all three as contented as they could possibly be.

Father and son often ran together until both were out of

breath, the father due to past days of confinement and the son due to his short little legs. It was a joyous time for the pair, and for Liza who sometimes watched.

Mantis, Preying Mantis. Liza called him Manny, her little Manny man. It would be Justice's job as a father to make a real man out of him.

Justice, a natural athlete, was delighted to find that his son was as well. He taught his son how to leap through the air, to twist and turn all while flying through space, how to move with tremendous stealth, how to catch the smallest movement of another, and how to use his nighttime vision to find his way.

Justice hid from him, daring the kitten to find him. The two quietly climbed up and over large and small obstacles near the wharf, playing spies with counterspies in pursuit, and at other times pursuing an imaginary, invisible prey. He tried to startle Mantis when they traveled through the darkness, but his small son was quick to adjust to the unexpected pounce, the cunning of his father hiding, then chasing—all without making a sound.

One night, the two of them went even so far, just for fun, as to take a midnight swim along the dock. They swam and swam under a spectacular night sky while the reflection of a full moon danced upon the waves.

Then the two floated for a while. "Mantis, I came a long way to see the ocean and now it seems I can't get enough of it. Probably never told you, but I left my first home when I was just a kid. Hitched a ride on a rickety old farm truck. Yep. It was a long ride," he said with a chuckle. "I left and never looked back." He paused a moment in his telling. "I do miss my father sometimes. I'd love to take the two of you to meet him some-day. His name's Tyrus, and he's a most interesting cat. He never seems to understand the simple truth of it—that a cat is a cat is a cat—and was born to do the very thing for which he's been designed."

Justice noticed his small son's confusion, so he went on to explain. "Your grandfather doesn't even have a taste for mice. He only enjoys the chase. He's never seen himself as a predator, which is a cat's sole purpose for the life he has out on the farm. Here we haven't had to catch our prey... we can easily find our feast out on the docks in a fisherman's nets. But on the farm, that's a cat's job—to rid the place of mice.

"Your grandfather is an embarrassment to all his family because he never understood the true purpose, the design, of a cat, and it's only because of a farmer that his supper can be found. Promise me you'll always remember a cat is a cat is a cat."

His son looked as if his mind was spinning. "Hmm... a cat is a cat is a cat."

Quiet ensued. For a time, the two simply gave themselves up to the gentle movement of the waves.

"Some cats don't like the water, but I always have, just like you," They returned to Liza looking more like drowned rats than cats.

His small son grew larger, stronger, and lean as the two raced and played. Justice got a chance to stretch his knotted limbs. And free himself, too, of unbidden tension that at times arose out of nowhere.

He despised the murderous rage and the helpless feelings along with the bitterness and the red-hot temper that followed. They took him to a dark place, a blackness of head and heart he had to struggle to escape.

It was as if there were two of him. One, the contented husband and father. The other, full of the unrelenting, blinding fury that began when caged, helpless and frightened, that night on the dock. Never again could he trust the world around him. Humans had betrayed him then and ever since. It seemed unrelenting. And it was then he would tell Mantis hate-filled stories, stories meant to twist and mold him, to shape him into a powerful force of rage and distrust. As if his young son could redeem it all.

He doled out advice to his son. "Bad things happen out in the world. You can never trust anyone, Mantis. If I let my guard down when I'm in my other home, trapped in the attic, it's always a mistake. You'll need to watch your back. Never take someone's word at face value. Always, always be ready to fight, to kill if you need to. Remember, a cat is a vicious predator, worthy of fear.

"Never walk away from your destiny. Fight with all your might. Make a name for yourself and make your family proud. Remember something your grandfather long ago forgot. A cat is a cat is a cat." The growing kitten seemed to soak up every word.

***

LIZA

Liza watched with despair as Justice attempted to shape Manny into the vicious predator her husband hoped their son to be, helpless to stop the metamorphosis unfolding before her.

She also tried to shape her son, but in an opposite direction. She wanted him to see the beauty in the world, not the anger, not the hate. She showed him the stars and pointed out the different constellations so very high overhead.

Liza mourned for both her husband and her son. Each was becoming lost to her.

MANNY

For many days and nights, Justice was absent as mother and son explored their world. Manny wondered when his father would make his next escape and join them again. *Soon, I hope!*

They each missed Justice, but there were places to explore and much to learn and enjoy. (Creamy Cone was the place for their favorite nighttime snack!)

Manny had the endless energy of a kitten and often ran ahead, then waited for his mother to catch up with him. She seemed to move a little more slowly with each next adventure, but he waited patiently or raced back to her side.

Liza pointed out Sirius to Manny and told him that it was about twice the size of the sun and the very brightest star in the night sky. "Would you believe it? Placed side by side, it'd be twenty times brighter!

"In Egypt, Sirius is called the Nile Star, and sometimes it's called the Dog Star because it's part of the constellation Canis Major," she explained. "That's Latin for the Greater Dog. Oh! There are nights I think I could simply get lost looking up at the heavens. It's really a wonder-filled world everywhere if you just look for it."

His mother went on to tell him that he, too, was an amazing creation just like each and every star in each constellation—every single star in the sky. "There's a great design to all of it, to all of *you*. Take your whiskers—just one example. Do you think there's no reason for those long flexible hairs on your face?" she asked. "You were designed by a greater hand than *anything* you can see," she smiled. "Found in the sky, in the moon and stars above us—the Architect of the Canopy of the Presence. That's the understanding of many.

"You know, Manny, it's my belief that the one who designed it all—everything you can see with your eyes and so many things you can't—is everywhere, not just high above. I think the Architect, the Creator, is truly everywhere and in everything and in every one of us." She shifted her focus from her son's face to gaze up at the Milky Way, splayed dramatically across the heavens, and then again began to speak. "And nothing and no one is ever gone but lives on for all time... in us each."

Moonlight brushed the two figures in the softest silver. In the distance, they heard waves lapping onto the shore, their age-old rhythms in an age-old dance.

His mother turned her attention back to him. "Each little star has a job to do. Just like we all do. A purpose. That's right, Manny—you have a purpose." He struggled intently to understand. She seemed to notice his puzzlement "Well, let's go back to the whiskers—the very reason for them. Three reasons, my little Manny man: to feel our way around, to show our mood— I can tell a lot just by looking at you. And if you pay attention you can learn by looking, too. You can see anger, agitation, happiness, and contentment—just to name a few.

"Your whiskers help you get around in the dark because they're designed to feel the slightest change of breeze. Amazing, I think. Don't you?"

"What's the third one, Mother? You said three."

"Oh! This one is important, and I want you to remember it. Number three will truly keep you out of a bind, it'll keep you from getting stuck!"

She went on to explain. "You can even tell if you'll fit through a tight spot by those same hairs on your face. Manny, they're about as wide as your body, sort of like a natural ruler. Pretty neat, right?"

He quickly nodded. This stuff was interesting!

She abruptly changed the subject. "I need to show you the house where your father lives sometimes. I'll show you how to get there. Soon, Manny."

He saw that her eyes held a faraway look and suddenly he felt an odd, funny feeling like butterflies in his stomach. *Why is that?* he wondered. His mother looked so very serious then, and he vowed to pay close attention to her.

"Manny, your father's love for us is bigger than the night-time sky, but he holds a duty of the heart to Sophie, the young girl he talks about, locked away by grandparents, no less! He feels he holds Sophie to this earth, and he is all she has—and you have me, and I have you. Do you understand a little?

"Your father has at times been held captive in the attic of that awful house, too. There its very darkness has seeped a bit into his soul. Oh, but his is such a good, good heart. You see, he's there for the sake of the girl, to keep her safe. He has honor and he feels he has purpose. He'll always return to her. He'll never totally abandon his post."

All this seriousness was not lost on him. Was there anything he could do to help his father? Or maybe help the young girl?

MANNY AND HIS MOTHER WERE JUST BLOCKS FROM THE OCEAN. THE smell of salt water and fish hung heavy in the air. Their day ended with laughter, and lots of it, the kind that made Manny's stomach hurt and his eyes water.

Everything started innocently enough with "Catch a Falling Star," a song that they had sung so often Manny could sing it in his sleep. In fact, he often did. Or hummed a little of it.

Liza had the most beautiful voice and though the tune was first sung soft as a feather, when Manny joined in the volume soared.

He started laughing and couldn't seem to stop. When he at last caught his breath he told his mother, "Father had a great idea. You ought to hear us sing with the words we made up!"

"And how is that, my little Manny man?"

He hoped she would think their version was funny and that it didn't ruin her favorite song. "We only have the first part figured out, but we can sing it two ways," he said. "Okay. Here goes... Smoke a strong cigar or keep it in your pocket. Or... and I like this one, too... Grab a little mouse an' squish it in your pocket."

"Your father! What in the world am I going to do with him? With the two of you?"

Then they began to sing with made-up words and danced like crazy fools. And the silliness meter, if there ever were such a thing, would have set a record.

Justice was still absent, so for now it continued to be just the two of them. Manny and his mother slowly and silently walked back from the Creamy Cone dumpster.

Manny had gorged on three flavors of ice cream and half a sugar cone. Yum. But oh, he could feel the tightness of a very full stomach. Finally, he noticed that his mother had grown silent.

Why are we walking so slow? And why isn't she talking? he

asked himself. *I wonder what she's thinking. Wonder if she decided she didn't like the way we changed her song. I'll tell her I'm sorry.*

They were soon found again caught up in the heavens. They simply sat side by side, each lost in the wonder of the stars.

Long moments passed. Manny was itching for his mother to say something. She sighed finally and then began to speak. "Wherever you are, look up into the sky. See how it stretches from one horizon all the way across to the other? And on a night just like this, see how bright the heavens shine? That's my love for you, always shining down." Her laughter was a soft melodious sound. "And you are the brightest star, Manny. That will always be you. We'll never really be apart."

What does she mean—we'll never be apart? I'd never leave her, never, ever, ever! Manny thought. She looked so sad. He had never seen her this way. Suddenly he felt frightened, though he didn't really know why.

He dropped his head and stared at the ground. He didn't want this conversation to continue, not in the direction it seemed to be taking, but continue it did.

"Manny, I need to talk to you. I need you to really listen and I need you to be brave. I have to leave you, my Manny man. I have to go away."

"Can't I go with you? I can keep up. I can run fast; I'll do anything you need me to. And—and I promise I won't mess up your favorite song, I'll sing it right. I'm sorry, I am," he cried.

"Manny, it's nothing you've done. No, you've been the best son I could have ever had and I'm always so proud of you. But there's some advice I need to tell you while I can. I may already be short of time.

"Do the important things right, but don't ever be afraid to be silly sometimes and have fun, just like with your crazy song.

Look for things to make you laugh or smile. Keep looking for the wonder and the good in the world and you'll find it.

"Enjoy the little things and the rest will take care of itself. And sadness can really only last as long as you let it, so... let yourself be happy again." She paused. "I must get a message to your father. You can help each other through all of it. I just need a little more time to make the arrangements. Just a little more time."

"I don't know what you're talking about, and I still want to go." Manny hadn't understood a thing his mother was trying to say.

"Listen. Listen, Manny! It's so late... I thought there was more time. Your father has never been away this long. Something must have changed, making it hard for him to return to us. But I need him now to be here for you.

"Manny, there's a tall skinny young man on the wharf. Joe... red-headed, you can't miss him. He knows where your father lives part-time in that attic with Sophie. Joe and your father made a game of it once and Joe followed Justice home. He knows of you and of me, too. Manny, he's a friend. Maybe he can help. My precious boy, I am dying. I don't know how else to tell you. Not today, but maybe soon. And right now, I'm just tired, so tired... " Her words trailed off. "I *need* a little more time."

Before he could catch his breath, his mother went on to explain that the very thing that was now taking her life was the same that had taken her own mother's.

Something that had now been passed down from mother to child. "Precious Manny, my kidneys are shutting down. They call it renal failure. I've had this a long time and hoped I'd be okay, but things are changing fast. I'm afraid I've come to the end of this illness. I was just fooling myself that I had time to make things right for you. I'm so sorry."

Manny struggled to comprehend all that she was saying. It was simply too much to take in. His eyes filled with tears.

"Please don't cry, my little man. Somehow everything will all turn out all right. It has to."

Neither spoke for long moments. Then she turned to him and held his face. "Manny, they were all wrong, those who named this star. You're my Sirius, my little one. Dog Star. Nile Star. Little Manny—my brightest star." She smiled. "Remember, my fine son, that you too have a purpose. Find out what it is. Always choose the light. Never the darkness. And never run from what you *know* is true." She drew herself up into the regal posture of a feline Egyptian princess. "Stand up for it instead."

He sobbed soundlessly then, his tears streaming down, whiskers sodden and droopy with them.

Liza spoke again. "You see," a crooked smile playing across her features, "we can still be together—we're together—high up there nestled amongst the constellations. And remember, my sweet boy, you are the brightest star of them all."

She drew Manny close and wrapped her arms so snuggly around him as if she would never let him go.

MANNY

One morning, Manny awoke to find that his mother had died sometime in the night. He knew it was true the minute he looked at her. She lay so perfectly still. And it was as if all the light and shimmer, all the life, had simply disappeared from her beautiful silvery fur. He saw that the light that was his mother had left, too.

He didn't know how to find his father; his mother had never said. She hadn't had time to show him. Manny's entire world changed in that single moment. His kitten days, his childhood, were gone in a flash, and his life as he knew it would never be the same.

And so, he did the only thing that he could think to do. He shut it all out, every bit of it, and he ran. He ran to nowhere because he had nowhere to go. And he ran and he ran and he ran until he could run no more.

26

MOON PHASES

MOE

MOE WALKED with quiet steps into the secret rocket-building area. He wanted with his whole heart to fit in and be a part of this great enterprise. First on the list, avoid blowing something up.

He watched on as Milo and Dahson worked to prepare for the maiden launch. The atmosphere was tense. Wonderful potential and brand-new possibilities lay heavy in the air.

The rocket was made of Tinker Toy pieces encircled by a number of firecrackers tightly fastened together with twine, their fuses twisted together into one fat stub. The boys had folded a large sheet of aluminum foil over and over to create their innovative heat shield between the explosives and the designated passenger section.

A worn 'Fire Chief - Strike Anywhere' matchbox served as the launch pad, while two wooden matches chewed to a calculated length secured its angle.

Dahson was reviewing his recent calculations and taking

another look at the rail line schedule, each test launch to be timed with an empty freight train, its rattle and its boom.

Moe swelled with pride. It was he who came up with the idea of covering up the noise of each rocket's liftoff with the explosive sounds of passing coal cars as they traversed a rough crossing nearby. He gave Dahson a thumbs up when he walked by him.

Moe then carefully examined the wobbly rocket platform. Lipton, the largest and oldest of the boys, did nothing but look on with disdain at the antics of his brothers. "Idiots!" he muttered under his breath as he stalked off. Moe, watching him leave, simply shook his head in wonderment.

Dahson made final calculations of the rocket's trajectory, marking with a short red crayon on a brown paper grain sack, his face almost touching the page, his yellow plastic frames balanced at the tip of his nose. Absentmindedly, he pushed his glasses back up where they belonged.

Then Moe looked on as Milo checked out a pulley system he'd designed to reposition the entire rocket if needed. The next moment, Milo swung through space like a crazed gymnast, a wild smile playing across his face. "Whoa! This is nice," Milo said, and Moe couldn't help but grin.

Moe next examined the twisted fuses of the firecrackers— the rocket power. He was in awe of the goings-on, and he couldn't restrain his natural enthusiasm a moment longer. He pretended to be supervising the entire operation. Of course, that meant dancing around and waving his arms, his cap somehow remaining on his head. He shouted, "I hope you know what you're—what we're—messing with: NITRO, TNT, and it could all blow."

He pantomimed a huge explosion, paused a moment, then looked with great seriousness at his brothers, who completely ignored him.

In the crazy mix of this, a large, shiny black insect crawled past, catching Moe's attention. "Dahson. Dahson! We still need an astronaut. How about sending a beetle like that one over there—or a stink bug? Either of 'em could take a tough landing and live to tell it."

Dahson looked up over his plastic frames now positioned like bifocals, blinked his eyes, and stared at him dismissively. "Moe. You have entirely missed the point. We'll want information. Trajectory assessments. Thrust, ease of landing, success of mission." He shook his head, and his glasses settled even lower, nearly falling off his face. He paid this no mind.

He did take a quick glance at the beetle. "Tell me. Just how are you going to get that out of a bug?"

The beetle moved away from the group at a determined pace, intermittently shaking his head.

Moe spoke up loudly. "If I wasn't stuck with chores, I'd go. It would be a hoot... "

"I'll do your chores for you," Milo replied at once, a bit of a smirk playing on his face. Moe's face fell and Milo laughed. "But I'd go. I would! I've dreamed about it for a long time, as long as I can remember," Milo said wistfully.

Dahson interrupted, "It won't work! You're both too heavy. The less weight our first rocket has to carry, the better. We need someone small, lightweight, and streamlined. We need—"

"Murfee!" Moe and Milo shouted out at the same time. All three nodded in agreement, Moe himself looking tremendously relieved.

MOE THOUGHT OF A PLAN TO REDEEM HIMSELF IN MILO'S EYES AND perhaps in his own. He quietly left the area hoping he'd somehow be missed and made his way to the classroom—and the *M* encyclopedia. After a bit, he found what he was searching for in the large book. "Moon and Moon Phases."

"Hmm." The lengthy article had him scratching his head. In fact, it honestly made his head hurt. But when he turned over a few more pages he found something that looked important, maybe pivotal to their project.

It was a colored diagram showing a full moon on one side, and a new moon on the other. Spaced equally between were half-moons, crescent moons, and one that made no sense whatsoever… waning gibbous, glory be. What was that?

But he had what he had come for. Vital information that could help them with their launch.

Such was his excitement that he barely remembered making his way back to his brothers.

"You are right to push this rocket launch forward as soon as possible. Now is most definitely the correct time," he told them. He dearly hoped he was sounding authoritative, and at the very least quite knowledgeable. "Scientifically speaking."

Dahson and Milo looked at him like he had crawled out from under a rock. Milo was the first to speak. "What are you talking about?"

This wasn't going at all the way Moe had hoped. He had important information, if only he could make them listen. "See, it's almost a full moon now—and we'd have the best chance with the bigger target, don't you think…" His voice trailed off.

Dahson blinked his eyes at Moe behind his spectacles then said, "The moon does not change size, the perceived changes are simply due to its lumination. It's all very simple." Both Dahson and Milo looked squarely at him and in unison shook their heads. Milo let out a long sigh.

Moe's previous excitement fully deflated like a punctured

balloon. His entire body slumped. *If I could crawl into a hole, I would. So much for trying to save the day,* he thought. He glanced over at his brother Milo and saw something like pity now traveling across his brother's face.

"Guess you were only trying to help," Milo said. "But you gotta use consistent and rational thought and reasoning. That's what Dahson always says. Our initial moon rocket is going to take every bit of that. Good judgement all the way." Milo turned to face Dahson. "We might be lucky with this first launch to land the rocket safely up on the roof—forget making it all the way to the moon. There sure are a lot of variables to consider."

Moe silently nodded, a sheepish expression playing over his features, then watched with amazement as Milo's face fell. "Oh my gosh!" Milo sank down to his knees and held his head in his hands. "What was I thinking? No better than Moe's logic. Sorry, Moe. I've made fun of you all the while I was getting ready to sacrifice Murfee. It's a test flight! What if she landed on the roof and couldn't get safely back down into the loft? Oh! I would have never forgiven myself."

Dahson, peering over his yellow eyeglasses, asked, "What in the world are you talking about?"

Milo spoke with care. "Guys. It's nuts to send Murfee up on our first rocket, even if it's only to the rooftop and not clear up to the moon. How do we get her back home in one piece? For now, manned space flight is out."

"Maybe we could try the moon trip later when you get it all figured out. It'd take a lot more firepower. You know, for a rooftop destination we could attach a really long piece of twine. An astronaut could use it to climb back down into the loft," Moe offered.

Milo appeared starstruck. "I think, brother Moe, I have sometimes underestimated you. Thanks."

Moe looked like he had swallowed a bug. Then, when he recovered, pure ecstasy lit up his face.

"Hmm..." was all that Dahson could say. The three stared off into space. *What new challenges lay in wait?* Moe was sure not one of them knew.

27
CATCH A FALLING STAR

JOE

Joe returned to the wharf, finding his friend on the pier, incapacitated still. Joe began to first hum, then sing, "Catch a Falling Star," and after a long moment got Justice to smile. Joe relayed to Justice that he had watched his and Liza's midnight wedding on the courthouse steps, toothless, white-haired Old Tom officiating. Joe spoke with reverence of the profound experience of hearing Liza sing. "I listened for the first time with my whole heart. Justice, I had never done that before," Joe said. "Your wife taught me that, a lesson that's with me still. And I'll never forget any of that."

28

MISCHIEF, SHORT AND SIMPLE

POE

With great effort, Poe flew into the Mouse family classroom. He was clumsier than ever due to one bulging cloth tobacco pouch draped over a crippled wing.

He emptied his treasures out on the floor near the front of the room. A shiny copper penny, a small mirror, a ribbon, and a long metal spring. A second trip brought items from his latest stash: Milo's magnifier, and Murfee's cape and sword. He surveyed it all with pride.

This was a new plan, a good and cunning plan. He'd expose Murfee Mouse to her entire family and ruin Murfee's reputation for good. She would turn out to be the thief they'd been searching for. Oh! What a smart crow was Poe. Here in the classroom, they would all see her deception. Then he would simply sneak off with her cape and sword when they were all caught up in the awful thing that Murfee had done.

Finally, he'd have both cape and sword to call his own. He

found himself chuckling. "Oh, that Poe is a mighty smart crow! And Poe is Poe is Poe. Hero is Poe."

He arranged his ill-gotten gains with care under the open front cover of the large, bluff-colored leather *M* encyclopedia, leaving only a portion exposed... the scarlet edge of Murfee's cape.

Now to get them all here and draw them into his plan. The crow scratched his head, the light coming in from the cupola above coloring his feathers a shiny, oily, purple and black.

THE CROW WATCHED FROM THE SHADOWS, HIS FAVORITE PLACE, A SAFE place, as unbelievably Milo and only Milo came into the room. *Oh. The gods are smiling down on Poe.* He held his breath in joyful disbelief. This was sure to drive a wedge between the littlest mouse and her best friend, brother Milo. What unbelievable luck. *Lucky, lucky is Poe. Poe is the luckiest crow!*

MILO

Milo walked in with purpose, thinking about moon phases. Maybe there really was information in the *M* that they had missed and that could help with the rocket mission.

Something caught his eye... a sliver of scarlet peeking out from under the large book. Struggling, he pushed the heavy front cover up and over. That piece of scarlet—it was Murfee's cape. And next to it a miniature plastic sword.

Under the cape, he found concealed a whole pile of loot, all lost treasures of the Mouse family!

Milo sunk to his knees. "No, no, no. Murfee can't be the

thief. Maddy's special penny. Her Lincoln wheat penny. Mother's mirror! Why... why would Murfee have Mother's mirror? And one of Minree's ribbons. Dahson's spring. My magnifier!"

He looked physically ill. He couldn't—he wouldn't believe this! He would have trusted Murfee forever. She was great—for a girl. She was his friend.

He stood and picked up his precious magnifier. He turned it over in his hands. "I had it all wrong. Thought findin' it would be the best thing ever. Now I find out the best thing—well, I just lost it."

Not knowing what else to do and somehow still wanting to protect his sister, he struggled with the book's cover until all the treasures were hidden once again, the cape included. Looking brokenhearted and cradling his precious magnifier, he slowly left the room.

***

POE

Poe peered down from his rafter perch. Though it had not quite gone as he had planned, it was going to work out just right. Maybe better than he had hoped.

Soon Poe would have the magic. *Magical magic is Poe. Hero is Poe.*

29

OF MOONLIGHT AND SILVER AND VAPORS OF LIGHT

MURFEE

Murfee was done though it was only the middle of the day. Feet dragging, she wandered throughout the loft, avoiding everyone as much as possible. She merely wanted to lie down and sleep for the next week—forget sword practice, forget dreams of adventure.

Mouse Marvel. The Red-Caped Crusader. Guardian of the Galaxies. Who was she kidding? She was having trouble keeping her eyes open, and her mind, though tired beyond belief, kept returning to her unrelenting fear of cats. Images of Moe's monster-sized, shadow-puppet cat devouring one little mouse kept popping up in her mind's eye. Magic and wishing hadn't done a thing to stop her from imagining the worst. What kind of hero did she really think she would be?

All that remained of her grand ambitions was a deflated ego and a heavy heart. The tiny mouse was mentally and physically exhausted. Much worse, she had given up on herself.

Murfee walked to the place where her dreams first took

flight. Nothing or no one could stir her heart now. Someone else would have to come along to save the day. It wouldn't be a one-inch mouse.

Maybe Milo could wear the magic cape and rescue them all. Live out her fantasies, have her dreams. He was the worthy one, worthy to wear the cape. She herself, despite all her yearning, all her best efforts, would never amount to one single thing. She was too afraid of cats.

She struggled up a tower of hay bales. Halfway up she stopped to catch her breath, then pulled and clawed the rest of the way to the very top before plopping herself down with a heavy sigh. "Forget all the big ideas, Murfee. Think small. You gotta think small. You gotta remember—you're just an inch." Those were her last thoughts before she fell into a deep slumber.

Murfee dreamed of moonlight and silver and vapors of light, like nothing she'd ever before encountered. A watery mist moved through a room that was missing any sort of ceiling or walls, but the path she was walking felt solid and reassuring. She wasn't at all afraid. Still, she struggled to make some sense out of any of it. Where was she?

It was the very strangest place, one that defied any real understanding, still, Murfee felt very much at peace.

"Why did you give up on your own dream?" a deep male voice called out. "You know you have within you everything you'll ever need to succeed—or do you? Do you know you are special, Murfee Mouse?" he asked kindly.

She found herself too tired to try to come up with an answer. The scene dissolved into nothingness and on and on she slept.

30
LIFT OFF

MOE

THE BOYS REMAINED hard at work at the building site. Moe stood nearby, ready to be of some kind of help. A new problem had popped up. How would both drag and an increase in the rocket load affect the maiden flight? A large spool of twine, the reason for these new challenges, seemed to dominate the space and had Dahson muttering under his breath, rapidly recalculating his previous assumptions. Moe watched on as his scholarly brother moved his specs further up on his nose and shook his head. Discarded pieces torn from an old brown paper sack were covered with Dahson's red crayon scribbles. They looked like a giant pile of leaves, a virtual mountain of crimson and tan.

Moe waded into the mound of paper scraps and let himself sink down into its depths. He was having a most difficult time with the wait.

The constant thinking hurt his head. It usually did. *Shouldn't we just get on with it? There's a whole lot of firepower left in the crate so it's not like we're gonna run short. Get with it, guys.* At last, Moe consoled himself that Dahson would find the answers. He always came through.

"I don't know quite how to determine what that long length of string is going to do to our latest figures. I simply don't," Dahson said, dejected. At this, the world as Moe knew it had come to an end.

MILO

Milo was glad to lose himself to the rocketry and to forget for a minute his terrible heartache and his sister, the thief. After a moment, he spoke thoughtfully. "The twine is a great idea. It'll help anybody taking that first manned flight to get down from the roof. Still, it'd be good to have a parachute for backup. I've been experimenting with that. Maybe we could even use the safety chute to replace the long piece of string and decrease some of our rocket load. I'll be right back." He quickly left the room.

PEEP

Peep could barely contain herself. Boy, was she somethin'! She was on the way to the giant firecracker factory, leading the girls minus Murfee who was nowhere to be found. *Oh, well. She already knows about it because I saw her there before,* she thought.

To further defend her decision to expose a secret, she said, "If Murfee got to see this place, we get to, too."

Soon the five—Peep, the twins, Minree, and Maddy—

found themselves in something like a parallel universe, a true world of wonder. All were speechless, Peep included.

The three-story Tinker Toy tower rose from the floor surrounded by rockets in various stages of completion. In the middle of it all was the launch pad, and a rocket at the ready.

MURFEE

Murfee came in right on the heels of Peep and her entourage. She had only moments before decided she was ready for a rocket ride; her dream had brought her courage. Now, what was it the voice had said? Something about Murfee being special and having within all she'd ever need to succeed. Now she had to prove it to the rest of them. She had raced to the launch site to volunteer before she could change her mind. A slow smile spread across her face. Could it be true? Was this *the* moment her adventures took flight?

Time to be a hero—instead of an inch!

Lost in all these thoughts, she stopped in her tracks— brother Milo plowed into her back, a bulky bundle in his arms.

The next minute Dahson ran up and lifted Murfee into the air. "Just as I thought. Perfect weight, streamlined. Of adequate intelligence to carry out the assignment." He let her down with a plop. "Timely, too, as it looks like Milo has brought that all-important parachute."

Moe's eyes lit up. "Murfee! Oh, Murfee, it's great you're here!" He took both her hands in his. "You know, you've always wanted to get a really good look at the stars. Well, here's your chance!"

Dahson looked at her intently. "What Moe is attempting to

say is that we have a proposition." He thoughtfully pushed his specs up again to where they belonged.

Milo walked over and got in her face. "You're always talking about going on a real adventure. What do ya say?" He stared at her and all she could do was blink. "I can make sure you get your wish!"

Dahson spoke boldly. "It is perfectly safe. We've worked it all out. Our team has just recently assembled the necessary safety equipment for manned space flight. You have a parachute to get you home, and then, of course, we'll need your full recount of everything from the beginning of the launch."

Moe nudged Milo aside. "It should be the opportunity of a lifetime." He grabbed her by her waist and hummed a lively tune as he danced her a few steps around the room.

By now Murfee felt almost dizzy with all that was happening. She struggled to understand the glare her best bud Milo continued to deliver. Strangely, no one else seemed to notice the angry looks directed solely at her.

She knew he'd been upset about the loss of his magnifier, but she hadn't been around him much lately to even discuss it. Privately she'd searched for the magnifier, and she'd give him whatever support he needed. She always thought he had her back, too, but now she wasn't so sure.

Milo gave Murfee several rough pushes toward the rocket ship. Like a sleepwalker, she started to climb onto the matchbook launch pad, thinking she must be caught up in some crazy, crazy dream.

Dahson said, "Milo, Murfee has yet to accept this mission. I would say having an adventure is, by its very nature, a voluntary proposition. Given the precise nature of this endeavor, she'll have to serve as a statistician, and there should be some training..."

Suddenly, all the voices faded, and Murfee, the one-inch

mouse, saw herself as from a distance. This strange, out-of-body experience yielded a great prize. For the first time since she had vowed to become a hero, she knew for certain her opportunity to prove herself was now or never. She needed to take action—not sit around and think about it. The superheroes in the comic books had shown her that heroes didn't wait. Page after page, without fail, they faced challenges as they flew off into adventure—each and every time with some kind of risk attached. And heroes didn't grow on trees. They were special—just like her.

And if she was ever going to become the hero her family needed, she needed to start somewhere. It was time. Superman had to start somewhere. Batman and Robin. They all had to start somewhere.

Milo was staring at her again. How was it, though, that her favorite pal, her trusted brother, looked at her with such dislike? She'd done nothing to deserve that and it hurt! Here was a rare and amazing opportunity to simply fly—far, far away.

Here she had an opportunity to make or break, but without the powerful magic of the cape. The rocket could propel her up and out of the barn loft. *Hmm... what were the exact words in my dream again—something about me being special and having everything I needed already on the inside? A hero without the magic, right?*

She could do her part. She could do it. All she had to do was hang on for the ride and make sure to keep her eyes shut.

With renewed excitement, Murfee clambered aboard the homemade rocket ship. Milo Mouse reached across her and firmly fastened several twisted-twine safety belts. *If I'm going to change my mind, now's the time,* Murfee thought. *Oh, wait! This may not be the best idea I've ever had.*

Milo leaned down to pick up the parachute he had made

from a piece of a deep-red bandana kerchief. Standing, he attached this contraption to her back. "There's a real trick to this parachute business," he said, an edge to his voice.

While making a show of folding and refolding it, Milo spoke so that only she could hear. "I would never have believed it, but I have proof. Yep! I saw with my own eyes. My own sister —a thief. Got my magnifier right here, and pretty soon I'll tell all of them where their stuff is. Serves you right, Murfee. And thanks for telling the girls about this place. I trusted you. How could you?"

Milo's accusations sealed it for the littlest mouse. *What do I have to lose? Nothing,* she thought.

Milo looked her squarely in the eye and spoke so all could hear. "We'll want her to come down easy and on her feet instead of on her back all tangled up in the string."

Bug-eyed, Murfee nodded in agreement. She had an immediate vision of a tangled mess of string and rocket and mouse.

Her thoughts raced on. *Hmm. I wonder what Milo meant when he said he had proof. I would never believe anything bad about him. Nope! Not even now.* As her brothers and sisters looked on Murfee grabbed a firmer handhold on the rocket and squeezed her eyes tight. Moe shoved Milo out of the way and lit the fuse. Yellow-orange flames sizzled and popped. The firecrackers exploded, sending the rocket ship blasting up towards the small patch of blue seen in the roof high overhead.

31
ROOFTOP

Up, up into the sky Murfee traveled, leaving the barn behind her like a tiny air-borne missile. Firecracker fragments flew off in all directions, and the foil heat shield twisted away in the wind. The ride was amazing. Murfee was flying without the magic of her cape. She was a true superhero!

The rocket ship contraption began to spin crazily, and in a flash, a blur, just as she opened her eyes, she saw the barn roof rise to meet her. Crash! The Tinker Toy pieces, all that was left of the rocket, rolled down to the roof's edge with Murfee still attached. Her eyes were huge and terror filled.

The rocket jerked to a sudden stop when a piece of twine snagged a rough wooden shingle. The small mouse shuddered. She found herself looking straight up at a turquoise sky and huge cumulus clouds.

She muttered shakily. "Whew! Gotta watch out what I wish for. I'd like to get out of this in one piece."

Loosening the twisted-twine ropes that tied her to the ship

made the rocket shift, scoot, and make one partial rotation. It came to rest at the furthest edge of the roof, dragging her slightly with it and pulling her to her side.

Murfee stared down at the ground far below. Her vision blurred and her stomach gave a lurch. She clutched onto Tinker Toy pieces and the bits of twine that entangled her.

Again, the whole thing shifted a bit, resettling. Murfee tried not to move. As she closed her eyes her stomach quieted. "Opportunity of a lifetime... a fun-filled ride. Glad the guys thought of me," she said wryly. Then she remembered it was she who had accepted the challenge, so she could begin her secret hero quest. Milo's terrible words had propelled her, too, but it was she who'd made the final choice.

"Oh, Murfee Mouse!" she said to herself. "What *were* you thinking?"

MOE

Below, Moe gawked open-mouthed at the roof opening high overhead. The silence was heavy. A movement, a something, filled the piece of sky far above. Every one of Murfee's siblings, Moe included, held their breath.

One red bandana parachute floated beautifully to the ground. It landed in the center of their midst, billowed upward and outward, and then deflated with a soft whoosh. Murfee was nowhere in sight. With shocked expressions, their faces fell. Everyone was speechless.

He was the first to react. As usual, his thoughts poured out the moment he thought of them. "Guys, I think we're toast."

MURFEE

Murfee lay still as a statue, afraid to breathe. The distance to the ground was staggering. She felt dizzy and nauseous and terrified. A portion of the rocket ship hung out into space.

Murfee again closed her eyes. Then she opened them but forced her gaze anywhere but down, as she felt about with her hands, the rest of her body held rigid. "Look down and you're a goner, Murfee Mouse."

With extreme care, she again worked to loosen her safety belts, the twine that still held her tight. The rocket moved ever so little, now hanging precariously over the roof's edge, but somehow remaining balanced as she struggled to untangle the twisted cotton string. She clung to the roof as the safety belts pulled against her body.

Trying to stay calm, she used one hand to work the last wrap—just as the rocket slipped off the barn. Murfee was pulled to the edge as the rocket fell. She grasped at anything, finally grabbing a protruding shingle nail as the loosened twine of her safety belt finally released her. She hung on for dear life while the rocket fell down, down, down. She dangled for a moment while she steadied herself, then straining as hard as she could, pulled herself back onto the old, shingled roof.

Keeping her profile low, she carefully moved upward and away from the roof's edge.

Finally, she stood, let out a deep breath, and said, "I wonder if anyone has ever died of pure fright. Hmm, hard to know, they'd never live to tell it."

She held her right hand over her heart and sucked air deep into her lungs. She looked around at the forlorn countryside of the rooftop, and a sinking feeling set in. Murfee closed her eyes and shook her head.

POE

Poe silently watched on. The crazy crow, the late afternoon's light bouncing off his oily feathers and the point of his beak, hid behind the barn's cupola higher up on the roof. He peered around a corner, agitated.

He heard a sound behind him and pivoted, his nerves all on end. The Professor was sleeping on a branch of the huge maple tree. The owl looked powerful even as he slept. Poe looked from The Professor to Murfee and back, covered his head with both wing tips, and whimpered.

MADDY

All Murfee's brothers and sisters remained shell-shocked, with the exception of Maddy. She was furious. "What were you thinking?! You should have asked me! I would have told you it was pure insanity right off, *before* it went too far!"

At this, Dahson became animated and spoke with great enthusiasm. "Maddy, the calculations held true to all our projections. Did you see how cleanly she went through the hole in the roof?" Looking thoughtful, he turned to the others. "I heard the rattle of a passing train but not a single sound of a rooftop crash." Then he spoke in a sad and dejected tone. "Still." He looked at his feet.

Moe spoke up next. "It could look worse than it is."

"How?" Maddy asked, hands on her hips.

"Give me a minute."

Maddy scowled and shook her head. "Whose hair-brained

idea was it, anyway?" She looked around, angry and on the verge of tears. *Oh, Murfee! Where are you? Are you safe?* She let out a ragged breath.

"It was stupid of Murfee to agree to it!" Milo retorted.

All the rest exclaimed, "Milo!"

Maddy pointed out the obvious. "You forced her to get on that crazy contraption. You, Milo! All of you guys! Didn't you see she was terrified? She couldn't even look—she had her eyes squeezed shut!"

Maddy saw Milo angrily wiping tears from his face with the back of his hand. If looks could kill, hers would have left him deader than a doornail. *I'd like nothing more than to wring his neck!* she thought.

Moe spoke, "Hey, guys, it's gonna be okay. I've never known Murfee not to come out on top. Oops... I guess that's the problem." He scratched his head. "Yet what goes up must come down. It's a universal law, a fact of life. What goes up must come down."

Pip said, "Shut."

And Squeak said, "Up!"

Moe looked the picture of innocence. "Who, me?"

Lipton surprised them as he seldom said much since his tail-bending accident. "This isn't helping Murfee at all!"

Maddy turned to look dumbfounded at her oldest and biggest brother, "What?"

Dahson looked at Lipton over his glasses. "Lipton, what did you say?"

Lipton continued. "We know we have a problem. The question is—what are we going to do about it?"

Maddy watched as Moe reached up and patted Lipton on the back. "Jumbo's right, we're doing nothing but wasting precious time. What we need is a plan, a strategy." Moe stepped forward, full steam ahead. "I read all about medicine in the *M* encyclopedia. We need to break into groups. Let's see —we'll need a rescue team with a couple of paramedics."

Peep interrupted. "Moe! What's a pair of medics?"

"Medics help with triage, Peep. Treatment at the site. Priority care," Moe answered.

Maddy spoke with tenderness, "Peep, it's first aid in case Murfee's hurt."

Peep seemed to shrink in size and said in a small voice, "Oh."

"We gotta find her first!" Maddy exclaimed.

MURFEE

Murfee gazed up in bewilderment at the vast blue sky. She saw a cornfield that seemed to go on for miles. The small mouse was careful to keep her focus anywhere but down as she moved away from the edge of the roof.

She noticed the tall maple tree. It almost glowed in the light; its leaves rustled as a large flock of sparrows lifted from its branches and poured into the air. Murfee jumped back in surprise. The birds spun and spiraled, gaining altitude, then flew directly overhead. They flitted and danced in the sky and Murfee was mesmerized. Her entire face broke out into a smile, and she laughed out loud.

She ran, for the moment fearless, and landed with a thump on a metal flashing placed to funnel water where roof lines met. She rode it down like a banister, rolling off sideways when she got close to the edge. Next, she played a wild game of hopscotch and then spun like a top. She felt she could touch the sky. Dance and sing. She'd never felt this way before. The feeling was glorious.

A miniature whirlwind lifted leaves and bits of debris into the air. Murfee ran with reckless abandon into the whirlwind and grabbed a maple leaf which lifted her off the roof. She held on tight to the leaf and let it carry her back down like a parachute. She landed like a pro, her wild laughter echoing across the rooftop.

POE

Poe peeked out from the cupola, puzzled. He saw Murfee gazing in his direction as he again hid in the shadows, remaining unnoticed as Murfee resumed her play. The ancient crow waited a moment, then snuck another peek. Still, he went unseen.

MADDY

Maddy stood before her brothers defiant. "Guys! We need to go to Father right this minute and tell him what's happened. Mother, too. Murfee's life is at stake. You need to come to your senses!"

Milo walked up to her, a dark, crafty expression transforming his usual sunny features. "Well... I'm thinking we could figure this out on our own and I have an idea to buy us some time. We can tell Mother and Father we've got a secret project that'll take a few days. Top secret. That means we'll need two or three days free from school."

He stepped up closer and gave Maddy a small nudge. "Tell me, Tattletale. Are you going to be responsible for giving

Mother a heart attack? That's what you'll be doing if we do it your way." Maddy's face paled.

"Besides," Milo continued, "This will keep us boys out of trouble, cuz we're all into it up to our necks...well, Lipton excluded. He's never much fun."

Lipton interrupted in his deep tenor, once again surprising the group. "My guess—Murfee landed on the roof." He tilted his head back and stared at the huge expanse of the loft's ceiling, then let out a heavy sigh.

Moe nodded his head vigorously. "Great! All we need to do now is send a long piece of twine up there, Murfee can hook it around something and crawl right back down. We'll send one of us up to tell her what's what and give her a hand. They can both get back down the same way. Or... another parachute. Slick!

"Yep! Bring Murfee home without a scratch, nobody the wiser, if you know what I mean, never have to worry the folks," Moe continued

Milo and Dahson rushed to crowd around him and nodded their heads vigorously.

And with his new sense of self-confidence Moe's voice rose. "We could rescue her from the air. We'd need our second rocket ship and another astronaut volunteer." He looked sideways at the girls. "Someone else of the right size and weight. Why—it's a hero-making opportunity. Sure would be an honor to be selected—and to rescue Murfee. An honor of a lifetime—"

Maddy interrupted, "Just whose lifetime are we talking about, Moe? Whose life? Not in your wildest dreams." Her face felt hot and she forced herself to hold back tears.

As one, the girls scowled, folded their arms over their chests, and nodded. "You may have gotten Murfee to agree to your crazy rocket ride," Maddy said, then thought about her assessment. "Well, sorta agree, I guess. But you're not roping any of us into it. Not on *your* life. I can't believe you guys! Didn't you learn anything from this tragedy?"

Moe looked at his sisters with disbelief. "Girls, girls. No guts, no glory!"

He ducked and covered his head as five girls rushed at him and pelted him with forearms and balled-up fists, Maddy's attack the most ferocious of the bunch.

32
THE SOUND OF SIRENS

JUSTICE

AN AMBULANCE with loud sirens blaring arrived, roaring up to the door, its red flashing lights rhythmically circling round and round. Blessed silence ensued the moment the sirens were quieted but the red lights continued to announce the unfolding drama to anyone near.

Neighbors soon gathered in clusters in front of the house as Rosalie, dead from a heart attack, left her home one last time on a gurney. Theo walked by her side to the waiting emergency vehicle.

Justice listened unseen from the shadows, hearing people talk first about their neighbor's death and next about several of them seeing a light in the attic a month or so ago, with a young girl standing there. And maybe a cat. "Why didn't anyone look into it?" several asked. "There shouldn't have been a girl in that house. Someone should have made a child protection call. Somebody should have, just to be sure."

Justice moved away from the crowds and waited for a safe time to return unseen. He was worried greatly about Sophie. He had to get back to her as soon as he could but right now the place was being watched.

33
A GOLDEN MAPLE LEAF

MURFEE

Night closed around Murfee. She could feel the wind picking up and the weather changing. The golden sunshine that had welcomed and warmed her was replaced by strange shadows that danced across the rooftop.

All the new-found excitement about her grand adventure evaporated. In its place, fear and doubt set in. No longer was Murfee thinking about being a hero. Instead, her thoughts were of simple survival. How was she going to get home? What would she do if she couldn't?

The tiny figure looked lost and forlorn until she spotted something shining and glimmering in the growing darkness. In awe, Murfee tiptoed over to get a better look.

"Oh! It's another leaf and it's bea-u-ti-ful!" She reached down and touched a large maple leaf glowing in the twilight. Colored in yellows, gold, and bronze, it shimmered like gold leaf caught in the fleeting sunlight.

Murfee picked up the leaf and stroked the satiny-smooth surface like Aladdin rubbing his magic lamp. She folded it around her and attempted to duck underneath. Next, she tried wedging the stem and ends of leaf lobes between cracks in the shingles to create a small tent. This was a success! She now had protection from the elements. Murfee bent low, wiggled inside, and re-secured the tent's opening. The wind tugged at her small shelter. Outside, fat drops of rain splashed down.

The wind strengthened and the tent snapped with every gust.

She loosened a side of her leaf tent, looked out and up, and saw patches of a beautiful nighttime sky beyond the clouds. Raindrops hit her face. She saw stars overhead just briefly before the gathering clouds obscured them. A slow and steady downpour and erratic pelts of wind-driven rain followed.

Murfee refastened her tent. She left one small opening opposite the storm's onslaught.

The rain came down hard and steady. Murfee drew herself up, and with false bravado, she started to sing, "Fly me to the moon..." but her voice broke.

Trembling, she moved to the leaf opening and looked up. A lone star twinkled overhead and high above the storm. Murfee pointed to it and spoke with disgust. "All because of a star. All because of a wish. That wish... wish I'd never made it.

"Oh," she pondered. "Maybe it *was* the darn song. I woulda never guessed it. 'Fly me to the Moon.' I shoulda never sung it at the same time I was making a wish. Yep. The timing was all wrong. Just as I saw that falling star. I'll never make that mistake again."

She bowed her head but only for a moment. "If I could only find a falling star, I could make a wish to go back home." She huddled in the cold, holding her face in her hands. "I feel like I'm a long way from home and not a bit closer to the moon. It still looks so far away. How can that be?"

Murfee began to shiver. "I didn't really want to go to the moon. And I don't need a grand adventure. I'll never be a hero, not even close. I just want to go home."

The littlest mouse in a family of twelve, the one with the soft blue-gray eyes, just "an inch" of a mouse, lay down, wrapping her arms around herself. She tossed about restlessly, finally falling asleep.

She mumbled incoherently.

And she dreamed.

In this dream, Murfee stood on the moon. She opened her mouth to speak but nothing came out. At last, a dramatic understanding shone in her eyes. "I'm on the moon! Really, I'm on the moon. Boy. If everybody could see me now."

She stood stock-still—afraid to move. A look of wonder played across her face. Star-studded sky, the solar system vast, and beautiful Earth—all seen far, far, away. The lunar surface was amazing. She turned in a full circle looking about and was drawn back to the stars and planet Earth.

Suddenly a tiny wrinkled old man not even four feet tall stood in front of her, obscuring the view. He wore green billiard shades pushed back on his forehead and an old gray double-breasted suit. "Whad ya do? Get lost in the stars? Never you mind—it happens to folks all the time." He shook his head.

"Huh?"

In the tone and cadence of a newscaster, he continued, "A tour will be starting in about..." He stopped, looked down, and tapped his Mickey Mouse watch. Murfee had seen one exactly like it in their treasured encyclopedia!

He returned to his normal voice. "Hmm... Fifteen minutes, give or take a few. Walk this way." He went ahead of Murfee with a step—shuffle—shuffle—hop.

Murfee did her best to imitate him.

The little old man stopped moving, looking both thoughtful and puzzled. "You know—the strangest thing happened just this morning." He now had Murfee's full attention.

"We get mostly mice touring our facilities, but just before you arrived—a cat—and *quite* a large cat—stopped by my booth."

Murfee's eyes grew wide.

"The cat wanted to tour our blue-cheese factory. It's only operational during a blue moon— seasonal work you know— but they say it's good pay." He looked at Murfee. "Say, you want the tour or not?"

Murfee had changed. Her eyes were fear-filled and her voice quivered. "Umm... I just came to admire the view..."

She was again drawn back to one amazing view of the galaxies, Earth, and the stars. The sky was luminescent, pure magic. The old fellow cleared his throat. She stuttered, "A cat. A quite large cat, you say?"

In the real world, a cat yowled. Murfee jumped up still asleep, eyes panic filled. "Help me! Help! Don't. Don't let Tyrus get me. Help!"

Instantly she came awake, breathing hard and fast. Eerie shadows, cat-shaped, darted and danced across the sides and ceiling of the makeshift leaf tent.

The wind groaned. The tent whipped about in forces threatening to destroy it. She peeked out, looked high into the heavens, and cried out, "SOS!"

No sooner than she called for help, a lighted firefly zipped into the small space, illuminating it with a soft, pale, yellow-green glow, changing her small shelter from dark and forlorn to one of enchantment, the cat shadow absorbed in the tiny firefly's light.

Murfee's eyes shone. "My own little star." She quickly looked out and up, far above her beautiful maple-leaf tent, and smiled.

34
A CHANGE OF PLANS

POE

POE WAS PUZZLED by the illuminated leaf-shelter. When he realized Murfee had company and was nice and safe without his help, his entire body drooped. He'd planned to rescue the Littlest Mouse and bring her to his castle. He would be her hero and he would keep her forever.

Now it appeared she'd been rescued by another. Unseen, the old crow flew from his home, the old barn's cupola, and soundlessly circled the cornfield, then the barn's perimeter. He landed on a section of the rooftop out of sight.

He remembered his plan to destroy Murfee and he began to shake. His head bobbed unnaturally as he talked to himself. "Get yourself together, Smart Bird." He gave himself a vicious slap, stretched to his fullest height, then reached up to smooth the feathers on the top of his head. Soon he would claim Murfee's magic cape and sword and all the power that went with them. His troubles would be over.

With steady, silent flight, he flew to one of his hiding places and gathered the two precious items. He returned to the cupola, put on the cape, and preened. Murfee was no match for Poe!

35
TWINK—OR—WHAT'S IN A NAME?

MURFEE

Murfee watched wide-eyed as the visitor to her makeshift leaf-tent continued to emanate an otherworldly light. Her eyes grew wider still when the tiny bug spoke. "My name's Twink."

"Wink?" Murfee's eyebrows raised in puzzlement.

The tiny firefly vigorously shook her head no.

"Blink?"

"Twink. TWINK." By this time, the glow worm was yelling at the top of her small lungs. "My name is Twink! Twink!" Then she added in a whisper, "Twink. It's short for Twinkle. Really call me just about anything… Just don't call me Dot. Anything but Dot." Murfee leaned in to listen.

"Sometimes I get called Dot… and then I feel stupid and small, and my light goes out."

Murfee's eyes widened, and her words poured out in a rush. "Boy! I know what you mean. I get called 'Inch' and I hate it. Who wants to be an inch?" She knew names could make a body feel small.

She looked at the 'but a tiny speck' of a firefly, her new friend, and began to stutter. "Uh. For a mouse, see, I'm the size of a baby mouse," she stammered. "And for a mouse, well an inch... " her voice trailed off. "My name's Murfee. Nice to meet you," she said at last.

In the next instant, Twink transformed before Murfee's eyes into a beautiful glowing orb. She twirled and spun while Murfee watched spellbound. The itty-bitty firefly began to hum, and then to sing a song Murfee had never heard before, "Catch a Falling Star." Murfee soon was singing along until she knew all the words by heart, and she didn't feel alone anymore.

If only Murfee's new friend could stay with her until she could find her way back home.

36

AN INSANITY DEFENSE

Justice hurried to the attic, stunned at what he found there. It looked every bit like a crime scene. He wouldn't be surprised to see police tape stretched across somewhere in the space.

He watched on from the doorway as Sophie attempted to rehang a clock. Giving up, she sunk to the floor, covering her face with her hands. After a moment she looked up and let out a gasp seeing him there. "She's gone. My grandmother's gone. I'm afraid I'm the reason she died." She shuddered.

"Sophie, what in the world happened here? Temporary insanity?" After a long beat, Sophie nodded.

"I wanted bangs, so I cut them myself, but then I couldn't stop, so I cut all my hair—all the parts I could reach. But I cut myself with the scissors—I tried to clean it up."

"And the clocks? Sophie, you've got clumps of hair and blood and broken clocks... everywhere. This looks like the location of a true crime and we're gonna need to get out of here.

"I'm afraid the information I have to tell you is going to

make this mess even worse. Remember that night when the moon was so full and round and orange-red that we couldn't stop looking… then we saw a tiny poodle race across the back lot, followed by a half dozen people trying to catch up? They saw us in the window, Sophie. I guess it's all the neighbors have talked about it… a young girl and a cat seen looking out a window—an unknown girl trapped high up in the attic. With a family that doesn't have young kids.

"With all the attention of an ambulance and several police cars, we're suddenly in the limelight and need to get out of here—and fast."

He looked upon her with kindness. Her face flushed, eyes swollen from crying, hair sticking up crazy-like. His small master appeared dazed. He'd need to calm her, then try to bring her fully back to the present. *Maybe if I give her something to do—maybe that will help.*

"Let me see where you hurt yourself. Just one finger. Hmm… doesn't look too bad. Get the first aid kit out of the closet and I'll try to patch you up. Hurry."

Sophie began to whimper. "I never told her I loved her. I never even knew myself, not until now." She sat down on the floor and pulled herself into a ball, leaving her cat to wonder what to do next.

37
TRAPPED

Murfee sat at the top of the old barn roof, slumped over, her head in her hands. The littlest mouse was exhausted, hungry, and utterly, utterly lost. Her new friend, Twink, left with the rising sun, and Murfee felt even more alone than before. She took a few minutes to feel sorry for herself.

The beauty all around her begged for attention. The leaves in the cornfield rattled. Bees languidly buzzed about. The air felt soft on her skin and smelled fresh after the night's rain. The maple tree's leaves rustled in the gentle wind and flew in scattered clusters across the vast rooftop.

Tiredly, she looked up as another flock of sparrows landed in the maple tree. She picked up a single leaf as in a trance. The tiny birds flew back into the air, frenziedly whirling and dancing as one, then darted out of view. Murfee Mouse stared at the large tree. Then she saw the great horned owl sleeping on one of its branches. An awful expression came over Murfee's face, her hand flying to her mouth. She started to back up and stand at the same time but stumbled and nearly fell.

Clutching her maple leaf, she clambered to the nearby shelter of the barn's cupola and scrambled inside. There she cowered. Murfee shook and the leaf trembled in her hands. Her sense of humor remained intact though, as a weary smile played across her face. "Gotta be how they came up with that expression 'shaking like a leaf.'" Finally, she sat down with her back toward the cupola's inner wall, her legs dangling over the inside edge.

The cupola resembled a miniature house. Though old and weathered it was still beautiful, and it commanded the highest vantage point of the old farmstead. Its purpose was to provide ventilation down into the large barn's interior.

Before her lay a mouth of blackness, an empty space that dropped into the void. Murfee's fear of heights rushed back unbidden. Bile rose in her throat. *Just don't look down. Just don't look down.* Like a mantra, she repeated the words over and over in her mind until the nausea passed and her heart settled.

Murfee noticed a scattering of grain and nearby a metal roof flashing holding rainwater. For a moment, she forgot her predicament and enjoyed a drink and the simple feast of plain oats, the breakfast identical to the one she would have had if she'd been home.

"Can't go up and can't go down. Oh, well. Guess for now I have everything I need right here and nothing I don't. What I don't need—I don't need to be called a thief! And I sure don't need another adventure. Not if it means I end up like this."

She sat and thought. *Sure could use a little magic right about now. Or maybe one of Dahson or Milo's brains. Hmm... I wonder where I'd be right now if I had my magic cape and sword. I would bet money a superhero or a real brainiac could find a way out of this mess.*

Murfee felt dejected, then bored. She got up, stretched, then stood and peeked out the wooden slats. Standing on tiptoe she could see a portion of the cornfield and the top of the maple tree.

She sat down with an air of resignation, twiddled her thumbs, softly whistled off tune, then stood and did a couple of jumping-jack exercises. *Boy! I wish this day would end,* she thought, until she remembered her nightmare of the night before. She didn't want another one like that. Better to try and stay awake.

The twilight came upon her as she knew it would. Finally, when she couldn't keep her eyes open any longer, she slid into a most uncomfortable position and slept. She began talking in her sleep. "I'm falling... somebody catch me! Where did everybody go? Come back! I didn't do it, I'm innocent. You've got to believe me. Help me! Somebody HELP!"

Then she began to dream.

Murfee was in a moonlit meadow. The sky was Crayola-colored, Cornflower, Vivid Violet, Purple Mountains' Majesty, Blue Bell, and Goldenrod.

She jumped at a slight rustling sound. A transparent vision of a thin, bearded man wavered before her. He was dressed in a long ink-blue-black gossamer robe, layered over cloth of a similar color made up of dozens of golden twinkling stars, a few of them sizzling like firecracker sparklers.

She was reminded of fireflies, and especially of her tiny friend Twink. Murfee's eyes widened as they traveled up the tall man with his pointy wizard hat.

He spoke, "Why are you surprised to see me? You were just looking for me in the M *encyclopedia. Your brothers looked at a picture of the moon landing, then you found a picture of me, Merlin of King Arthur's Court. Wizard of Camelot." He peered at her until she fidgeted and squirmed.*

"I—I was? I think I would remember you," she said.

Then it came to her. "You! You're the voice from my dream. I remember now! You said I was special. And if you're right—and if I really am, well, maybe I really could be a superhero. I'd get out of this tough spot and go out to have the most wonderful and grand adventure... maybe on the moon or high up in the stars. But I'd race back just in time to rescue everybody and be sure to save the day." *She let out a happy sigh.*

"Dear Littlest Mouse, you need to get your head out of the clouds and out of the stars. Forget about an adventure somewhere high overhead. Your adventure is right now, you are living it. Don't ever wish it away. Life happens right where you are."

The air around the wizard sizzled and popped with each word he spoke. As beautiful as the stars, *Murfee thought.*

His deep voice continued, "Your courage has never been in the cape or sword. Your power has been with you all along. The hero is right inside."

Merlin's eyes remained locked on hers and Murfee was spellbound. "Think," he continued. "You know the way home. You know how to get home. Use your brain. Oh! And keep your eyes open, Little One, for danger lurks about in places you fail to see." And then, just like that, he was gone.

"Well! I never. He sure could have been a little more specific, wouldn't ya think?" Suddenly she felt herself falling.

She woke up with a start and was terrified to find herself hanging half out and over the void. Murfee quickly pulled herself to safety, and as soon as she calmed herself, mulled over the words and images of her amazing dream. Further sleep was not to be. Not this night.

Around midnight, under the beauty of the Milky Way, an exhausted Murfee began to sing. Her voice, though untrained and at times off-key, was the strange combination of defiance and innocence as fresh as the dew.

As she warbled "Catch a Falling Star," it was all heard, word by word, note by note, by someone hidden in the deepest blue-black shadows of the night.

MANTIS

Mantis was searching for supper, or at least a midnight snack, when he was strangely drawn to the small mouse's singing. The words and the melody of the song caused him to gasp for breath and clutch his chest. *That song... it's like it wants to take me somewhere,* he thought.

He fell into a crumbled heap but stayed hidden as both instinct and long habit demanded. Preying Mantis, the great mouse-killer, the annihilator, was reduced to nothing but a bag of bones.

MURFEE

Moments before dawn, Murfee collapsed into a deep sleep and the day started without her. She was startled awake when her friend Poe tapped her on the shoulder. She jumped to her feet.

"Poe! Oh, Poe, you're not going to believe the story I have to tell. I climbed aboard a firecracker rocket ship, the first mouse astronaut to the moon. The takeoff was spectacular, I whizzed straight through that hole in the ceiling, but somehow I didn't get any farther than right up here." She wrung her hands.

"I thought I was going on a great adventure but now I'm in trouble. My parachute went who knows where. I have no idea how to find my exit hole in the roof and even if I did, I'd still have to figure out a way to get home. I am most definitely in a dilemma of untold proportions. That's what Dahson would say."

Murfee embraced the old crow with great affection, then simply held him for a time, her body leaning into his. She stepped back, all smiles. *It's so good to have an old friend here to help.*

Poe's small beady eyes gleamed. With great theatrics, he held his head with the tips of his wings. "Poor, poor Littlest Mouse." He sighed loudly. "You must be hungry, probably thirsty, too. Look real close. See. Look here—see over in the corner. It's a place for rainwater. And over there, some grain to eat."

"I already found it. Thanks for sharing, Poe," Murfee answered easily.

POE

The crow worked to hide great disappointment. Murfee was spoiling his surprise and even making light of the provisions he'd graciously shared. He was wanting to be her only hero. Not that silly bug of a firefly, but only him, the smartest crow.

In a flash, he remembered his plans for her ruin. Discredit her. Call her a thief. Make sure she depended on him, and him alone. Then he could keep her. Because he wanted both her destruction and her company. She could be his little prisoner roommate. Forever.

But for everything to play out, he'd first need her trust. He'd lead her along for a while.

"Poe the Great and Majestic Crow is here to save you. Your

first-rate hero has arrived, you lucky little mouse!" The ancient bird bowed low.

"Poe can help you get home. Maybe fly you home. Just as soon as this is better." He held up his crippled wing and moved it back and forth to demonstrate. One lone wing feather loosened and lifted away in the wind. "It's a little floppy, but just you wait and see—it'll get better, and Poe can carry you home. Put you in his trusty ol' tobacco pouch and deliver you right to your door!"

The crafty crow was quick to take note of the doubt that crossed Murfee's small face as she looked at his impaired limb.

He felt great humiliation and shame wash over him, and in an instant became enraged. The stupid little mouse should feel honored by his offer to help instead of staring at him. He wondered if she would taunt him next.

Poe knew what he needed to do, for he was a very smart bird. The smartest, smartest bird was Poe. He must find a way to force her trust and make her swear her allegiance to him. Forever.

Suddenly the crow's wild, convoluted thoughts carried him back to a powerful vision of the teasing and taunting by the cruel boy, Carl Dunbee, when Poe was small, and Poe's imprisonment and near-death that followed.

For a moment his entire body was consumed with a craziness that threatened to engulf him, then swallow him whole. Sweat dripped off his oily feathers. He leaned over and whispered, "This is Poe's home. Nobody knows but you! Poe will share his special place with his little friend. Poe never leaves this safe place, not for long. No, never for long."

Murfee appeared astounded. "You mean you never fly high into the sky, never swoop over the cornfield to see it all simply for the pure fun of it? Never go visit your own bird friends?"

"Oh. Littlest Mouse, you're my only friend. Only need one."

Murfee didn't seem to want to let it drop. "You could fly all over the farm and practice using your wings more. Exercise 'em."

First, he was defiant, "Poe flies everywhere, places you don't even know. There's a lot you don't know and what you don't know can hurt you, Tiny Mouse." Agitation rumbled through him and held him in its grasp.

His body shook and he spoke in a scared-little-boy voice. "Poe was hurt. Then Lily came and saved Poe. But he called and called... and nobody came." Tears rolled down his face.

"Poe—"

"Fell out of the nest. Too little to fly. I called and called but they never came. So scared." Poe composed himself somewhat and began talking to himself. He no longer acted like he knew she was there. "That terrible boy found Poe... and—and put him in a cage. Poe was so scared. But they never came."

Murfee moved to stand in front of him. "Who? Who never came?"

"My folks, Murfee. And Lily. *Nobody* came. They never came." He broke down and silently wept.

"It's okay, Poe. I'm here... and I'll be your friend."

Poe shuddered and let out one last sob. She reached out and gave him a pat, and the crow pulled her close. "Poe, you could look for your family. I could look for Lily, whoever she is. Maybe they're looking for you. I'd help." She smiled up at him. "Mother and Father are probably searching for me right now and I need to go home. My heart hurts just thinking about everybody worrying. I miss everybody. I miss my family, Poe, and I bet they miss me. I have to go."

Poe's expression became dark and cold. "You can't go. Poe won't let you! And don't you see—there's no reason to leave. Never ever."

Murfee looked like she'd been slapped. She struggled to pull away from him.

"You can't leave Poe the Crow. You have to stay. I get to keep you!"

"Keep me! What are you going to do—put me in a cage like that mean boy did to you? Well! Isn't this the same?" Her eyes bored into his. "And your fancy little house—it looks like, like just a bigger cage." She gestured to the walls of the cupola. "A jail cell, bars and all." She reached out and banged on a slat of the cupola with a balled-up fist. "You could leave, but instead you just make up excuses. Well, excuse me, but I'm outta here."

She shoved him hard. Her voice dripped with sarcasm. "Move out my way, old friend. I'm going home. Don't know how, but I'll figure it out along the way." Murfee turned to leave, but Poe grabbed her by the tail to stop her. She stretched out her arms and tried to grab one of the slats to help herself pull away, but the boards were just out of reach.

Poe was unrelenting. "By now your family *knows* you're a thief." Murfee gasped. He continued, "Poe's the only friend you've got. The only one. Even if you find your way back, you can never go home." His voice took on a fever pitch. "And Murfee, it's the crow's job to keep you safe from The Professor. That huge horned owl living in the big tree. He is a scary bird. He scares Poe."

She turned back to him in a panic. Poe smiled and released her. "Poe, you know about that owl? I bet he'd like to make me his little late-night snack." She shuddered.

Poe looked aghast. "Oh! Poor Murfee. That's terrible. Just terrible! And that's just what Poe's been trying to tell you. Poe can keep you safe. Boy are you lucky. Poe is here to help."

Suddenly a crazed, contorted expression came over the old crow's face. He laughed manically then leaned down and spat out his words. "You will *never* leave me. You're not going anywhere. See, Littlest Mouse, it's never quite so simple. Nothing ever is."

He moved to pick up one of his stolen pennies from the floor with his beak and tossed it past the ledge and down into the black void. "Listen." With full concentration, they waited for a sound. After a few seconds, the penny hit the floor with only the faintest clank.

"Far down, too far down to jump and live. Poe can fly. Mice can't fly."

Murfee moved as far away from the edge as she could.

"And... there's a vicious cat. A wild mouse-chaser. He's on the prowl down below and he eats little mice like you."

MURFEE

Murfee stared down at the floor, trying to catch her breath.

She happened to glance over to the spot where Poe picked up the penny. In the straw, she spied a pile of trinkets that she easily recognized. They all belonged to her family. A bit of scarlet velvet and the tip of a pink plastic sword poked out of a nearby mound of straw. Looking more closely she spied a second pile of grain. More oats.

Murfee's eyes became saucers. Poe followed her gaze. His eyes narrowed. In two long strides, he gathered up her beautiful cape, tied it around his scrawny neck, and scooped up her pink sword. Scarlet fabric swirled and danced around his bony figure, the crow now a grotesque, ghastly vision.

He towered over her. "If Poe lets you go, you'll hurry-scurry back to your precious little family, and tell 'em everything. Tell 'em who's been stealing from them. Poe will look like the bad guy and they'll run him outta town. Uh-uh!" His eyes glazed over. His body contorted, and looked twisted, crippled, wild. "You can *never* go home."

He drew himself up to his fullest height, the feathers on his head shining blue-black in the light. Looking furious but in tight control, he said, "Now, the cupola can be your little cage if that's how you wish to see it. Poe will bring you tasty molasses-covered oats and trinkets— pretty shiny things."

'Molasses-covered oats.' Her mouth instantly watered. Murfee remembered eating them once when she was younger. She had rolled a few around in her mouth, then held them on her tongue until they dissolved—nothing was as sweet as molasses-covered oats. A dreamy expression now lit up her small face.

POE

Without thinking, Poe glanced back to the stale-looking, run of the mill oats he had gathered there and Murfee followed his gaze. He pointed with the plastic sword. "Don't worry, tiny mouse. Those are just ordinary oats, but Poe knows how to get the good stuff. A neighbor's silo is full of it. Only Poe knows because Poe is a very smart crow."

He stepped closer, pinning Murfee up against the boards of the cupola. Poe took a quick look back at his pile of grain before turning to glare at her. "You are a most miserable, ungrateful mouse. You don't know how lucky you are. You've never known hunger, but your family soon will. They're running out of food, minute by minute." Murfee gasped. "Haven't you figured it out yet? These oats came from your family. Yes, from your food stores in the loft." He cackled. "With hard work, in little more than a week, Poe will have taken every morsel. Oh! That Poe. Powerful is Poe."

The crazy crow took great pride and delight in the telling of his treachery and theft of the Mouse family's food supply.

He wanted to strut. He wanted to pound on his chest. He wanted the world to know of his cunning, but with a huge effort, he restrained himself. There was much more dirty work to be done before he could reveal his genius. The timing was everything.

With great drama, he transferred the plastic sword to hold it loosely at his other side, then lifted the tip of his good wing to his chin. *Try to remain cool. Don't tell the Littlest Mouse about Poe's plans*, he thought to himself, but everything was building up and was too much for him to hold inside. He had to let it out or he would burst. "Mice must be stupid. There is a mountain of grain in the old saddle room, growing even bigger every day. All because your family's food supply somehow finds its way there." He smirked.

"Stupid mice! None of you will ever find that gargantuan mountain of oats because you're fools and think the tack room must be haunted." Poe then mimicked the strange ghostly moans that had kept them away.

MURFEE

Murfee shivered in spite of herself. *Get it together*, she thought to herself. *It's the only chance I have to bring Poe back to his senses. I've got to stay calm.* A sudden breeze puffed through the cupola, stirring up the dust. Her nose start to itch. Mid-sneeze, she captured a movement out of the corner of her eye and high over her head. She looked up, and her breath caught in her throat. She gasped at the images of her superheroes impaled on nails. As the pages trembled in the wind, each picture was strangely brought to life. Superman, Batman, and Robin, like moving pictures but somehow terribly wrong, frightening, and ghostly. Then she spied the comic book image of Two-Face in all its grotesqueness. Half normal faced, half green, a bug-eyed creature ready to devour any and all who cross him. Wild hair and a wild look in one of his eyes. Something like her old friend, Poe. Demented in part. All the breath went out of her.

The oily crow stepped closer. "If Murfee is nice and stays in the cupola, she'll be a lucky, lucky mouse and, like Poe, she'll never have to starve. Poe will never go hungry, never again." A self-satisfied expression crossed his face an instant before his eyes turned black. He started pacing back and forth and muttering to himself.

"Poor Poe... no. No! Prince Poe. Prince Poe. This is the Kingdom of Poe. Hero Poe. Bow to Poe. Beg *him* for food." His eyes narrowed. He stopped his pacing abruptly and turned to face her. "Lily loves her Birdie. She does. Always has, always will."

Murfee's mouth fell open. "What? Birdie? Who's Birdie?"

Poe's face melded into a look-alike of Two-Face, his most beloved of the superheroes, the monster's portrait on the wall directly above him. The old crow bent over her menacingly and spoke in a high-pitched voice, one that quivered with unleashed fury. "Tease you and taunt you. Forget to feed you. Dolly will find you. She's always watching. She'll find Poe."

His head jerked and his persona changed once again. In a trained-bird voice, he said, "Bad Bird! Bad Bird! Awk! Stay in the cage. Stay safe. Stay safe. Awk!"

Murfee tried frantically to get his attention and bring him back to reality. "Poe! You're sick! Not right in the head. It's me, Murfee! I'm your *friend*, remember?"

The crow looked right past her, right through her. "Poe! Look at me!" But he no longer recognized her; he looked vicious instead. Terrified now, Murfee made a tremendous leap through the nearby slats and out onto the roof. She hid behind the cupola and held her breath.

Murfee watched on as the crazed crow left his home, talking just to himself, the beautiful cape transforming him into a strange Dracula-like figure. "Bad Bird! Bad Bird! Get back in the cage. Awk! Awk!" His eyes were unseeing, and to Murfee he looked nothing like her old friend, Poe.

Murfee darted back inside. No longer did the cupola feel like a wonderful, temporary shelter, but at present, she had nowhere else to go.

One thing she knew for certain, she needed to take stock— then decide on a plan. For the first time in her life, she could see clearly. Every childish dream fell away, dissolved before her like clouds crossing the moon. Cotton candy wisps fading into nothingness.

This fear of heights... she'd better get over it. Or simply endure it. She'd better get tough.

38
RESCUE PLANS DOWN BELOW

MILO

Milo slipped out of bed before anyone else was up so he could be alone and gather his thoughts. Sleep had been out of the question. Every moment was filled with worry about Murfee and her safety.

"Murfee, come home. Just come home. Whatever happened, I don't care. We'll figure something out, I'll help you. I promise." Tears that had begun to form in the corner of his eyes now dripped down his face. He brusquely rubbed them away. *There must be something I can do. There's just gotta be.* Looking determined, he stood up and walked from the room.

THE RESCUE TEAM

The sun shone a golden yellow; it was good day for a rescue. A second rocket ship stood ready, aimed with precision at the hole in the roof high overhead. Dahson meticulously folded Murfee's parachute. He studied the result, then muttered something to himself before unfolding the chute and methodically starting over. Looking satisfied at last, he gave the small bundle several gentle taps, then, eyes unfocused, solemnly stared off into space.

On the floor, Pip and Squeak finished a colorful banner that said, "MURFEE, WE MISS YOU." Long and short pieces of crayons littered the space. Dahson turned to look at the twins and the mess they had made and shook his head once again.

Maddy and Minree packed a bundle consisting of oats and a few kernels of wheat and corn. Both banner and food were handed off to Dahson who loaded them and the parachute into the rocket's cargo bay.

Moe staggered in, his arms heavily laden with firecrackers large and small. He set them down carefully, then proceeded to add a number of the largest ones to the rocket's base. "More thrust. That's what we need." Milo deftly removed the excess explosives.

With great ceremony, Moe Mouse lit the match. Once again, the sound and the explosion were spectacular.

Milo flew backward. Huge puffs of smoke belched outward and filled the large space. The injured mouse groaned and took his time getting up, his hair standing on end.

As the smoke thinned, Moe came into view, covered with soot and ash, his hair singed and blackened. Readjusting a now sooty and tattered version of his cap, he attempted a small, crooked smile.

Rocket pieces were strewn throughout the room. The unmanned spaceship had exploded on the launchpad. Murfee's survival supplies would never reach her now.

MILO

Milo, Moe, and Dahson sat on the top rung of the Tinker Toy tower, legs dangling, each looking glum, each seeming oblivious to the beautiful light beams that poured into the space from the cupola overhead.

Milo peered down at one of their few remaining firecracker rocket ships. He shook his head, a tuft of hair on his forehead wilder still. "I know I'm mostly responsible that Murfee sailed out of the loft; I pushed her into taking the flight. I want to be brave and bring her back, and I'll never give up, but for now, I'm beat."

Moe, soot-covered head to toe, said, "I think we need a whole nuther plan. We're going about this all wrong, and we can't take much more abuse."

Dahson, not a scratch or smudge of soot on him, hair neatly combed, took off his glasses and stared into space. Appearing nearsighted, he said, "Limited personnel resources is definitely a problem and has been in the past. Serving as both your chief astrophysicist and statistician, I find I must tell you that it continues to be simply essential—"

Milo said, "Just speak plain English, Dahson!"

Dahson shook his head. "If I'm to continue to fulfill my function as the brains of this project, I'm just going to have to safely stay out of the fray."

Milo and Moe stared across at each other with identical expressions of disgust while Dahson remained oblivious, rubbed his nose, pushing his glasses back up on his face.

MILO

An exhausted group of eight sat in a circle and brainstormed ideas for Murfee's rescue. Milo looked up just as Moe tore into the room. His brother seemed in a panic.

Moe's precious tam was no longer to be found, Milo learned. No matter that his brother's cap was almost ruined in the last few explosions, that it was tattered, torn, and covered with smoke and soot, Moe's cap seemed to define him, and he was inconsolable. Had he taken it off for a moment? Moe said he didn't remember doing that. "Has anyone seen it?" Moe cried. "I've lost my Scottish tam!"

Should the group stop long enough to help the poor fellow? They'd been unsuccessful in designing another rescue plan. Perhaps it was time to take a break, returning later with fresh minds and a way to bring Murfee home. Milo found himself agreeing.

All of them began to look for Moe's cap. They turned over every leaf of paper, every scrap of rocketry, crayon, and firecracker. After the unsuccessful search, the group sat in a huddle, trying to decide where to look next. They scattered then as if rejoining a giant treasure hunt.

Milo felt drawn to the classroom and the *M*. He had absentmindedly lifted the large book's cover when he made a shocking discovery. Here was every stolen item of the Mouse family minus Murfee's scarlet-colored cape and sword. Then he saw the lost tam, soot-covered and worn, its sad condition the result of too many explosions gone awry.

Milo's breath caught in his throat, for he knew his grand error. Murfee couldn't have done it. She'd been long gone by the time Moe's cap was taken. Someone else was the thief. Someone else stole his sister's sword and cape, too.

Oh no. It was Murfee who was blameless and he, Milo, was the one who had sent her flying up through the roof. The one who had blamed her, who had called her a thief. She was in danger because of him, and only him. He sat down heavily and cried. "What will it take, Murfee, for me to bring you home?"

39
FLOOD GATES

MANTIS

MANTIS FORCED himself to stay on his feet. Most of the day he moved as if in a daze. One tiny mouse on a rooftop in the dark of night bravely singing her heart out had nearly destroyed his.

"Catch a Falling Star." How was it possible that a song, long forgotten, had brought him to his knees? Mantis was deeply ashamed of himself for falling apart. Self-disgust clouded his thinking, even his vision, but he shook it off. No time for that and no more dopey sentiment, if that's what this was. No more remembering anything. Just conquest and anni-hilation.

For crying out loud, he was Preying Mantis, the mouse-killer, the Destroyer.

So on to the task at hand, a savvy follow-up to what he'd gleaned from conversations overheard between that great horned owl and that wildly crazy crow.

A family of mice lived in the loft. A family of twelve, minus one, from what Mantis had figured. For it was his belief the diminutive mouse he'd seen and heard in the night had once been part of the dozen in the barn. Eleven was enough. His stomach would be full.

Those mice would be terrified once they spotted him, and hard to capture. It would be interesting to see if he could catch them all, not even let even one escape. He dearly loved the challenge.

It was easy enough to gain entry. The huge cat peered into the last opening he needed to crawl through and got the biggest surprise of his life. A strange little creature, one wearing a soot-covered cap, blasted past him in a blur. Mantis had never seen a mouse move so fast. *Was* that a mouse? Or was he simply seeing things? It had him doubting himself and shaking his head.

Stranger yet, the melody began to dance through his head again. "Hm Hm Hm-mmm ..." and in his mind, he chased the kite-tail of a dream, of a song.

What were the words to it? Those he remembered from his childhood made no sense. "Smoke a strong cigar. Or keep it in your pocket." Immediately he heard laughter in his head, his mother's laugh. He knew it was hers, for it too sounded like a song.

He knew instinctively he couldn't afford to lose himself again. His life depended on mental sharpness and lightning-fast reflexes, and right now he had neither.

With his mind back on the hunt, he reexamined the small opening he'd have to maneuver to get to the family of mice. He poked his head in a bit further but found his whiskers touching both sides.

Whiskers. His mother's lesson to him on whiskers...

Thinking about her, for that small moment, unlocked memories like opening a hallway of doors, and instantly took him back to his childhood. He could hear her words, her voice.

"Your whiskers. Do you think there's no reason for those long flexible hairs on your face?"

He recalled how his mother had pointed out the different constellations flickering high above their heads.

"You were designed by a greater hand than anything you can see. Each little star has a job to do, just as we all do. That's right, Manny—you have a purpose, too. This third reason for your whiskers is important, and I want you to remember it. Your whiskers will tell you if you'll fit through a tight spot to keep you from getting stuck."

But his beautiful mother died, and he had run. Mile after pounding mile he forced his body forward and away until the catch in his side became too painful, and the last breath left his lungs. He'd had to shut it all out—both good and bad, every bit of it. It had been the only way he *could* breathe.

Mantis had been chaperoned by the constellations, their stars his nightly compass. His father's training allowed his body to put away the countless miles, until Mantis was worlds away from the place where he'd left his broken heart.

Unknowingly, two inner voices continued to guide him. His mother Liza and his father Justice held places deep in his heart and their lessons remained.

The floodgates opened, and Mantis remembered it all.

It was his undoing when he recalled those words to her favorite song. For it wasn't "Smoke a strong cigar." He knew. He remembered. It was "Catch a falling star." The very words the little mouse had sung from high on the rooftop. A magical song about catching the starlight and saving it, of keeping it until you needed it.

He could hear his mother's singing so pure and clear,

shivers raced down his spine. He thought back to the nights of staring into the heavens, her arm wrapped around him tight.

He recalled the words she'd spoken shortly before she died and left him forever. Words of advice she handed out like precious silver and gold, ones he had never treasured but instead forced himself to forget.

"Manny, they were all wrong, those who named this star. You're my Sirius, my little one. Dog Star. Nile Star. No! Little Manny, my brightest star."

She had smiled. *"Remember, my fine son, that you too have a purpose. Find out what it is. Always choose the light. Never the darkness. And never run from what you know is true."* Sitting up straighter, she assumed the bearing of a princess. *"Take a stand for it instead."*

What would his mother think of him now? What was his purpose—destruction? Was he searching out the family of mice for a meal or simply for his pleasure?

Unseen, the large cat quietly made his way out of the barn, his attention totally distracted from the present world, but rather enraptured and entangled in the past.

40
SHE KNEW

JUSTICE

"Sophie, listen to me. You've got to get yourself together. We don't have much time."

He continued, "Look... with the eyes of your heart at this beautiful place the two of you have made. She loved you, Sophie—more than just a little."

"I never even called her grandmother. Some days I hated her."

"Your eyes lit up when you showed her one of your paintings or excitedly told her about the 'who done it' in another one of your mystery books. I watched the two of you break out in laughter or a smile at the very same moment.

"Sophie, she knew."

41
CRYING WOLF

PIP AND SQUEAK

PIP AND SQUEAK walked hand-in-hand to the long silver kitchen ladle, climbed up to the raised handle, then managed to slide down the spoon's length, hands still clasped. They landed with a soft plop.

The twins wore identical dark under-eye circles. They hadn't slept a wink in the night—a consequence of the boys' scheme. As part of their brothers' plan, Pip and Squeak had been separated for the first time ever.

Murfee's siblings were painfully aware that their parents' nightly bedtime nose count could get them in big trouble. Murfee's predicament would be exposed, and Mother might never recover. Plus, as the boys stressed, they were surely close to bringing her home.

At bedtime, Pip and Squeak were usually counted just once, then multiplied times two. Now instead of the twins in their own bed, one of them went to Murfee's spot to serve as her replacement and to be counted as the Littlest Mouse. When a parent came in to check that all ten were safe and sound in the sleeping place, the number would come out just right: ten.

It was essential that all nine get to bed early. And that no one act even the least bit suspicious at bedtime or any other time throughout the day.

The second part of the cover-up was the fib they told Mother and Father Mouse about their surprise project. Top secret. And the folks believed them. So far, so good. That left them free to be gone from the classroom and common living space each day, free to devote all their time to Murfee's rescue.

The girls worried that their parents should be told that Murfee was in desperate need of help. But they had vowed to never inform their parents of any trouble. They worried whether their mother could handle the news.

Murfee's siblings took turns checking in with both parents and making assurances that they were all doing fine. With any luck, the next thing they knew, they'd be bringing Murfee back safe.

Pip and Squeak said the only reason they had agreed to their part of the arrangement was their belief that it would help somehow. Neither had been able to sleep.

They walked back to the slide and sailed down it again, landing easily in the straw. "Murfee's lost and we're having fun," Pip said. Squeak reached out to touch Pip's face. "It's okay, Pip." The twins stood. Pip dramatically swept her arm in a wide arc. "After you, Squeak." Hand-in-hand the two left their fun behind.

DAHSON, MADDY, AND MINREE SEARCHED THE LARGE *M* encyclopedia for medical advice as Milo rested nearby, gingerly holding his head. Lipton sat a short distance away watching quietly. Dahson looked over the rim of his spectacles as he scrutinized Milo from head to toe.

"*Medicine* was really no help at all," Dahson said. "Perhaps we should look under *Migraines*."

Lipton's attention was turned inward. "Hard as it is to believe, guys—the answer is not always in a book."

For a time, they each looked lost in thought. Finally, Milo broke the silence. "My noggin's fine. What we need now is some action." He muttered under his breath, "We're coming, Murfee. Hang in there, only a little longer."

He stood on shaky legs as Moe Mouse raced into the room in full panic. The group simultaneously rolled their eyes. And for the very first time in his life, Moe could not speak. When his words finally did pour out, he was met with both ridicule and disgust.

"Have you lost your marbles?" Milo bellowed. "Moe, we've heard it all before and this is no time for a ghost story."

Surprisingly, it was quiet Minree who came to Moe's rescue. "Guys, can't you tell he's scared out of his mind? Moe might think he's an actor, but *this* performance would win an award. No offense, Moe. Listen," she pleaded. "Just give him a chance."

MOE

Moe Mouse took a deep breath then started again. Everything was at stake, and it all depended on him to save them. "I'm telling you... it was the biggest cat you will ever, ever see. No, not the size of a cow, but truly, guys, he was the size of a big, big dog. You've never seen such a thing. And—and he was trying to squeeze through a hole and get to us. I know I get carried away with my stories, but I always know they're made-up stuff. I know that. I do. This time I'm tellin' the truth!"

Dahson was the first to respond. "Dear Moe, I understand why you are acting this way. None of us has paid much attention to you of late. And if the truth is known, this probably goes back to your place in the family. Your birth order."

"Huh?" Moe was totally lost.

"You're the quintessential middle child," Dahson continued. "That's what this is."

"You can't keep calling wolf, Moe. Someday it will get you in real trouble," Milo said.

Moe tried one more time. "Guys, I know it sounds like one of my stories. But this terrible cat is nothing like Tyrus, the old cat that chases mice *just* to chase them. Or Tyrus the Terrible, the cat with two sets of eyes, one in the back of his head. I'm tellin' you and you gotta believe. This one is a real-life killer and I bet he'll come back! You gotta believe me. You just gotta." But no one did.

Moe slumped over in defeat. He'd lost any credibility he had and any chance to warn them about the danger of a real-life monster-sized cat.

42

DOES POE SELL HIS SOUL?

POE

POE WAS ECSTATIC. He had his very own roommate trapped in his very own home. How could life get any better? He preened. He danced, and for a time, attempted to sing. Poe. The greatest, greatest crow.

But his celebration ended abruptly when, in the middle of the day, the great horned owl came to call.

He instantly began to whimper and shake. The owl grabbed him by his neck and shook him relentlessly. As Poe's body became limp, the owl at last loosened his grip.

Poe slowly opened his eyes. The oily black crow vaguely recalled The Professor demanding that Poe help with his plans to kill the cat. Oh! Poor, poor Poe. Suddenly it was Nurse Betty staring back at him. The doll's eyeballs were huge and unblinking. If he could look away, he might stand a chance. Maybe.

The Professor again asserted that Poe was needed to save the lives of a mouse family of twelve. Poe didn't dare tell him that he had one of them already captured. Oh no! Poe was a smart crow. And Poe is Poe is Poe.

Then Poe remembered that his own life was at stake. That cat was after him, too. The pure terror of this moment somehow burst through his pea-sized brain. This time the crow could not allow himself to ever forget again. This time he'd have to remember all of it, *his* life depended on it. Still, he couldn't stop his shaking, no matter how hard he tried.

THE PROFESSOR

The Professor struggled to calm himself, he released his hold on Poe and took a step back. He was deeply repulsed by the crow but knew he needed him. Evidently, the situation required a different tactic. Hmm. How to get the demented bird on board? What was Poe's weakness and what would he want most in the world?

The great horned owl did his best to look most serious and wonderfully kind at the same time.

Everything depended on these next few moments.

"Dear Mr. Crow, you know that I can't do any of this without you. Could I let you in on a little secret? Yes?" He had Poe's total attention. "Things will change for you quite rapidly after this operation. You'll become a part of our brotherhood, a sort of family. We'll never let you down and we'll protect you —not that you'd ever need to be protected. In fact, you'll be celebrated, you'll be the most powerful crow. We'll consult with you on all our plans, and you'll have the final say on every operation. Why, your title will be Exalted Counselor of All."

The owl paused for several long beats, all the while looking at Poe with a most reverent expression. Finally, he asked earnestly, "Would you like that?" Poe gave no reply.

———

THE PROFESSOR FLEW TO ONE OF HIS FAVORITE LOOKOUTS, A DEAD, twisted, and blackened tree that rose up out of the ground like a strangely beautiful art form. Its vantage point was priceless.

The century-old tree was a stone's throw from the old barn and of a similar height. Here, high on his perch, he could spy upon everything and everyone down below. The huge maple tree, the cornfield, the farmhouse, the small apple orchard off in the distance. His was a laser vision and from here he could see it all. These were moments to savor. And it was here he was most able to search out his prey.

But this day the vicious bird was unusually unaware of his surroundings, lost in his own thoughts and wondrous imaginings, his mind spinning with his devious plans.

The great horned owl felt a delicious sense of power whenever he could make someone else feel weak and afraid, and he'd long thought the only way to true power was the theft of another's. Though the terrible predator appeared to ooze power and authority, often it was nothing more than what he could convince each victim to give up on his own.

The secret ingredient to his success was the presence he created, and he used his words to indict, intimidate, and demean. He'd long excelled in subterfuge and illusion, and his was a false bravado.

The owl owed it to something else as well. He was quick to discover his victims' Achilles heel, their vulnerabilities, but their true talents as well. Very likely he was the only one to see the cunning and intelligence in the crazy old crow.

How Poe would be able to get an entire family of mice up

and out onto the old telephone wire, he had no clue. But this he did know; Poe would figure it out. He would do anything to keep himself safe and hidden in the shadows. Added to that, now the crazy bird thought he'd been promised protection. A family. And a title. What an easy mark that foolish crow was. His death would be the sweetest. The powerful great horned owl languidly blinked his enormous, beautiful eyes, then narrowed them to slits.

The Professor reveled in the horror soon to unfold. He was so incredibly proud of the game he'd created that he spoke of it out loud, revealing details both big and small.

When he saw that all twelve were on the wire, he would bail out of the sky, hit the wire, grab the one-two-three mice that had bounced up into the air, swallow them whole, and swiftly go back for more. If any slipped past his talons, why, he'd just dive for them on the ground.

It was his morbid interpretation of Jacks, an age-old game also known as Knucklebones, usually played with five small objects, or ten or more in the case of Jacks, with the pieces thrown up and caught in different ways. Knucklebones. He liked the sound of that.

It had come time for *him* to be the one to decide the rules of the game. In his demented version, *he* was the grim reaper, ready to swoop down for the kill. Life or death, his alone to decide. Mice would fly into the air where he would catch and devour them one by one. The great horned owl chuckled to himself. As always, he had a plan B. If the old crow failed to play his part and the mice failed to show, The Professor would simply change the game. Poe the Crow would be the one to not survive and *he'd* be nothing but bones.

Details, large and small. Wonderful it was to speak them all aloud. The Professor's eyes gleamed with the juicy gore of it. The horrific vision in his head.

"Bones. Bones and more bones. Mouse bones." His eyes narrowed to slits.

***

POE

The ancient crow went over everything again in his mind. Could he trust the words of The Professor? Somehow it sounded a bit too good to be true. He could do nothing but pace. Could it be his own life was at stake?

There had to be a way out of this terrible situation. Maybe he could fly away. Hide out somewhere for the rest of his days. But what about his roommate? His roommate forever?

He had another dilemma. The mouse family numbered an even dozen. What if The Professor counted them one by one and Poe's captive, the Littlest Mouse, was noticed missing? Oh, no! Twelve was not eleven, and eleven was never ever the number twelve.

This was a truly terrible dilemma. He had the tiniest mouse as his prisoner for life, and now he was about to have to give her up. Lose her. He couldn't stand it; he wouldn't let it happen. He wanted to keep her.

Poor, Poor Poe!

***

MANTIS

Mantis the cat was tracking all movements of The Professor. Earlier, the graceful feline climbed up to the top of the towering maple to watch the massive bird. He'd witnessed the exchange between the owl and the crazy crow. More importantly, he listened as The Professor disclosed his true plan to wipe out an entire family of mice. The huge cat climbed down to the ground and moved deep into the overgrowth. There he could quietly ponder the meanings behind all that he had seen and heard.

POE

Poe paced. He cowered. He paced again, then slumped down and covered his head with his wings. Nothing helped. The more he thought about it, it became plain as day that The Professor was no more than a dangerous predator with ruthless plans to kill and destroy everyone and everything in his path. Including Poe.

The owl only said what he thought would sway him. Lies. Nothing but lies. And he would never be family. Never be a protector of Poe.

Oh! If Poe had a friend—a friend, he would know what to do. He'd tell Poe, he'd tell him what to do. But he'd never had a friend. Never ever.

But then he remembered all that Murfee had said to him. "Why! It's Poe. My good friend Poe! I'll be your friend. I would help you. I'd help you find them." Strangely these words and her small voice threaded through his mind. Was he going crazy? Please! Say it isn't so.

Poor, poor Poe.

Like a hard nut that finally cracked, Poe's mind let in some love as well as some hope. If even just for a little while. And somehow, he remembered the spark of a feeling he suppressed when tiny Murfee hugged him and held him tight.

Brand new thoughts took shape and for once in his life he

thought about someone else with a deep feeling of protective-
ness, and something one could only describe as true affection,
the care for another, and the sacrifice of self.

Like the blossoming of a flower in time-lapse photography,
a name came to him now with the scent of lilacs and sunshine
and the sound of laughter. Lily. Lily—the name floated, then
expanded through his consciousness. Lily. He remembered the
little girl who had loved him so.

Oh! Too much for Poe. He'd have to forget most of that if he
wanted to stay safe. So smart! Such a smart, smart crow
was Poe.

There just had to be a way to save the little mouse while
keeping himself out of the way.

Suddenly, he had a stroke of pure genius. He'd go find that
terrible cat. Poe would get the powerful feline to stop The
Professor. The cat could do it! He'd seen that the two were
enemies. Vicious, they both were.

And they deserved each other. Hmm. Maybe they could run
each other outta Dodge and then everybody else would be safe.
This was a genius plan. Only he could have come up with such
an amazing plan.

Wow! He had to be the smartest, smartest crow—that Poe.

———

POE FOUND MANTIS WITHOUT A HITCH. IN HIS EXCITED STATE OF
mind, he felt no fear of the huge predator. Instead, he was
giddy with the idea of getting rid of both cat and owl.

His newfound confidence was truly wonderful. Hero is Poe.
He puffed out his chest, and in his most stately voice said he,
Poe, was bringing important, life-saving information. "Cat,
Powerful Poe the crow is here to save the day.' He exuberantly
added, his voice rising, "Your worries are over, Cat."

Mantis replied calmly, "First of all, crow, I'm not one bit worried. And second, my name is not 'Cat' but Preying Mantis, or Mantis for short. You can call me that."

Poe didn't care about what this giant cat thought or what he chose to be called. What did it matter? He just wanted to get on with this, his most ingenious plan. He immediately began spinning a story endlessly rehearsed, completely unaware that Mantis knew the truth of the crazy crow's encounters with the great horned owl who called himself The Professor.

The oily crow told his own twisted version of the owl's dastardly scheme. The Professor planned to kill or drive away all the mice and small prey, leaving Mantis to slowly starve or force him to move away from the old farm. To slowly weaken Mantis so that he could destroy him, too. Poe was careful not to mention, that in truth, he was part of a scheme to lure the cat to his death. Oh! Smart Poe!

The only solution was for the cat to attack the owl before Mantis became hungry and weak. He should immediately attack. Kill the great horned owl now. No, not maybe. Today was the day. With not a moment to waste!

The crazy bird made it sound like it was really the cat who would come out on top because of the crow's most clever plan. Mantis could be the hero by getting rid of the terrible Professor once and for all.

MANTIS

Poe had to dramatize it all, but Mantis easily tuned out the ravings and the rantings of the crazy crow. Strangely, his thoughts drifted back to a picture in his mind he couldn't seem to shake... of a brave little mouse singing her heart out high up on the old barn roof, "Catch a falling star." He'd been watching her to see what she'd do next.

As Mantis thought back to that moment, his heart gave a lurch. That was truly something, courage like he'd never before seen. He'd witnessed her fear, also her spunk, and a glimpse of her hero's heart.

He decided right then, as Poe continued his tale, that the teeny mouse was in fact a giant. And that size had nothing, absolutely nothing, to do with anything.

Then for Mantis, the real clincher, both the beautiful song and the spirit of the mouse, suddenly reminded him of his dear mother.

An amazing review of his life began to dance through his mind, and quickly brought him back to his earliest memories, his very beginnings.

Still, the crow droned on about The Professor's final plans to make the cat tremble and cower in shame as he begged for his life, before torturing and killing him. Surely this powerful feline wanted to fight back!

Mantis slowly came out of his stupor. As he brought himself back to the present, he decided he could take no more. He got right into the face of that psychotic crow and told him everything he'd just heard was nothing but a pack of lies.

Poe began to sputter, it appeared that he was trying to figure out how to redeem himself and get Mantis back on board.

Poe began again, and the large cat listened. The looney bird finished with a pantomime of all the tragedy to come. Mice terrified, cat attacked, cat dying, Poe witnessing it all. Maybe being attacked, too!

He bobbed his head, paced back and forth, choked himself, then collapsed to the floor.

The final death scene was stupendous. It might have felt sad if it hadn't been so comical.

Mantis was unmoved. In fact, it was all he could do to keep a straight face.

Melodramatic Poe ended his enactment with huge crocodile tears as he begged him to help him stay safe. The greasy crow wanted nothing to do with The Professor and his plans to kill the cat. Poe worried that the vicious bird would kill him if Mantis escaped.

Mantis again tuned him out. The huge feline became strangely silent as he struggled with brand-new thoughts about himself and the world around him. Like tectonic plates shifting on the ocean floor, the ground surely moved beneath his feet.

Who was he? What did his life mean? Did he have a special purpose? Was there another path to take? And the plan that was forming in his mind sounded crazy beyond belief. On and on his thoughts raced.

Mantis watched as Poe began to squirm. When he began to speak, the crazy crow looked like he could not believe his own ears.

Mantis said they were all in trouble—Poe and all dozen mice. And he wanted to help.

———

POE

Poe's eyes narrowed. His two beady eyes bore into the cat. He muttered to himself, "What is his game? Does this vicious feline think Poe is a fool? Poe the crow is nobody's fool."

Too much! Where to turn? Who to trust? Poe wanted it all to go away and he squeezed his eyes shut.

Again, the cat got clear up in his face and demanded he listen. "Listen like your life depends on it—because it does." At last, Poe opened his eyes and tried to look alert.

Mantis wanted Poe to do just as The Professor had asked. Poe would have to get the Mouse family on board. All twelve would need to walk out onto the wire and make their pledge.

He would have to convince them somehow to do just that. It was then Poe remembered that they were one mouse short, and out of pure necessity, he told the cat about the littlest mouse, Murfee, who was stranded up on the rooftop, and who was now living as his guest in the cupola.

Much to his dismay, Mantis told him The Professor's *real* intentions and laid out his own newly formed counterplan to destroy the great horned owl instead. A plan to save Poe *and* the mice, every one of them. A mid-air attack. Owl and cat. Mantis was willing to gamble it all.

The ancient bird was astounded. The idea was nuts. Impossible. Unbelievable! And why in the world would a cat want to help a mouse? Most likely lose his own life in the process.

What was the catch? Whatever made him think he could trust a cat?

MANTIS

Mantis grew quiet for a moment. He knew this was going to be a hard sell and was having great difficulty understanding it himself. Why did he care? Why in the world would he risk all that he was for a family of mice? How to even begin to explain the feeling that this new path was right. That even in the face of death he was finding his real self and from that, his life.

"The Professor is ruthless and it's a ruthless game he'll play. He'll kill them all, every single one of them! He'll chase them and catch them and swallow them down, you know he will," said Mantis.

Poe nodded empathically. "You're right, you mighty cat. It's a whole family that's in trouble. All but Murfee, she's the only one safe. Murfee's a real nice little fella and I don't want her to get hurt."

"Hurt! If you don't help and do your part, you're going to get all of Murfee's family killed! Even if they never venture outside of the barn. Never step out onto the wire. The owl will find an open loft window. He'll swoop in without making a sound and won't leave until he finds them. He'll kill them in the night. I need your help."

The shiny black crow had a quick reply. "Oh, Mantis, you're the one to stop that owl. You can stop him. Not Poe. Poe cannot do what you ask. He stays in the shadows. Poe stays safe. Always. Always he does. Cat, it's all up to you."

Mantis knew truer words had never been spoken. A terrible weight rested on his shoulders; it was every bit up to him. Was he Mantis-the-annihilator, or Manny, as his mother had told him, someone with a very special purpose? A true hero, his mother's brightest star.

What would be required of the large feline, Mantis the cat? Hero stuff. That's what was being asked of him. Either life-changing or tragically life-ending. Destroying any chance he had to retrace his steps to find his father, or ever meet his grandfather.

Poe appeared unaware of the large cat's inner struggle, and flew away with his distinctive, awkward flight, leaving Mantis to wild thoughts of all that lay ahead.

43

A LEAP OF FAITH

MURFEE

Puffs of a cool breeze pushed through the slats of the weathered cupola. Bits of straw and several of Poe's lost tail feathers floated upwards only to waft back down onto the wooden ledge. Murfee's maple leaf slowly lifted up, out, and over the black void, spinning, then twisting like a small top. Rising, rising, turning as in one graceful dance, then beginning to drift toward the blackness below.

She saw that she was about to lose her precious leaf. The tiny mouse threw herself forward, almost toppling into space. She barely grabbed the stem an instant before her maple leaf was lost to her forever.

Murfee had worked diligently to overcome her fear of heights. Now she could lean over the edge of the opening, stare far down into its depths and not get the least bit sick. She knew getting rid of her paralyzing fear was her first step to freedom.

Sitting down, she drew a shaky breath. Her treasure and

her purchase had been nearly lost. But both the leaf and she herself were safe once again. At least for now.

Still, she found no pleasure in that thought. She just wanted to go home. She wanted to lay her head down at night and know that the morning would come. That the sun would shine. And that the twins would find her and be in her hair. That she could count on Maddy being Miss Bossy and Peep being in everybody's way. Minree and her quiet beauty. Lipton and his rare but oh-so-soft smile. Mother and Father and Crazy Moe. Everything and everyone she'd always taken for granted. Did they miss her maybe just a little? She dearly hoped so.

How *did* she end up here—high on the old barn roof? Maybe she had started this journey by wishing to see the stars, but Moe and Dahson set everything in motion. No! Milo was the one who pushed her to climb aboard the rocket. Without his anger and accusations propelling her, she would have chickened out.

Milo's words replayed in her head. "We'll want her to come down easy and on her feet instead of on her back all tangled up in the string." She distinctly recalled visualizing a twisted and tangled muddle of string and rocket and mouse. "Wow! Guess I sorta knew what was coming. But what kind of best friend puts that image in your head? Was he wanting the rocket to crash and burn? Seriously!

"And why such a hateful look? If you can't trust your best bud, who can you trust?" She chewed on her lower lip. *What else has my favorite brother gone and done since I've been up here on the roof?* she thought sarcastically. *What lies has he spread? And a thief. I've never stolen anything in my life.*

Lipton... Lipton will know better. But he might not speak up. He might hold all his thoughts in his heart and not say a word to defend me. Same goes for Minree... she's painfully shy, too. Hmm... Mother and Father—they'd never believe Milo's lies about me—or would they?

Which of Murfee's lifelong assumptions were solid? Which ones could she stake her life on? Well, her trust and belief in Milo were shot to smithereens, much like the rocket she'd ridden, its pieces scattered to who knows where.

Murfee shifted her sitting position and let out a soft sigh. For the moment she was safe and she took some solace in that. She reached out and patted the beautiful maple leaf she'd placed beside her. Tangible. Touchable. For right now that would have to be enough.

A light, cool breeze moved through the cupola and she shivered in spite of herself. *Will they label me a thief? Maybe they forgot all about me. Maybe I can never go home, I have no home. No... that can't be right.*

Murfee considered her options. If Poe stopped acting crazy, maybe she could make a deal with him. And if his wing *was* strong enough, he could fly her home.

If she made a pact with him, what would be the catch? Mischief at the very least. Shaky promises, an alliance to be kept in the dark. Or worse, simply another prison, captive in another time or place. There would be strings attached to any arrangements with Poe.

On the other hand, for now she was safe where she was. Murfee could move deep into the crevice she'd found—the tiniest of openings leading into a hidden space of the cupola, a space within one of its walls. There maybe she could rest. Be invisible, be hidden from all that sought her ruin. It would be a great plan except she hated a confined place. The crevice was dark, musty, and almost airless. Eventually, she'd run out of the supplies she'd stashed there.

But still... maybe hiding there could buy her the time she needed to make a better plan.

Back and forth she argued which path was best. At last, she shrugged her shoulders. She'd simply have to trust that a way would show itself and that everything would turn out all right.

Murfee thought back to all that had happened since landing on the rooftop. She had come through so much uncertainty unscathed. *It's really against all odds I've made it this far,* she thought. *Something else must be at play here, something much bigger than me.*

The tiny mouse had a sudden bolt of understanding. She'd never really been alone. Deep into the storm, she'd called out her SOS to the Architect high above and in flew Twink.

The oh-so-needed belief in herself came to her in the form of a dream when Merlin of King Arthur's Court, the kindly wizard, told her she knew the way home. Without the magic, without a cape or sword. She had the brains—*she* knew.

And in fact, she did, she'd just been shown. It was her precious maple leaf. She'd already used one to lift herself off the roof in the small whirlwind, flying free just like the little birds lifting and twirling and dancing in the sky. Those tiny birds—they'd shown her life. Joy and real freedom.

She'd never have it here, simply surviving. And she knew in her heart it would never work to make a deal with that psychotic crow.

She stood up, awkwardly carrying her precious leaf, and moved close to the very edge of the mouth of blackness. "I'm going home. All I have to do is make the jump," she murmured.

Murfee bent low and peered into the darkness as if she could see her family waiting. She picked up a small hard corn kernel and gave it an easy toss into space.

"Shhhh… listen… " she said to herself as she strained to hear it reach the floor far below. But she heard no sound.

For a time, frozen in place, she continued to stare down into the nothingness. Legs numb, arms suddenly heavy and nearly lifeless, bloodless. Oh! She forgot about that cat. Tyrus —old and toothless or a wild mouse-chaser, a mouse killer? She wished she knew.

Murfee heard the screeching cry of a hawk flying overhead and it galvanized her into action. She stood, grasped both ends of her leaf, held it high overhead, and attempted to step out into space. But not one part of her moved, not even the slightest fraction of an inch.

A frightful wind found its way into the cupola and stirred up the dust and sent several small feathers high into the air.

Murfee teetered forward and back for what felt like long moments, finally falling back onto the ledge, clutching her maple leaf, and crab-walking and crawling to the back wall of the cupola.

There she collapsed in tears. Unbelievable. The hero that she had been working on becoming, where had that part gone? Could it have totally disappeared?

Wide-eyed, the littlest mouse worked to steady herself. Would she ever have the courage to jump out into endless blackness? Murfee shivered at the very thought. "Got goose bumps on goose bumps. That just can't be good. It just can't."

44
FIGHT

SOPHIE

SOPHIE SEEMED TO BE FADING, her mind unfocused and dazed. At last, she confessed her deepest fear—leaving the attic and going out into a terrifying world "out there."

"I don't remember. I won't know how to act. I'll be afraid all the time and I'll stick out like a sore thumb and get us both caught. I killed my grandmother—they'll know that. Then they'll take you away somewhere and I'll be all alone. I'm better off staying right here and never going out there." She motioned to the attic door. "Justice, I've never been so afraid, ever. If I could just go back to how it was before, I'd never complain. I wouldn't give Rosalie a heart attack and I would stop asking for bangs and for all the clocks to stop." She turned away.

"Sophie, Sophie, Sophie. You didn't kill your grandmother. You didn't give her a heart attack. Get that straight in your head. Sophie, you've got a family to fight for, remember? Fight for your father, maybe for a mother you don't know anything about. Fight for your family even if you can't find a way to fight for yourself.

"Join me. We'll fight for our fathers. Fight for Lane. He might be needing you. Have you ever thought about that?

"I know I need to find my father, Tyrus. I left him without so much as a goodbye. I'm hoping he can find a way to forgive me, and maybe give me answers I seek— answers about my son.

"Don't you want answers? I know I do."

45
CONQUER THE MOUNTAIN

LIPTON HAD FOUND a quiet place to be by himself. As usual, his thoughts were of Murfee and his fear for her. Did she know she was constantly on their minds? Did she know she was missed fiercely? Was she hurt, did she need their help, had she even survived?

There was something terribly wrong that Mother and Father didn't know. Was the secrecy really needed or was everybody simply hedging their bets? Maybe protecting self-interests? And what, if any, was his own responsibility? He fought with these thoughts constantly.

True, none of the crazy scheme had been his, and he had voiced his opposition from the start. Oh. But here's the rub. The question that would not let him rest. Could he have stopped the whole idea of building a rocket ship to the moon? And more to the point, could he have vetoed the proposal for manned space flight?

Was he also in part to blame—no—maybe even more—

maybe all? He was ashamed of himself—for his lack of courage and for the part he'd played lying to their parents. For he had recognized the potential of danger, but he'd been so wrapped up in himself that he hadn't stopped his brothers. He could have brought sanity into the mix.

He heard a noise like something dragging. *What was that? And now it's stopped. I hear it again! Maybe it's a cat. Maybe Moe did really see a monster cat!* His heart began to beat hard in his chest. "LUB DUB LUB DUB LUB DUB." And the fear that was so often his companion, in the night or in the light of day, came back with a roar.

Ever since his accident, life hadn't been the same. The pain that never left him was a part of it, but the self-doubt and the distrust of himself and his world were much, much worse.

His injury wasn't really anyone's fault, though he would have loved to have found someone to blame. What had happened in an instant had changed his world forever, and there was never a way to go back.

Lipton Thomas Mouse, giant-sized Lipton T., had been damaged both inside and out. He was now nearly always afraid, and nobody knew.

There they were again. Strange sounds. Scratching, dragging sounds. A thump, another thump. Then something like the sound of breathing that he knew was not his own. His breath caught in his chest, only to escape in pants.

Such a big and burly fellow he appeared to be, but in reality, he was nothing more than one extra-large scaredy-cat of a mouse.

Everything became deathly quiet, and that made it seem all the worse. How much more could he cower, tremble, or shake? Shame moved through him like liquid heat and almost brought him to his knees. Murfee might be fighting for her very life and here he was in a panic, maybe over nothing more than branches moving in the wind.

Would he take a risk for Murfee if he could help her? Could he sacrifice himself for his treasured little sister? He hoped he would. He prayed that he could.

It's only the wind. Only the wind. Branches blowing in the wind and scratching the side of the barn or the rooftop. Unless it's what Moe tried to warn us about—one monster-sized cat.

Lipton willed himself to just breathe. Breathe. Breathe. His heart slowed to a softer, slower rhythm and he found himself once again thinking about his sister Murfee.

Would he be able to move past his own struggles to save her if he could? *If, and that's a big if, I could get out of my own mind long enough to help her, how would I? What could I do?*

The wind blew hard lifting and rattling the shingles on the roof high overhead. The disturbance made a strange whistling sound as it found its way through cracks in the old walls. It finished with the definite thump of a large branch crashing onto the rooftop. *Branches of the maple tree up on the roof!*

Lipton's eyes grew wide with a sudden understanding. If Murfee were somewhere up above and he could reach her by climbing up the maple tree, could he help her, maybe rescue her?

With excitement that both energized and somehow calmed him, Lipton Thomas Mouse quickly made his way down to the main floor of the barn to leave the safety of its walls, and then to prepare to scale one ancient, colossal, towering tree. Mount Everest to a mouse.

46

SECRETS IN A HIDDEN DRAWER

JUSTICE

"Pack light, Sophie. Put it in your backpack. A couple changes of clothes. A couple lightweight sweaters you can layer—it can get cold at night. We've got stuff to gather up from downstairs, too. Hurry."

"What's a backpack? And I want to take some of my maps. Maybe a couple books."

"Your book bag. Your grandmother gave it to you on your birthday before last, remember? See, it's got straps on one side and you wear it on your back. You'll have to carry all of it—I'm not going to be any help, so pack light."

Sophie looked longingly at her stacks of books.

"You don't understand the seriousness of this. Do you want someone to come and take you away?" Sophie eyes grew wide. Justice quickly changed the subject in an attempt to redirect her thoughts. "Okay. One map, then we gotta go.

"Oh, and your envelope of cash—your money from this birthday and the last ones—and Christmas. We might need that. Grab that small flashlight and your compass, if you want. Oh, and some of that cat food you've stashed somewhere close. Yes, Sophie, the smell reached me before I even started up the stairs.

"Now for the tricky part. In the study downstairs, Rosalie has a secret drawer with a hidden release latch... I think I can show you how to unlock it. We'll need a couple of those small water bottles she has in the fridge, fruit bars, and your grandfather's cap."

"Why the cap and what's in the drawer?"

"Sophie, your hair looks wild, and we don't want any extra attention. You look a bit like a boy dressed in your painter's bibs. That flat tweed cap of Theo's might add to the disguise. Oh! Grab one of those stiff hairbands that your grandmother made you wear, the one you always complained about. Maybe it'll hold your hair back." He struggled not to laugh. "We can only hope."

"Those darn things make my head hurt. Justice, what about Theo? Maybe he'll come back and take care of me—do you think?"

"I watched your grandfather lose it. I saw him pack a small bag of his own. I heard him on the phone talking about bus schedules.

"The drawer may hold answers about your father. Sophie, we can't afford to get caught. Now, let's go!"

47
STRANGER THAN STRANGE

MANTIS

THE LARGE FELINE climbed to the top of the old wooden windmill tower with easy grace. Mantis allowed himself a short moment to enjoy the simple beauty spread out before him.

Golden sunlight gilded angles and edges, making the old farmstead a spellbound fantasy. He wondered how it was possible a place of such serenity could be hiding horrific forces soon to be put into motion, an end to it all, perhaps this very night.

Such beauty and innocence surrounded him, crowded him from all sides, and filled him, taking him back to when he was a kitten. Those long days of running and jumping, nights of strolling down the wharf, swimming in the moonlight. Singing at the top of his lungs. And laughing, too, sometimes until he hurt. How did he not know it then? How did he not count it all as treasure? What he'd give to travel back to that time. For a week, a day, for just one fish dinner with his family under a ceiling of stars.

So different now. Life and death lay before him. Instead of beginnings, this day was likely a time of goodbyes, a leave-taking.

But not this minute. Not until the night fell. For now, he would take air deep, deep into his lungs. He'd notice the dew drops, the rhythm of the leaves, and the tall grasses kissed by the sun. He'd think of his mother. And of his father, too. No tears. There would be no tears. Not one.

MURFEE

Murfee was crouched down at the outside corner of the cupola ready to slip inside or to make a run for it, whichever the next challenge might require. Thankfully, she had not seen a glimpse of her old friend, Poe, nor of the great horned owl that she'd noticed in the early dawn sleeping high up in the maple tree. But, oh, was she tired. How much longer could she stay vigilant both day and night?

"Murfeeeeee," drifted out over the spaces. Hearing her name, she gasped. *Good grief! Now what?*

The small mouse turned pale when she saw that it was one monster-sized cat calling her. In her panic, her mind began to race. *Oh no! There really is a cat the size of a dog with maybe eyes in the back of his head.* Instinctively, she took two halting steps backward.

Heaven, help me! I need a little break—can't take much more of this. Still, I don't think cats can fly, and he's not even near the roof. Maybe I can make a run for it. But to where? Oh boy! Got my goose-bumps back. Goosebumps on goosebumps! she thought.

"Hey! Over here. On the tower. Yep, it's me. A cat. And you gotta get over your fright, tiny mouse, because I have a whole bunch I need to tell you. We don't have much time!"

"WE!" Immediately anger replaced every bit of fear and Murfee drew herself up to her fullest height. "We? Whadya mean, 'we'? I haven't noticed much help up here. And if my white knight did come, I really doubt he'd look like an over-sized cat!"

Where it came from, she didn't know, but anger spilled through her. She started to shake, her face turned red, and she felt ready to explode. Murfee Mouse had at long last reached the end of her rope.

The large cat seemed to pay absolutely no attention to this, but instead made a formal bow and introduced himself. "P. Mantis Cat. You can just call me Manny, if you like."

Murfee could do little but stare. *That cat's no big deal,* she thought. *He can't even begin to get me. I'm perfectly safe right where I'm at.*

She took several steps forward. "Your name's not impor-tant, Cat. I've got a question for you, though, and you're gonna have to answer it before I even start to listen to what you came to say. Everything depends on how you answer it, too."

Her eyes searched his. "You're a cat," she said. Manny held her steady gaze. "And most cats eat mice, right?" She waited for him to speak, and when he didn't, she asked again. "Most cats eat mice, right? Just what is it that you eat, Cat?"

"Well," he began after some hesitation. "When I was young, I lived at the seashore, and I ate fish, lots and lots of fish. And when I was on my way here, I ate just about anything I could find... lizards, rats, birds, insects even. Garbage when I couldn't find anything else, sometimes even grass. Squirrels, bugs. Protein's the important thing—my mother always said. Ummm... moles and voles."

"Voles," her voice came out in a squeak. For a moment, she lost all speech. Then she continued. "I saw a little fellow, a small vole starting on his own adventure—just like me. His mother stopped him. She gave him an awful sassing, and it looked like he was going to stay safe in the corn field. But then later... I heard an awful sound... a screechy screeching sound. Something really not right." For a moment her eyes glazed over. She shook her head to refocus.

"He didn't get to go on that adventure, did he? That sound. Something I'd never ever heard before... That wasn't you, was it, Mr. Cat? Tell me that wasn't you—you didn't eat that little vole... and then you can talk all you want, and I'll listen. Tell me right now."

"Murfee," he said quietly, "I am a cat. And cats eat voles and cats eat mice." His eyes remained fixed on hers. "A cat is a cat is a cat." The tiniest mouse in a family of twelve, the one with the soft blue-gray eyes, gulped. She got very quiet, began to stare off into space, and for a time looked perfectly, perfectly lost.

When she recovered, the one-inch mouse drew herself up to her fullest height. She'd hear him out, yes, but she wasn't going to be swayed by anything he said. She made a mental note that none of what she had just learned would give her bad dreams in the night. She was done with being afraid. Done.

"It's going to sound strange, and it's not at all logical that I should care—your whole family is in terrible danger from the great horned owl," Manny went on to say.

Murfee looked about to faint. So much for not being afraid. She looked petrified. "My family! All of them? Mother and Father. All my brothers and sisters. The big owl in the tree? Please, no!"

She looked away and stood still as a statue. It was a long moment before she could collect herself and even then, her mind continued to race. At last, she again faced the huge predator.

"Oh! Mr. Manny, I wish you were more like that cat down in the lower part of the barn that hates the taste of a mouse. He only eats whatever the old farmer feeds him, and—and I hear he's quite content with that." She became thoughtful. "He must be a really nice kind of cat.

"Years ago, the farmer's kids, two young boys back then—Tom and—and Terry, I think, played with him and loved him. Heard he never scratched. Just played nice—and he didn't eat mice! That's the way I heard it, anyway."

She shook her head and pursed her lips. "It doesn't sound at all logical forming any kind of alliance with you, I'd have to watch out for the both of you, an owl *and* a cat!"

MANTIS

"Just hear me out, Murfee Mouse. Then you can decide." When he saw her small nod, he went on to quickly fill her in on The Professor's wicked plan. Yes, he himself was an eater of mice, but what The Professor, the great horned owl, had planned was diabolical and just plain wrong. "My mother would never forgive me if I didn't at least try..." His voice trailed off.

Murfee looked at him questioningly. "I don't understand."

A wistful look crossed his face. "You kinda remind me of my mother, which I know is stranger than strange. Murfee, it was the song. It all started with the song." He paused to gather his thoughts.

"I heard you singing 'Catch a Falling Star,' my mother's favorite and—and you sounded a little bit like her, too. I'd forgotten her. I'd lost so much... and you brought it all back to me. Now I'm remembering." A dreamy expression softened his features.

"The ocean. And fish heads, and boats, and nets, and even a midnight swim in the moonlight." He was lost to her now, awash in memories once locked away. He spoke as if in a deep, deep trance. "That song carried me back to those special times when I was a kitten. So long ago. A time when I was safe and loved... when I was small. And the sound of the waves, the times with my father. All of it."

His eyes refocused and he looked at her intently, willing her to understand the depth of his words. "You wonder why a cat would want to help a family of mice. Well, I don't know how else to say it but, you see, I have a purpose. Each star has a distinct purpose, too. And when you know the truth, you can never run from it. My mother told me all of that."

Murfee listened in earnest.

"Small mouse, I had made destruction my purpose. And now, I have to follow my conscience and I have to make a choice. I know it doesn't make a lot of sense to you, but I don't have time to explain it all. Instead, I'm going to have to be blunt. The Professor wants to kill your whole family. You too, if he can find you. The Professor wants to kill you all. Make a wild game of it, with his demented version of Jacks."

48

THE STUFF OF HEROES

MANNY

MANNY WENT on to explain the details of his scheme to battle the vicious owl and to save Murfee's family—maybe save them all. They would have to act as if they believed the lie the owl had contrived and go out onto the wire and wait. Expose themselves to real danger. It was the only way.

But Manny would be ready, too. He would be prepared to launch his attack, targeting The Professor from his position high on the old windmill tower.

"Don't count on even seeing Poe. I think he's hiding out until this drama has played out. In fact, he's trying to play this from both sides, and you *cannot* trust anything he says. We need to get you to your family. See if you can get them all on board. Hurry, Murfee. We don't have a lot of time."

Murfee chewed on her lower lip. Then she asked, "What do you mean with this 'we' business, P. Mantis Cat?"

"Murfee, you and me. That's the *we*. Hard to believe, I may be your only help. You'll have to trust me."

His large eyes silently pleaded for understanding. "When I saw you high up on the roof singing that song, I had a sudden thought—that size doesn't have anything to do with anything. Little mouse, it's your help I need and yours alone. Only with you on board will the plan stand a chance. And Murfee, I have a few ideas about how to get you down off the rooftop. I think I know a way," he finished.

MURFEE

Murfee's mind was spinning. She knew the way to go home! *She* knew. All that was needed now was her courage. The courage to take a huge leap of faith down into the black void and down into the loft.

Her mind was filled with worries for her family and of the part she must play to save them. She turned away, then turned back. "Well, Mr. Manny, it's hard to believe we're gonna form any lasting kind of friendship. You are a cat, and I am a very little mouse. I should be terrified down to my toes."

She continued, "But I've learned on this trip that there are real reasons to be afraid, and I don't think this is one of them. Strangely, I am not afraid of you—as long as you've had something else to eat or drink. 'Cuz, did I hear you right? You do, you really and truly do—eat mice?"

With the cat's slight nod, Murfee's eyes widened and she gulped. But she took note of the kindness that radiated from him. She once more became thoughtful. "You've given me the very best reason to find my courage. I do know how to get back home, and this time I think I'll be ready. And I'm going to take your word for it that you're here to help. Somehow, I believe you. Together maybe we could put an end to all of this.

"Oh!" She started to leave but turned back to him with a deadly smile. "Promise me you'll make sure you're filled up—drink your milk. By the way, you'll find some down in the dairy barn. Just look for the food dish of that old cat. Father said he only drinks milk or slurps up scraps that come from the farmer's table. Moe thinks his name might be Tyrus, the mouse-chasing cat. I bet he'd share."

MANNY

Manny was speechless. His words become all tumbled and jumbled. "Ty—Ta—Tyrus... Tyrus. Tyrus. You think his name —is Tyrus? And he never eats a mouse, just wants to chase 'em?"

Murfee mutely nodded.

Could it be? Was it even possible his grandfather Tyrus was the cat she spoke about? Right here on this very farm? Had Manny traveled all these many miles only to return to his father's childhood home? Had his own feet somehow carried him there? He tried to wrap his mind around the idea. What were the odds of that, of finding his grandfather? Of finding family?

Another thought ricocheted through his brain. He knew the way home! He could retrace his steps. Find his father. Maybe bring him back to the farm... if only he had more time.

"Earth to cat! Manny, you say you want to follow your conscience. Just know there may be a terrible cost to that."

"I do know. Trust me, Murfee, I do." His next words over-flowed with hope and longing. "I have to ask; did you hear anything else about the cat named Tyrus? Did he have a son... a son named Justice? That's my father's name, see?"

The large feline looked off into the distance and the small mouse slipped away without his notice.

"His father's name was Tyrus. Is it possible I've found my way to where my father was born?" P. Mantis Cat was left talking to himself as he stared off into space.

Suddenly he sucked in his breath. He had forgotten to tell Murfee about the two guys he had seen slinking around the farmstead. Did he need to warn her about them, too? The huge predator knew how to slink, and that's exactly what he'd call it —they were always glancing around furtively, too, and poking around where they didn't belong. One of them walked with a shuffling gait and a distinctive limp. It looked like he wore some sort of leg brace. The other was taller and seemed to be the boss of the two of them. Manny wished he had questioned the small mouse about what he had seen.

Weird. Every time he thought about those young men, a great unease moved through him. They never did anything, never tried to take anything, and never seemed to be anything but two overgrown kids creeping around. Still, it was secretive, that's what it was.

Maybe they had jumped off a passing train, the tracks not so far away... just passing through. Maybe that's all it was.

Well, it wouldn't matter any which way if he couldn't stop the great horned owl and his horrific plans.

MURFEE

A plan had taken shape, and it would work, or it wouldn't. But it was all they had. Now they each had a job to do, and there was no time to waste.

Murfee closely examined the vent-hole opening down into

the barn. She turned back and slowly picked up her precious maple leaf. Could something so fragile in appearance hold up without tearing apart—all the way down? Could she keep her firm hold on it? If it took a tossed penny so long to hit the barn floor... she didn't even want to know the math. A mouse-eating cat might be waiting. Waiting and watching. With two evil slits for eyes that took everything in, eyes that could see in the dark. She'd dreamt about him. He lurked at the corners of her mind each night before she escaped into sleep. A vicious, most terrible cat.

Poe! He was the one that set this all up and you could never trust that crow. Maybe this was his sick way to send her to her death. Manny the cat didn't know Poe like she did.

The oily bird was power-hungry and insane, a terrible combination. She should have told Manny that, yes, he himself had been played.

Here she was safe. She could stay here. Maybe it was a good thing in the end. She had her hiding place in the inner wall. Poe's food storage was close by. She could deceive *him* and make it look as if she had at last escaped, then sneak out to take a drink and eat when she was sure he was gone.

Her family hadn't tried to find her—no second rocket ship had traveled the same path she'd taken up through the hole in the roof. Did they believe Milo that she was the thief—not Poe?

Murfee didn't need that. She didn't need them. Milo was her best friend. If he believed Poe's lies, she didn't stand a chance with all the rest. To be shunned by everyone—that would be the most unbearable of all. Survival. She had that here. Stay safe, stay small.

She'd been lying to herself—she needed to face that. *She* was a liar; she wasn't a hero and would never be. She'd never even be a somebody.

Perhaps the raw truth was she had no family, no home but

for the prison she found herself in. Certainly, she owed nothing to no one, and no one could count on her.

***

Murfee had never felt so low. Less than an inch. Was she taking the true coward's way out? What if she could save her family? What if she was the only one who could? First, she'd have to survive that long fall with nothing but a leaf to slow her descent. Was that even possible? Did a mouse-eating cat lie in wait? Would Murfee be traveling a road to betrayal or be bringing help?

If there ever was a time for her to be a hero, it was now. She'd have to trust that Manny's plan was the right one and that it would work, and that she would in fact survive.

Trusting was the risk she'd need to take.

Her heart raced and her head pounded. Had anybody ever had their whole noggin explode? Sheesh, maybe she'd be the first.

Manny was getting ready for his crazy part in their scheme. He didn't show any fear, and yet his role and his ability to survive it all looked next to impossible. To fly off the windmill tower and attack the large bird in mid-flight? What was he thinking? What was at stake for him?

Murfee's hand flew up to her mouth and her large eyes grew larger still. The family that *he* loved wasn't at stake. He'd never met Mother and Father. Never held Peep as a tiny baby. Raced down the silver spoon with the rest of her sisters. Not one ride on Lipton's broad shoulders.

Only the words of his own mother and the promise he'd made to her, if only in his heart. To follow truth. To step up, to rise to his true purpose. Murfee hadn't really listened as he talked longingly about his family. She hadn't cared about that.

A thought exploded in her head. He was the real hero, not the littlest mouse. It was he who was risking all for a family of mice. And she hadn't even said thanks.

Manny said she could be brave. That size *didn't* matter. It better not because she had a job to do... an important part to play... to save a family of mice. Hers!

A leaf for a parachute. Dear Lord, she'd need a parachute for her parachute, a spare and she only had one.

MURFEE THOUGHT WITH DEEP SATISFACTION THAT SHE HAD USED SOME of her time in the cupola wisely when she'd practiced getting rid of her terrible, debilitating fear of heights.

Thankfully, she didn't have to worry about dizziness or nausea stopping her now. But that was the least of her worries.

She planned to step out into the terrible void. Into what looked like a bottomless nothingness. Right now, what she wanted most in all the world was simply to live through that nightmare drop. Beads of sweat broke out on her forehead and her heart gave a little lurch. Skipped a couple beats, left her pale and feeling faint.

Murfee returned to the edge of the hole and peered down. Looking nervous and uncertain she stepped away, holding her maple leaf close. "I can do this, I can."

All at once her legs gave out and she sat down hard. The maple-leaf parachute lay at her side. She wished she could take every one of her wishes back, everything she had set into motion. Be home like none of this had ever happened. It wouldn't matter if she was ignored or teased. Murfee would never be discontent again.

Had her wishing started it all? Brought danger into her

family's midst? There was no way to know, and it didn't matter if it had because she couldn't take any of it back.

If only she had a little magic. She'd wish for that. Magic could make everything right again. But Poe had taken her velvet cape to where, she didn't know. Her sword, too. It would be impossible to find them in time.

Time! She was running out of it. So much depended on her. Lives depended on her. Earlier, she had sorta wished for her family to be in danger so she could save them. She'd be the hero. What a fool. She was nothing without the magic.

Who was going to save her family? Maybe the cat could be the hero. Murfee squeezed her eyes shut and slumped down in defeat.

She lay down by her leaf, too tired to cry, and was half asleep when the wizard of her dreams returned, Merlin of King Author's Court, still dressed in a robe of stars. He made certain he had her attention before he began to speak.

"Littlest Mouse, surely you know by now neither courage nor power will be found in a velvet cape or a sandwich-pick sword. The magic *is you*, and your hero is right inside."

Murfee came wide awake in a flash. She stood and, assuming a warrior's stance, picked up the maple leaf. She moved to the very edge of the black. Resolutely grasping the stem end of the leaf with one hand, the furthermost lobe of it with the other, she held the leaf high, closed her eyes tightly, and willed herself to jump.

Instead, she shuddered. She opened her eyes, took a step back, and began again talking to herself. "Do you s'pose Poe was right about a cat being on the prowl? Guess I'm about to find out. Now's the time for courage. Come on, where's your courage, Murfee Mouse? And remember, you're much more than an inch." Her knuckles whitened as she tightened her grip on her makeshift, maple-leaf parachute.

"Boy, it's a long way down."

Abruptly she moved back to the opening and lifted the leaf high. A grim smile settled over her features. Her eyes widened as she jumped out and into the void. "GERON—

"—IMOOOOO." Murfee disappeared down into the loft.

Her golden leaf parachute wafted gently down from the cupola high overhead. She drifted through the dark for what felt like an eternity. She couldn't see above or below as she gripped the maple leaf. She finally noticed some light below, growing as she floated down. At last, her feet touched down like a feather, the leaf settling over her head. She'd made it! She wanted to jump for joy. She hadn't gotten sick and the leaf held up.

She peeked out from under her parachute and then exhaled deeply. Soon she was running toward sounds coming from another area of the loft, her maple leaf slung over her shoulder. She was returning to her home all in one piece, unharmed.

———

MANNY

Manny couldn't change much of what the night would bring. He did have the element of surprise, though, which could be game-changing. It was also pivotal that he carefully select his position. That might make the difference of life or death for the Mouse family and give him a better chance of survival.

As for himself, he knew the odds were nowhere near in his favor. He'd have to put that out of his mind. Focus! Manny checked out different heights and distances before making his final choice. He'd done his best. Now all that was left was the wait.

49
A BATTLE IN THE SKY

MURFEE

MURFEE HURRIED to her brothers and sisters, the maple-leaf parachute draped over her shoulder. When they first spied her, they stared with their mouths agape, as if seeing a ghost. Murfee took advantage of the momentary silence and put up a hand like a stop sign and a finger to her lips. "Shhhhhh…"

They were as still as wax sculptures until Milo Mouse broke down and cried. "Stuff it, Milo," Murfee said. "We've got trouble, and I don't have time for dopey sentiment. If you're gonna help, you gotta come right now. Everything else has to wait." Immediately, words began to pour out of Moe's mouth, then the rest of them chimed in. Cacophony reigned.

"ZIP IT. All of you." Murfee glanced over to Milo's crushed expression. Unsmiling, she said, "I'm sorry, I am, but we all have no choice if we're going to have the slightest chance of staying alive. All our lives are at stake, Mother and Father's, too. The owl wants to torture and kill every single one of us."

Moe squeaked, "Owl?"

Before Murfee could answer, Peep interrupted. "Have you seen Lipton? Was he with you? Is he coming?" Not getting a reply, Peep plopped herself down, stuck her thumb in her mouth, and tried not to bawl.

The boys and the twins began to question Murfee all at the same time until Maddy emitted a piercing whistle that threatened their eardrums. "Listen! Give her a chance to talk. SHUT UP!"

"Lipton's not with me. I thought he was with you. Maybe he's with Mother and Father... have you checked?" Murfee asked.

Suddenly looking sheepish, Maddy said, "They don't know. We haven't told them about either of you missing. We thought Lipton would just turn up and the boys thought they could bring you back before Mother and Father found out about your firecracker rocket ride." She dropped her head and looked down at her feet.

Murfee was dumbfounded. *My folks never missed me?* she thought. *They never even asked about me? Who did my chores? What about the bedtime count?* Things were worse than she could have ever imagined—she wasn't even important enough to be missed at night. But the clock was ticking. Far too little time for self-pity.

Her oldest brother was missing. Was he in harm's way? She said softly, "I'm sorry, but I haven't seen Lipton since the day I flew out of the hole in the roof."

Maddy jerked Peep from the floor and made her take her thumb out of her mouth. "Shape up. Now's not the time to blubber."

Without a word, they gathered into a tight huddle. Each turned toward their new leader. Murfee told them the details of The Professor's horrific plans. The great horned owl planned to kill every one of them, but a very large cat named Manny was ready to help. They'd have to be brave and do their part, too.

Moe interrupted. "A cat. *The* cat? Murfee, I met that terrible feline, stared him straight in the face. Nobody believed me, but he's real. He's huge, he's vicious, and he's a cat! *You* want us to trust him, a cat?

"Murfee, seriously, did you land on your head?" Moe demanded.

They talked all at once until Maddy yelled again to listen.

Milo asked quietly. "Murfee, do you really trust this Manny Cat? Cuz if you do, that's good enough for me." She stared intently into Milo's eyes before slightly nodding her assent. Everyone raised their hands to show they were all on board.

"Okay, everybody," Murfee said. "It's risky but here's what we're going to do. I've got a plan. I'll need everybody's help."

"Do the folks need to be a part of this?" Maddy interrupted.

"We better leave Mother and Father out of it. I think that's for the best," Murfee answered. "Everybody agreed?" They all shook their heads yes.

"There are no promises, even if we do everything right. There is a lot to be asked of each of us. Hopefully we'll find Lipton Thomas while we're at it," she added.

They all solemnly nodded, then Moe shouted, "Everybody, get ready to roll!"

Murfee laid out her strategy. The initial steps of the plan were quickly executed with each one given a job to do and not a moment to waste.

Dahson began his calculations. His talents were essential and his concentration was absolute. The rest of them worked in tandem to roll a huge spool of twine into position. They hoped the simple weight of its massive bulk would ensure that it wouldn't slide.

All this action took place at the window opening overlooking the old windmill tower. An abandoned telephone wire snaked across the span from window to windmill. This was the site where all the drama would unfold.

Everyone, minus Brainiac Dahson, helped Milo gather up his arsenal of pulleys and ropes. Harnesses quickly took shape, and the eight chosen to walk the wire were outfitted with them.

Dahson, with his near-sightedness, was given the task of stabilizing the telephone line by lying face down upon it, straddling it, arms and legs wrapped tightly around the near end of the wire. Upon further reflection, he was outfitted in safety gear, too. Everyone crossed their fingers that none of the rope, twine, or pulleys would be seen from high up above.

Details of the plan were repeated over and over again. Now all they had to do was wait.

Quiet, graceful Minree was the first to volunteer for the vital high-wire job, and she was the logical choice. She moved with a fluidity they all admired. Had Murfee ever told her so? Sadly, if things went wrong, she'd never get the chance.

Dahson looked worried. "Minree needs a better balancing pole, one with some flex. But you've got the length right." He looked up at their questioning faces over the top of his spectacles. "Flexible. It all has to do with the center of gravity and the need for a ready adjustment of the pole while she walks."

Milo said, "Dahson, it's all we've got. It's gonna have to work. Right, Murf?" He looked over at his sister. She nodded and gave him the slightest smile.

Preparations were complete. The sun slipped away. Hopefully, The Professor had been sleeping and hadn't noticed a thing. Perhaps he would not show up at all!

THE PROFESSOR

But the great horned owl was wide awake. He now narrowed his eyes to slits as he looked about and listened to the sounds of the night. He felt the wind shift. He watched the moon as it seemed to dance in the sky. Normally he experienced a surge of proprietorial pride as he took it all in, this kingdom that was his, but this time he did not. Instead, the magnificent bird felt a rare sense of unrest, of being a bit unsettled. This was a new experience for him. Never before had he wondered about an adversary. Never before had he ruminated about a situation he was in. But now...

What evil strategies did that miserable feline hold deep in *his* heart? The Professor thought back to the time of his confrontation with the big cat. He clearly remembered threatening him. He recalled feeling powerful with a fearless confidence that was heady. He remembered a recklessness, a superiority that pumped through his veins and delighted him deep in his soul. What had happened since? What was the light of the moon telling him? Tonight, its moonbeams seemed to bring a warning. Death. Was it his?

MANNY

Manny imperceptibly stretched, attempting to release the tension in his muscles. A visible shiver moved over his body. Fear or adrenaline? He'd love to know the answer, but in the end, did it really matter? One would die. One would live. All of his life had prepared him for this. Liza, his mother, had prepared him for this. He was glad she wasn't alive to see the battle before him, her heart would have been in her throat. But she could have been assured that her lessons to take a stand for truth would soon bear fruit.

Another thought came into his mind. Was it possible she was looking down from above and was holding him in her heart? Focus! Focus, Manny! That's all that was needed now.

POE

Poe the crow was in the middle of a panic attack. So many things could go horribly wrong. It was vital he kept his eyes open, at least to witness the end of the fight to see which one survived. Poe would want to assure the victor of his allegiance and of his usefulness without delay!

What in the world was he thinking, getting involved in this mess? Well, actually he'd been pulled into the drama by the owl's demands, so again he himself was the helpless (and wholly innocent) victim. Sheesh! Why couldn't he be the hero for once? Just once. Now if his heart would quit skipping beats, then racing, he could calm down and think. What if he found he needed to make a rapid escape?

What if both owl and cat met their untimely deaths? He, Poe the crow, could then save the day and come out on top. Hmm...

MURFEE

Murfee was filled with remorse. What had she been thinking, risking the lives of brother and sister alike? Why hadn't she gone immediately to her parents, to her father? Was there some part of her that wanted the limelight, some part that so coveted attention, that it rose up and demanded instead the hero worship found in her dreams? Some part that had betrayed her in the end and would get them all killed?

It wasn't that she didn't trust the cat and his motives, she didn't trust her own. Death was waiting this night and her own childish dreams of adventure and heroism were already at its door.

MILO

Milo's heart was breaking. He alone had started the tragedy about to unfold before him. What he wouldn't give to take back hateful words he'd said to his littlest sister. She never would have taken the rocket ride. She wouldn't have gone missing. Maybe they'd still be safe from the great horned owl.

Words. Couldn't be taken back. The unrelenting guilt he felt brought a heaviness to his chest and he felt sick. Maybe his heart would stop and he would die on the spot. But then, that was the least of it.

MINREE

Minree stepped out onto the wire. She moved with the agility of a seasoned tightrope walker, holding a length of Tinker Toy to serve as her pole. Her task was to take the far end of the string of twine all the way across and anchor it to the windmill tower. Not only did she have to walk the entire span with only her balancing pole to help her, but the twine was unwieldy, and the wind had begun to blow. Her siblings played out the string continually to give her the slack on the line she needed.

The wire swayed with each gust, and Minree struggled to keep her body loose and responsive. Still, she made steady progress. Not until she wrapped the end of the twine snuggly around a wooden brace did she let herself take in a full breath. *Whew!*

MURFEE

Holding onto the twine as a guide rope to steady herself, Murfee moved silently into position. Darkness had come quickly, but the waiting that followed felt endless. Murfee held on tightly to her leaf parachute; the talisman gave her courage.

MADDY

Maddy tried to be mad, if nothing more than to distract herself from the terror she was feeling, but it didn't work. Her pulse pounded in her throat and her eyes filled with tears. Where did they come from?

Her entire life had up to this point been one of order. Doing things right, instructing her brothers and sisters to make sure they did the same. Making sure she was known to her parents as the one they could depend on—the good one. Perfectionism and obedience, even to the point of tattling to earn extra points. Lining up her siblings in ramrod order. That was her place in the family, and she'd thought it had served her well. Control, that was dependable. Rules, they were like a foundation for living. Now there was nothing she could count on. Even the moonlight seemed to be adversarial, exposing each of them high above the ground, vulnerable morsels suspended in space. Her world dropped away under her feet.

DAWSON

Dahson was having great difficulty carrying out his assignment. His ever-present glasses were left behind, and though his vision was quite good, he'd gotten used to the idea that without his specs he could barely see a thing.

Maddy helped him earlier, before they had taken their positions on the wire. She'd suggested that he leave his frames, and she'd placed them on the upper surface of the massive bundle of twine.

Dahson struggled to stabilize himself atop the rounded surface of the old telephone wire. He felt lost and adrift without his glasses. The world around him was nothing but a blur so he closed his eyes. His heart pounded and his stomach twisted in knots.

MURFEE

Murfee saw that Manny was in position, but she hadn't seen The Professor. All this time waiting, and she'd not caught a glimpse of him.

She had a terrible thought. *Had* Poe played a double-cross, a payback for Murfee's escape, with devious plans to have her and all her family destroyed? Had he formed an alliance with The Professor? Maybe he told the owl to wait until every mouse on the wire was ready to collapse with little or no chance of escape. If so, she and her siblings would most likely meet death this night.

Or instead, was *everything* a lie? Maybe the story about The Professor was something the crow had dreamed up to terrorize her family and make Murfee pay.

Could Poe have changed the mind of the cat? Turned Manny back into the predator he'd *been* not so long ago? Was *he* positioned to kill.

No. This one thing she was sure of—his true intentions to help. P. Mantis Cat was the one with the true hero's heart.

Something *had* changed in the owl's plans. She just knew. What had that nasty crow done? She hadn't seen him since his wild departure from the cupola where he'd held her prisoner. Since the day his mind had finally taken leave of him, she'd not caught a glimpse of him.

Perhaps the truth was much simpler. It could be The Professor had found the count to be off, only eight mice balancing on a high wire— four short of the expected twelve.

It was then Murfee spied her oldest brother, Lipton, hidden in the branches of the maple tree, apparently trapped there for fear of The Professor she now glimpsed waiting nearby. Lipton and Murfee silently exchanged glances. Her big brother looked totally surprised seeing them and their crazy high-wire act. His eyes widened in panic.

Murfee held her breath hoping Lipton would go unnoticed and everything could unfold according to plan, but Peep slipped. The baby in the Mouse family dangled in space, hands flailing, just one foot remaining on the wire. Her safety harness was all that was keeping her from a terrible fall.

Lipton leaned out as if he could save Peep, but he too found himself helplessly grabbing nothing but air, and without his own safety equipment, he began tumbling down through branches and leaves—down and down, immediately drawing the attention of the great horned owl.

The Professor looked pointedly at where Lipton now lay, just as Murfee knew that he would, and their entire scheme went up in smoke.

But they were prepared! It was now or never. She'd draw the owl's attention, force his hand, force him to act. With his lightning-fast reflexes, it was her hope The Professor would attempt to catch her in midair if she jumped and Manny could in turn attack the owl. It was the only plan she could come up with on the fly, but she'd better act quick. Time to risk her own life, not just the cat's.

Wait, Murfee. Think it through, she thought to herself. Maybe there was a possibility for everyone to survive without making herself easy prey. The powerful winds continued to buffet and bounce all of them on the wire, making each a difficult target. There was still a possibility to tear back to the safety of the loft. But Lipton was certain to be killed if something didn't change, and fast.

Manny's plan to leap from the windmill tower, destroy the vicious owl, and save them all required the owl to focus his attention on the wire. Instead, The Professor's stare was directed at Lipton Thomas, spread-eagle on the ground below.

The only gamble Murfee could see to save her brother was to draw The Professor's evil eye to herself, thus giving Manny a chance to attack.

Diving for the ground, she was certain to be an easy mark for The Professor. But maybe it could give everyone else a chance to escape and make the owl a target himself. Did she have the courage to endanger her own life?

Would Manny succeed? An airborne attack seemed next to impossible. So much was at stake in these next few moments. And Poe, where did he fit into all of this? Had they all fallen for his ruse? A deadly ruse that would get them all killed?

Murfee's thoughts returned to the sacrifice the large cat was getting ready to make. What was it that embodied a real hero? She herself could find out. She'd have to act fast to save Lipton, to save them all. And she knew just what she had to do.

MILO

What is Murfee doing? This wasn't in the script! Milo was appalled at the scene taking place before his very eyes. Murfee had taken off her safety ropes and was preparing to use her leaf parachute one last time. He wasn't ready to lose her again.

His mind held a silent scream. *No! No. Murfee, NOOOO!*

He watched on as Murfee, looking straight ahead, paused for a fraction of a second, and jumped. Her descent, at first graceful, was interrupted by a strong gust of wind that forced her sideways, flipped her back up into the air, then down to the ground in a rush and a thump.

MANNY

Manny's entire life came down to this—a choice of the two voices that weaved through his soul. One of light. One shaped of the dark. A choice his alone to make.

Regret pierced his heart. Almost certainly he would never have the chance to meet his grandfather or see his father again. But he'd made his decision, the right one, and he'd carry it out this night.

The large feline had seen Murfee's signal that everyone was ready. Eight small mice, eerily exposed, were suspended in space in the beautiful moonlight. That surprised him as he'd expected all twelve of the Mouse family. He watched the owl poised to begin his nightmarish version of Jacks. He observed The Professor redirecting his focus to one rather large mouse falling out of the giant maple tree.

Manny sneaked a look back at the group of mice on the wire and watched in amazement as Murfee lifted her maple leaf high before parachuting to the ground.

Murfee's movements brought The Professor's evil intentions back at once to the remaining seven of the bizarre high-wire act. The deadly game had begun.

The mighty cat saw the owl take flight and he launched himself forward like a missile-fired rocket, a nuclear warhead, like the great warrior that he was. Out. Out, into the beautiful night.

He thought of his mother calling him her shining star. Surely now he was no bright shining star in the sky, but a meteor flaming and plummeting down and down to the planet Earth.

The wind rushed, whistled past. Everything played out in slow motion, yet there was no time to react.

Manny and the owl met in the air and tore into each other

with talons and claws and beak and teeth. The large bird used every bit of his tremendous strength in a failed attempt to lift them both high.

His giant wingspan worked like a brake, and for a time, the two, locked in a death-like grip, hovered in space. Then they dropped like a rock to the ground far below.

SURVIVORS

Like dazed survivors of war, each of the seven mice made their way back across the abandoned telephone wire to the shelter of the old barn where they joined Dahson, with his death grip on the wire, eyes shut tight. Several helped him up. Maddy handed him his yellow plastic glasses which he quickly placed upon his nose.

Unspoken, the group hurried down through the barn and out again into the night. They raced to their fallen comrades and rejoiced to find them both struggling to their feet. "I don't think we're any worse for wear," Lipton said, and he looked over at Murfee and grinned.

Dahson got everyone's attention when he doubled over and threw up his lunch, but he quickly recovered. They retraced their steps to their home on the highest floor of the barn.

MURFEE

Murfee was the first to walk back to the loft window. Moonlight lit up the outside world as if it were day. Two bodies, warriors both, lay motionless far below. For a moment, Murfee allowed herself to be a scared little mouse. She let go of all the bravado, all the courage. Tears streamed down her face that she didn't brush away.

Milo walked over to stand by her side. He put an arm around her; she did the same.

"Oh! Milo. He was really something, he was a hero. Strong and true. The best. A very fine cat."

AN EXHAUSTED MURFEE COLLAPSED INTO THE SLEEP OF THE DEAD along with the rest of the kids, but within the hour she was wide awake again. Adrenaline coursed through her veins as she relived her short rocket ride to the rooftop, and everything that followed.

How naïve she had been when she first set out. Her thoughts raced on. It was one thing to want a hero's quest and quite another to live it. So many things could have gone horribly wrong. Did Murfee still need to prove herself? Home was safe. She *was* sure about that.

She took in the darkened loft with new eyes. How was it possible? Only days had passed, and yet nothing remained the same. Things looked the same. She looked the same. But everything had changed.

Childhood dreams of magical, carefree adventures dissolved like tendrils of smoke rising toward the heavens only to disappear in the first strong wind. Maybe Sami Sparrow and all her escapades needed to stay between the pages of a comic. Perhaps the real magic was of her own making, in her own heart and mind, the courage found deep within.

Murfee's adventure could have turned out like the small vole's journey out into the wide world. In too many ways she wasn't very different from him. Clueless sometimes to the dangers all around. Another adventure? With what she knew now?

———

252

MURFEE CALLED A MEETING EARLY THE NEXT MORNING. HER SLEEPY-eyed brothers and sisters followed her to the nearly abandoned rocket site. Once there, she confidently informed them it was time to let their parents know about her firecracker rocket ride to the barn roof, and all that had happened since. She'd be the one to tell it, she alone had earned the right. Murfee added that if the kids were in trouble, it would be good to get it over with. Her brothers and sisters agreed with everything she said.

Murfee started to leave, but Moe got right up in her face to stop her. He stepped to her side, took off his tam, then waved it high in the air until he had everyone's attention. "I know something I bet none of you know and maybe you'll believe me for once. I saw Father packing a knapsack like he was getting ready to go somewhere. Maybe he already left. Oh, and Mother was crying. What's up with that?"

"Why didn't you tell me? When was this?" Murfee wanted to strangle Moe or at least call him a choice name or two, but there wasn't time. Besides she didn't think name-calling ever made much of a difference.

Could she catch Father before he left?

50

HABEAS CORPUS AND QUID PRO QUO

MILO

Milo waited along with the rest of them for Murfee to return and explain how everything went with their folks. Grounding for the next year seemed a distinct possibility. Maddy thought the boys would be lucky at that. Milo was ready for whatever punishment he had to take. Maybe that would help him feel a little better about his terrible part in putting Murfee's life at risk. Not one of them, Milo included, could understand Murfee's frantic departure.

MURFEE

Murfee flew into the music room, breathing hard. Her mother stood near the now silent radio, crying into a piece of lace. "Where is he?" shrieked Murfee, her eyes full of worry. "Who?" her mother replied.

"Father. Where is he? Where's Father? I've got to stop him!" If only she'd have come sooner. Ultimately it was her fault if he never returned. Not even Sami Sparrow could help her now.

Murfee gasped when Quintin Cornelius walked into the room and began speaking to his wife, seemingly oblivious to Murfee's presence. "It'll be important to keep the kids busy, so they won't worry so much. It'll help you too. I'll leave after we put them to bed tonight."

He took a step back, looking startled to see Murfee standing a short distance from his wife. His face paled and his hands shook. Next, he scooped her up in his arms and hugged her fiercely, then set her gently back down.

Murfee nervously looked from one to the other. Her story tumbled out in pieces. "You don't need to leave, Father. There's a hidden supply here. In the loft. Oats. A mountain of them! Poe told me… he didn't mean to. After the rocket ride. On the roof. You can't trust that crow. But I'm home now. The parachute worked." Both parents gasped.

Mother began to weep. Between broken sobs, she talked to herself. "I don't have the right to have children if I can't protect them. I fooled myself into thinking my safety lessons could make a difference." She closed her eyes and turned away.

"I was the one who made every bedtime count those nights my smallest was gone," she continued as a shudder moved through her. She turned and looked at Murfee and Quin through tear-filled eyes. "How can either of you forgive me? How can I ever begin to forgive myself?"

Beautiful Mother Mouse was inconsolable until Murfee explained the clever ruse designed to hide her absence.

Murfee herself had been relieved to her toes to find it was never a case that she hadn't even been counted, wasn't missed, and never loved, but rather it was all a part of her brothers' crazy scheme. She knew they all cared—that she really mattered. More than just an inch.

She struggled to help both her parents understand the incredible journey she'd made. She told them of strangely feeling she *had* traveled to the stars, to the moon itself.

Murfee told her parents of the challenges she'd faced, how she had grown along the way, and how she believed she'd never be the same. She spoke to them of the Architect's help from high above, her SOS, and her new friend, Twink. And, of course, of the gift of song.

Oh! The great beauty of an ever-changing sky, the towering maple, the birds that danced in flight. Of her dreams, and a bit of what they meant to her. The treasure of the maple leaf, her shelter, and the parachute that brought her home.

With a sadness that surprised her, she spoke of Poe and his descent into madness. Of his great instability and of his heart-breaking tale of woe. She warned them also of his thievery and mischief-making. There was a mountain of grain right here in the barn. The crow had been steadily adding to it by his thievery of their own provisions.

The Mouse family would never run low on food supplies again!

She told them about The Professor, the vicious owl who set the last of her escapades into motion. Mother nearly fainted when she heard this.

Murfee told them about a cat named Manny, a cat who gave all to save a family of mice. She spoke passionately of his courage and of the truth he had shared of his own journey and the lessons he learned. The amazing choice he ultimately made. The cat was truly the hero, something she hoped they'd never let themselves forget.

She left nothing out, for she'd decided that real ignorance of the dangers surrounding them was the biggest threat of all.

The courage of all their children working together to save their family of twelve, she told of that, too.

Lastly, she reminded them that all ten were safe. In fact, the ultimate safety of the entire family was the result of *all* that had transpired.

It was her heart's journey that had taken her to the moon and back.

Mother started to cry again, and the only thing that seemed to comfort her was wrapping Murfee in her arms.

It was enough. It just had to be enough.

———

Murfee moved to peer out a window and down to the ground far below. She needed to look—to really see—to face it all. She made a startled sound, and all her brothers and sisters came on the run.

The cat and the owl were both gone, almost as if it all had been nothing but a dream.

She heard Dahson as he muttered under his breath. "Habeas corpus... and quid pro quo."

"What are you saying?" Milo blurted out. "Dahson! What did you say? Speak louder. And in English. Dahson, please!"

"Show me the body—and tit for tat."

"What?"

Dahson had started to walk away. He turned, took time to better secure his yellow specs higher up on his nose, and answered Milo somewhat absentmindedly. "Oh... well. Show me the body—Habeas corpus, and quid pro quo, tit-for-tat. Ask Poe. I just saw him near there. He'll know."

"Quid pro quo?" Murfee asked.

"Yes! Yes, ask Poe. Make it a trade for something shiny.

He'll tell... short and simple. Clearly, it's a simple matter of... habeas corpus and quid pro quo."

Murfee wondered, *And now, where is that crow?*

———

Murfee struggled to make some sense of the disappearance of her missing friend and of the great horned owl. She'd heard a cat had nine lives. But could the same be said of a fowl?

And friend? She was surprised that she even thought of the large cat in that way. Theirs was a friendship never meant to be. She knew this, but she found herself missing Manny already.

She wouldn't mind if she never again saw the oily bird, Poe. He was the embodiment of trouble, and she had only bad memories of him. *Where was the old crow?*

51
BEYOND THESE WALLS

MURFEE

MURFEE STARED through a large window in the barn loft; her sisters were busy playing nearby. A meteor trailed across the heavens, and Murfee was mesmerized by it amongst the splendor of the stars. She appeared dumbfounded, and her mouth remained for a time in the shape of a tiny O. She turned to see her father and mother quietly watching her sisters at play. Mother looked over at Murfee and smiled.

Twins Pip and Squeak, Peep, and Minree were now taking turns sliding down the beautiful but tarnished silver spoon. Three brightly colored bobbins of thread, stacked up nice and neat, acted as a small stool to give them purchase, and the straw gave them a soft landing. Maddy stood nearby trying to catch her breath.

A large and shiny black beetle scratched his way across the floor. Sounding a bit like the voice of the Merlin in Murfee's dreams, he turned and spoke directly to Murfee Mouse, "There's a big world out there, just waiting. I promise."

Maddy shushed him, then made a menacing move toward the bug. Abruptly the beetle changed direction, zigzagging to the other side of the space.

Murfee peered out the window. Clouds scuttled by, revealing the large orange orb of the moon. She watched as a flock of tiny birds lifted into the air, only to land once more, high in the maple tree.

She turned back to the beetle, and there on its ebony surface Murfee saw a reflection of the spellbinding beauty of a falling star. *Do I dare make another wish? Adventure takes risk—I know that now.* Her thoughts returned to the small vole and his death, and she felt a moment of sadness that he never got a chance for a grand adventure.

Her attention was drawn back to the spectacular view of the night sky, and for the next sliver of a moment everything seemed suspended in time, the entire world holding its breath, just as a starstruck Murfee held hers.

Her soft blue-gray eyes were liquid saucers with their own reflection of the galaxies, of a Milky Way splayed high over-head. Finally, she let out her breath and sucked air deep into her lungs. In that very instant the soft nighttime noises and the gentle breezes returned.

Mouse Marvel, the littlest mouse in a family of twelve, a mighty inch, the Red-Caped Crusader, Guardian of the Galaxies, opened her arms wide as she twirled in a circle, and began to sing, "Catch a falling star..."

JUSTICE

Justice struggled to remain patient though time was rapidly getting away from them. The very end of his tail twitched.

He watched on as Sophie stood rigid and unmoving at the threshold of what had been her home—the only home of which she had any real memory. Still, there was no time to waste.

"Justice, I don't know about this. I'm starting to think we're safer right where we're at. Someone will come to help. Someone will..." She turned to look up at the attic landing. "Adventures can be found in books. The ending is always good and there's usually a surprise rescue at the end—don't you think?"

"Come on, Sophie. It's okay, I've got you. Time's a wasting and trust me—we'll be sure to find adventure out there." Sophie stood up straighter. She gave a small, forced laugh and Justice was filled with admiration for what he knew to be his young master's hero's heart.

"Grab your backpack, my brave friend. We've got a train to catch!"

BONUS SECTION
BACKSTORIES, OUTTAKES, AND MORE

BACKSTORIES AND OUTTAKES

HOW AN ATTIC BECAME A HOME—SOPHIE'S STORY AND THE SECRET FILES THAT STARTED IT ALL

Sixteen-year-old Lane had had it up to here. *Why'd we move to this stupid place, anyway? So, what if Mom's great-aunt left it to her? This old mansion should be bulldozed to the ground. No excuse to pull a kid out of school, from friends I'll never see again, to move clear across the country. From a place with a great skate park to what?—this neighborhood with not a kid in sight.*

And now I'm grounded. Can things get any worse? Mom's gone today and I'm to stay in the house and unload some more boxes. "Ugh."

What was he grounded for this time? Using his dad's computer. *Seriously! And in my defense, he should have put his laptop away where it belongs, not just leave it out in the open.*

He picked up another load from the stack in the garage and stepped into the house. "My back is killing me. Child labor, that's what this is." He glanced down at the top of the box. It was marked 'office.' He set it down, then scooted it with his foot across the living room. He looked through the doorway to his dad's desk. *Hmm... what's this? Dad forgot his laptop again and left it up and running.* Lane rushed over and sat down. Why hadn't the computer gone to sleep? Instead of a blackened monitor, his dad's company's web page was still up. The HOST Corporation. *'Communication made simple—on a global scale' filled the screen.* Not even their newest employee—Dad—could easily explain what that meant. *And the letters* H O S T *are abbreviations for something but what do I care?*

"Communication made simple... I'll make it simple, hand me back my cell phone. Five weeks is surely long enough." Unwillingly, he was forced to acknowledge the reason for the loss of his smartphone, and perhaps the real reason they'd moved—his getting into a whole lot of trouble at school. His intentions were good. He just wanted to see if he'd passed his English test. He wasn't trying to change his grade and he hadn't. But he couldn't seem to help diving deep into the school computer—payroll, employee review, and closed school board meetings, and then from there to breach the firewalls of city and state records—and his goose—as his mom would say —was cooked.

I'll take a quick look—ten, twenty minutes tops, hey—I'll even time myself. It's now 9:44. What's this? A menu tab marked miscel-laneous. Takes me to the company logo—nothing else. But when I move my cursor over it a password field appears. Hmm... the user field's already filled in with the name HOST but the password field's blank. "Nine characters." He scratched his head and then scooted his chair closer. "Maybe the word HOST is a clue."

Better be smart about this. I'll give myself three tries, then I'll retrace my steps and log out.

Oddly he kept thinking back to his biology class and the company name. HOST. "Parasite—that's eight. Symbiosis—

that's nine letters." Drats. PASSWORD DENIED. "Two more tries, wouldn't want to get Dad in any kind of trouble. I'm guessing it's not case sensitive. I'll try it backwards. s i s o i b m y s."

An entire world opened up before him on the screen. And for once, he was speechless.

Like a blind man, he rummaged around for a thumb drive. He inserted it, highlighted all file names, then used control C and copied them to his memory stick.

"Gotta get out of here. Internal alarms are sure to be going off all over the place." His hand flew up to his mouth. *Can they trace this back to Dad? There were idiots guarding the gate—this was way too easy. Cyber Security must be run by some gray-haired old man down in the basement... but when I downloaded those files...*

He was stupid. He'd put himself and his parents in real danger. There was nothing left to do but run.

***

Roughly Seven and a Half Years Later— The Company Picnic

THEO

THEO, LANE'S FATHER, WAS MOVING UP THE RANKS OF THE HOST Corporation. It was an innocent moment in time at the yearly company picnic, an annual event that he had before somehow managed to avoid. Now he was being asked to step up to the microphone to be introduced as a member of one of its newly formed divisions.

He gestured to his wife to stand at his side as he stood before the company hierarchy and their families.

"Theo, what an asset you've been to the firm." The firm's

president held out a welcoming hand to them both. "This must be your wife. It's so good to finally meet you. Sorry to say, we've never heard about your family, though we've gone on and on about ours." He looked out at the gathering. "We all owe him a big apology, right?" He waited for the obligatory applause to die down. "Theo, let me be the first to apologize to you for letting you keep your light under a basket. We want to get to know you.

"Now's a perfect opportunity to tell us a little about yourself. Have children, grandchildren? Your chance to brag a bit about them. Take your time, you've earned it." He handed Theo the mic.

Rapid-fire thoughts went through his mind. *How do I explain that I have a son... there are reasons I've never talked about him... a runaway son, not at university, not making his mark on the world. Not traveling abroad, but on the lam... far as I know.*

Theo paused, took a deep breath, then began. "Where do I start? This—this is my wife, Rosalie. We've been married for what feels like forever." He turned toward her with a sheepish grin, and this time the laughter of the audience was genuine.

"It's just the two of us, but as I'm sure my wife would agree, we feel most fortunate today to be counted as part of the family of the firm." At this, real clapping began as Rosalie tightly squeezed his hand.

<hr>

A Few Short Months Later...

SOPHIE

DRESSED IN ILL-FITTING, WORN-OUT CLOTHES. TIMID AND CAUTIOUS, nervous and watchful. Large, expressive eyes dominating a small face, her head crowned with a wild head of gorgeously unmanageable copper-colored hair, Sophie was hurriedly dropped off by her father Lane to her grandparents, who could not afford to make her presence known. Sophie talked little. Especially in those days and weeks right after her father left.

Like a malignant growth, the mesh of lies grew until there was no going back. No way to untangle the mess of it and make it all right. Forever the three of them in the stately mansion—only two—Theo and Rosalie, husband and wife—known to the outside world.

THEO

Theo heard his wife's footsteps, sat up in bed, and looked at the clock before putting on his robe and slippers and walking out into the hallway. There he found his grieving wife. "Tell me."

Covering her face with her hands, muffled sobbing reached his ears along with several indecipherable words. "You've *got* to tell me or there's no way I can help. You're making yourself sick. Rosalie, you're going to wear out the floorboards. Tell me."

She sort of collapsed into his arms. "We can't go on like this. It's wrong. It's always been wrong. I heard her. I can hear her. She's been crying. And... and why wouldn't she be? It doesn't matter that I'm making the attic into a special place with toys and paints and books. All kinds of books. A computer that teaches a child how to read. None of this matters to a lonely child." She rubbed her eyes and nose on the sleeve of her silk robe.

"I understand how this happened and I'm not blaming

you. And I, I too played my part." She shuddered. "I knew from the moment I laid eyes on her it would be foolish to let myself love her, even a little. Back then I thought Lane would return in just days and grab Sophie right out of my arms and break my heart. So, I didn't. I didn't let myself love her... and he didn't. He didn't come back as he promised. I thought he would. He promised he would." She reached into a pocket, pulled out a tissue, and blew her nose. "And how do you explain to a little girl why she's hidden away in the attic?

"It was innocent enough at the start. For the first few days—no, more like a week—that precocious five-and-a-half-year-old was plumb tuckered out, and she mostly slept. Who knows what she'd been through? We hadn't seen Lane for years. We didn't have a clue he had a child. Our grandchild."

Her eyes held a faraway look. Her voice softened into a whisper. "Answer me this, why all the secrecy? Why'd Lane act so nervous—why'd he seem to always be looking over his shoulder? His and Sophie's clothes looked like they had come out of somebody else's hamper. Theo, I hardly recognized our own son! And Sophie's mother, what about her? We know nothing about her and she must be worried sick. Theo, at the very least, Lane could have told us where he was living and how to contact him.

"And why did he make us promise not to tell anyone about her. 'Keep her safe'—those were his very words. What does that even mean?"

She visibly shuddered. "Right after he dropped her off, I'd often find her sleeping. Maybe she was in shock, I don't know. Theo, she always looked scared. Her eyes searched around the room, and they darted away if I drew near."

He smoothed wisps of hair from her face. "Rosie, we're in this together. I'm right here. It will be all right if we just wait it all out. Any day now Lane will show up out of the blue and it'll be as if this never happened—though I'll never understand why he left Sophie in the first place. Or why all the secrecy? You know I'll keep her safe—I'll keep both of you safe.

"But he'll be back. I mean, how could he not? She's a little cutie. And that hair!" He looked to see if he had brought out a smile. He hadn't.

ROSALIE

Rosalie turned her head away and continued talking as if he had not said a word. "So, I'd creep into Sophie's room like a shadow. But it became a rhythm of sorts, me slipping in and out. Theo, I've become not much more than a ghost.

"Sophie has known me as the one who comes in to clean or to bring food or supplies. Books and things. Turn on a lesson on the computer. Sometimes make small talk like one would to a stranger." She turned to her husband with a light in her eyes. "Theo, she's coming out of her shell. Now she almost begs to come and stand next to me, lean into me, reach out and touch my hair... talk to me."

Her brow creased. "How many weeks or months has it been since she quit asking when her dad is coming to get her? How long has it been?"

She went on in between sobs. "And Theo, she's so bright. And she likes to learn. Do you remember when her daddy was that way? I do." She squeezed her eyes shut for a long moment.

"She's started calling me Rose," she said, smiling. "I think she just wants a friend, but I'm nothing you'd want to love. Poor little sweetie." Her face fell. "Theo, what have we done?"

Several More Years Have Passed...

THEO

THEO USED TO LIVE FOR HIS WORK IN RISK MANAGEMENT. GLOBAL market vulnerabilities, national and international trends. World events and national news. The numbers were just a small part of it. It felt like 3-D chess and the job was fascinating. He reveled in the vast world around him. Now it felt like he was doing nothing more than drowning in data.

Nose to the grindstone. Head down. The only difficult part, he at last realized, was that he was never done. Columns of numbers swam before his eyes from daylight to dark, and often deep into the night. And the next moment he checked, the sums—losses and gains, receipts receivable, receipts outstanding, debt tabulations—had changed once again. Why, any newbie CPA could fill his shoes. *When had my job description changed and why? That's what I'd like to know.*

Work life did provide him an escape from a home at times seemingly drowning in grief and confusion. Sophie was still living in the attic. They'd never heard from Lane since the day he'd dropped off his daughter. Rosalie was up pacing many nights. It was all too much—this cloud that hovered over them. His job was to keep the two of them safe and never for a minute did he forget it.

WEDNESDAY NIGHT, WEARILY LEAVING HIS OFFICE, HE PULLED ON HIS coat and picked up his briefcase, then turned off the light only to discover he seemed to have misplaced his keys. He felt around again in his trench coat pockets, then in his suit. Had he put them in his desk? *Maybe, I took a ride-share this morning.*

Oh. That's right, the car's in the garage for a tune-up. These long hours are making my head fuzzy.

He was startled when a door slammed. He heard steps coming down the short hall. They paused right outside his darkened office.

"Stop your obsession. Theo is a patsy. We don't have to worry a thing about him. Keep him swimming in figures. Treat him like a lowly accountant with limited access to all internal files. Load up his hours and his workload. He doesn't have a clue." Their combined laughter chilled Theo to his bones.

"Does he ever wonder how he ended up with his fancy office—on the *top* floor? What an idiot. He thinks he's a world-class executive." Something in between a laugh and a sneer followed. Theo found it hard to breathe. "Little does he know…"

"How many years has it been since the computer breach? Roughly ten years?

"Funny how nobody even knew he had a kid. Well, it's worked to our advantage. Nobody will be any wiser when the kid disappears for good."

Theo worried they could hear his trembling. Blood pounded in his ears with every beat of his heart—a whooshing sound surely loud enough to make his presence known, too. *Leave. Just leave. I haven't done anything—neither has my son.*

"We need these loose ends tied up. No one should've seen those files, and now they're downloaded to who knows where. If we ever catch up with that kid… well, let's just say we won't have that worry hanging over us, that's for sure. And I think we're getting closer. Got a lead."

Theo waited for what felt like hours before quietly leaving to catch a late-night cab. Only this morning had he thought things could not get any worse. How very wrong he had been.

The First Two Loves of Father Mouse

FAYLENA

Faylena Mouse was visiting her cousins for the summer at their vacation home. Their home until the time the humans (who legally held the title) came for their own visit to the estate.

The beautiful country place seemed to go on forever, as did the loud and wonderful parties. So very different from anything she had ever known.

It seemed a large and fun-loving group, but she often found herself sitting alone. Tonight's party was again loud and lively. The dancing flowed from the house through the open French doors and out into the gardens.

A soft rain began—not one of them seemed to mind. The dancers moved into the shelter of an alée of flowering lilacs. The lacy, intertwining archway seemed to go on for miles. Soft breezes blew through the gardens, mixing all the scents.

Several partygoers commandeered the radio, and just as Faylena began to tap her foot to one tune, the channel changed, and another song poured out. It was a little disconcerting.

Quintin went unnoticed until he cleared his throat. She turned and saw his approach.

Hmm, not my type, was Fay's most immediate thought. *Not the most handsome of the bunch. Doesn't look like the brightest, either. Maybe I can give him a quick brush-off.*

"They're getting ready to play our song," he said with a straight face. "Would you like to dance?"

Maybe there's more than meets the eye. Could be. Oh, what the heck. At least he seems to have a sense of humor. What do I have to lose? she thought as she stood to take his outstretched hand.

The soft pitter-pat of raindrops was turning into a torrent. The pair ran into the ancient gazebo where they took seats on the wooden bench that encircled the space. Large puddles were quickly forming into miniature lakes. A weather forecast announcing a zero percent chance of rain blared from the radio and made them both smile.

"About as likely as cloudy with a chance of meatballs," Quin said, laughing. The young mouse reached out and brushed raindrops from her face. "My name's Quin—Quintin. Ohhhh. It's Mama Cass—it doesn't get any better than this. Listen." He scooted closer. "'Dream a Little Dream of Me'... and nobody can sing it like she could."

As the rain lessened, he stood and took her hand, then pulled her to her feet. They danced atop the bench high above the puddles. Quintin sang along in a clear tenor voice.

The storm clouds moved on, exposing a ceiling of stars, and the two sat side by side and began to share their secret hopes and dreams. Faylena said, "I've known from the time I was tiny I'm meant to travel the world to find my adventure. Colorful stuff I could write about—maybe someday put in a book."

Quin's face broke out into a wide grin. "I've always wanted to get married and raise a family. Two or three. Maybe four. I've wanted to be a father, have ever since I was young."

They sat quietly for a time. With halting speech, Faylena began telling of a lonely childhood and a very sheltered life. From the time she was small, she lost herself in books. They took her on adventure after adventure. Around the world, those stories had taken her. She'd known little else.

"I want my life to matter. I want it to have purpose. Maybe to leave the world a better place. And have a real adventure. Does that all seem like too much to ask? Or am I only fooling myself?" Shyly she turned her gaze to his. He seemed to be waiting for her to continue.

"I've never felt like I've mattered, not really. And what's crazy about my dream is that I'm a bit of a coward, too often afraid of shadows. Things that go bump in the night... birds and cats... *anything* that makes a sound in the dead of night. I don't know if I'd take that adventure even if it were given to me all laid out for me to follow."

QUINTIN

Quin slowly reached out and took her hand. "You could go on a fine adventure with me. I'll keep you safe from anything that makes a sound in the night."

"And cats?" She pulled away.

"From birds *and* cats. I'd keep you safe from everything! And we could have an adventure as big as a nighttime full of stars." He looked up at the Milky Way. Then he turned back to her. "There's such an unbelievable world just waiting to be explored... you know, maybe we could travel."

He paused. "After the kids are grown up and gone." Then he burst out in a laugh. "How crazy is this? We've only just met and now it sounds like I'm planning out your entire life. Sorry."

He took in a deep breath. "Marry me. We'll have our own stories to tell. And I promise both our lives will matter. Somehow, we'll make a real difference in this world—our lives will count."

Quin's chest felt as if it would explode when she took his hand and held it tight. Neither spoke for the longest time.

Quin at last broke the silence. "My auntie showed me just how big the world could be... she showed me the wonder of the stars!" Quin swept an arm across the heavens and let out a sigh of deep contentment.

But then his face fell. He squeezed his eyes shut. "I wish with all my heart you could have met her. Aunt Wilamena, I mean. She was my family. She was the one who let me know my life could one day be great and full of adventure. Oh! If I could be a parent anywhere near like she was to me... I'd have a whole bunch of kids and life would be swell."

He opened his eyes and looked far up into the star-studded sky. Reaching out, he tenderly touched her face, "She would have loved you."

It was getting late. Someone turned off the music. One by one the partygoers began to disperse. He watched as she turned to go back inside. "I'll see you tomorrow, right?" she asked.

Quintin grinned. "Tomorrow it is. I'll pick you up at noon, if that's okay with you."

She smiled. "Noon it is." He walked her to the door, and with a hurried kiss on his cheek, she was gone.

As outside lights were turned off a quietness settled like the dew. Quin sat in the dark on the bench in the gazebo, at times swinging his legs, at other times simply staring off into space. How long had he been lost in thought? He noticed the moon resting in a different place in the sky from when he'd first sat down.

A gentle breeze danced about. Striations of moonlight slipped past branches of the willow tree only to move about on the gazebo floor with the grace of a ballet. To Quintin Mouse, it seemed a fitting ending to a most astonishing night. Oh! What he would give to share the news with someone that he'd just met the love of his life. If only his auntie were still living! She would have thrown him a small party and for certain she would have sung him a song, a serenade. Maybe there would have been dancing, too.

His auntie, his only real family. She had saved him,

bringing him hope when he needed it most. His mind took him back to those days long ago as a lonely child struggling to survive a nearly impossible situation until she came onto the scene and saved him.

Young Quintin Mouse had been ready to release all his childhood dreams and let them travel to the boneyard of dead and foolish things. *I should do what I'm told and nothing more, there's no hope for anything better—that's how I felt when she came into my world.* Auntie seemed to understand young Quin Mouse's desperate need for encouragement in his present circumstance, as well as his hunger to learn about and understand the world around him.

Quin's family life had been chaotic for as far back as he could remember, but now it was significantly worse. Mother delivered her third set of triplets, and the home was bursting at the seams. One of the new little ones had colic and wailed night and day, barely pausing to take in the next breath. Everyone's ears hurt. Mother, tired and angry, was quick to take out her bad temper on anyone who came near. Father said he had just about had it and things had to change. Chores were piled onto Quintin.

Nothing I do, though, as hard as I try, ever satisfies either of them. He had long been the one on which they chose to take out their frustrations and he always wondered why. *Why is it always me?* He tried to stay out of their reach. He tried to stay nearly invisible; easy really, because it seemed he *was* invisible. But when tensions escalated, they often sought him out, and he could be sure of a berating. So... mostly he hid.

Sometimes he disappeared to a forested area nearby. There, deep in the trees, the only sounds were those of chirping birds and a gentle, bubbling brook. He walked carefully there, so as not to break the spell of this enchanted place.

One evening, as he raced into his home for supper, he nearly ran someone over. Both mice, he the young and agile one, and she, stocky and old, struggled to stay on their feet. Quin's eyes grew large. *Bet I'm in trouble now.* But this stranger only smiled back—with a joy that lit up her entire countenance. It was like she wore laughter on her face. Aunt Wilamena—here to help his mother.

But, instead of his sister Wilamena creating perfect order, as Quin's father had hoped, she brought laughter into the home, games and silly songs. How was it that only Quin took notice? Perhaps it was due to the volume of sound that the household generated. Perhaps the noise level had dulled all their senses.

Wilamena was quick to expand his possibilities. Wonders of wonders. A peek at stars and entire universes! But much more than that, she made him feel loved, and he loved her for it.

Chaos continued to exist. The baby continued to wail, and Mother and Father stayed frustrated and angry. Thankfully, in the midst of total madness, Auntie and he somehow managed to make their daily escape. When it was just the two of them, Wilamena told him dreams of the life she wished for. Her secret desire was to travel to the very stars high above. To do this, initially, she needed to become a scientist, specifically in the area of astrophysics. She would need to gather foundational knowledge of the Earth and stars.

He felt privileged to learn of her secret longings and was beyond thrilled to at last have a friend, and he told her so.

She said that actually, she'd nearly stopped herself years before from having any hope of being a part of the world, let alone allowing herself such mighty aspirations. She told him of a time she herself hadn't wanted to go on. Quin was aghast. Surely not.

Auntie had been told she was stupid and that she'd never get her head out of the clouds. Her name on the schoolyard—'Gotrocks'—she with nothing but rocks for brains.

Sadly, for a time she believed this. For a long time, she did.

"How did you change what you thought about yourself?" he asked breathlessly. Aunt Wilamena was the wisest, to his thinking, and he felt bad for her, though he soon found she had no need for his pity. Aunt Wilamena was doing just fine.

Quintin quieted himself as he listened intently to her answer. Auntie had discovered a fascination with flying creatures, bees and birds, bugs even. Airplanes leaving their jet trails high overhead had her head spinning. The stars splayed out across the heavens nightly took her breath away. "Too bad I had nothing but rocks for brains. But the idea of a rocket ride to the moon—perhaps the best way to study the stars—seemed never to leave me."

"It was the fireflies that changed my heart," Aunt Wilamena continued. "These small things looked like nothing but itsy-bitsy nondescript bugs until the evening fell and they each took to the sky. They illuminated the worlds around them." Her voice trembled. "Did they one by one make the decision nightly to bring beauty and wonder into my space? Was it that within each of them, this treasure of light was waiting in readiness to be revealed? What was *my* treasure?"

Her eyes looked off into the distance as she reminisced. "Surely a brain that held only worthless rocks would have no need for starlight, fireflies, or even begin to desire a trip to travel the galaxies. But I did, so surely, *I* was a wonder, and had worth, too." Her laughter was melodious.

His auntie went on to tell him of parents who long before had shared their steadfast faith in the Designer of this world, and His care for each of His creatures here on earth. The Architect high overhead was with her, too! She began to have faith in the heavens and faith in herself. Quintin wondered if his own childlike faith had brought him his auntie.

He was almost knocked off his feet with what she told him next. "I know you won't believe it when I tell you now, but you are a lucky little mouse.

"Yes," she continued, "I know it doesn't feel like this today —in a house filled with noise and frustration—and anger taken out on you—perhaps it is in fact the loudest household I've ever encountered—but everything is going to work out for you in the end."

He squeezed his eyes shut. Without a whisper, she stepped closer to hold his face in her hands. Young Quintin surprised himself as hot tears rolled down both cheeks. He was surprised too when she started to sing:

> It's a lovely day tomorrow
> Tomorrow is a lovely day
> Come and feast your tear dimmed eyes
> On tomorrow's clear blue skies.
> If today your heart is weary
> If ev'ry little thing looks gray
> Just forget your troubles and learn to say
> Tomorrow is a lovely day.

Quintin was filled with confusion. He didn't want to doubt the words of the song but believing seemed as unreachable as the farthest stars overhead. "I don't understand. Maybe... I don't know." He took in a deep breath, then slowly exhaled. Aunt Wilamena had shared with him. *Can I trust her with my most secret feelings and thoughts?* he wondered.

"It's hard every day. All day long and sometimes nights,

too. You see," his eyes pleaded for understanding, "I'm always wrong. I'm to blame for all of it. If a fight breaks out or someone gets hurt. Always... always it's me. If something is spilled or broken or if one of the bigger ones picks on one of the little ones and makes him cry—"

"Quintin, listen. Do you remember telling me of all of your close calls going into and coming out of the woods?" He nodded slightly. "How many times have you escaped trouble... once you told me about an owl, once or twice a cat. Other times, too. You, my fine nephew, are for certain favored by the Architect and watched over by above. Your path is golden."

This time her eyes pleaded with *him*. "Your father didn't mean to yell at you today as he did. It's a lovely day tomorrow. Remember that tomorrow is a lovely day." She grabbed up her walking stick and motioned him to follow.

FAITH. MAYBE THAT'S WHAT LED THE TWO OF THEM TO A TREASURE trove—the town library, a place brimming with books, tomes that held many of the answers they sought. It seemed quite by accident that they discovered it. One particular night started with what was to be only a side trip through town before their visit to the nearby woods, but an open door, unattended, and a lighted hallway seemed to call them and guide their steps, drawing the two of them into the library itself. Later, the discovery of a side vent that opened directly into the room. On those nights when the ancient librarian remembered to lock up after she left, their nightly visits continued without interruption. Coincidences, one after another, left the place theirs. Was it by pure luck—or some crazy coincidence—or was it something more?

The small-town library became their motherlode of knowledge. Wilamena and Quintin found it relatively simple to push the chosen tome off the tall shelf. *We can read whatever we want.* He was in heaven.

The impossible part came with having to return the book to its proper place. The pair instead used the painstaking process of scoot, scoot, scooting each textbook deep under the bottom of one of the tall book towers scattered throughout the room.

Over a period of some months, not one of the chosen books remained in its rightful place according to its previously painstakingly arranged Dewey Decimal System. They could not seem to be found anywhere at all, leaving an entire section on the solar system, lunar exploration, rocketry, and physics of propulsion as supposedly as barren as the lunar surface of the moon. One night, Quin and his auntie watched on from the shelter of a mouse hole as the white-haired librarian bit the end of a #2 pencil, looking dumbstruck and nervous as she checked and rechecked her records of library loans. What wonderful times those were.

HE'D NEVER FORGET THE DAY HE LEARNED SHE HAD LEFT HIM. HE heard raised voices in the kitchen. "She's not coming," his father shouted. Quin heard something fall to the floor with a clatter; his mother begin to whimper.

"You'll have to learn to do without her. Wilamena is not coming today, so she's dead to me for all I care. Dead!" His father's voice rose higher still. "When has she ever really been here for me when I needed her? I need her now!" Another crash. Young Quintin burrowed deep into his covers.

Dead. Wilamena's dead. She can't be! His mind began to drift away. *Never coming again? Dead.* Blood pounded in his ears.

She's never coming? Ever? He fought to make sense of it. How could he live without her?

QUINTIN LEFT HIS CHILDHOOD HOME A FEW DAYS LATER TO MAKE HIS way in the world, ill-prepared for the hard journey that lay ahead. *It wasn't planned,* he thought. *I simply could not stay another day in that house. Anything I faced had to be better than that.*

He had started that day with a pre-dawn visit to his beloved woods. Maybe he'd find her there, alive, and well. Maybe he'd hear her singing or laughing or making crunching sounds as she trampled through the leaves, excited to show him some wonder she'd just found. But there was nothing but bird song. At last, he knew... his auntie wasn't coming back. And without much of a plan he began to walk; he never looked back. His one and only friend was gone.

EVEN NOW, AS AN ADULT, SOMEHOW AUNTIE WAS WITH HIM STILL. He believed it was his faith as a child that brought Wilamena into his life. He strove to escape the memories of his childhood, the exception being those of her. And he hoped with all his heart to leave the pain of the past behind, and instead to carry on her legacy with every good thing he brought to another.

Aunt Wilamena, heavyset and slow-moving, but with the heart of a young mouse. She had dreams bigger than anything Quin had ever heard before. Dreams to explore the solar system, to travel to see the stars, and never a doubt but that she'd get there.

Off in the distance, a light came on, bringing Quintin out of his remembering. Stiffly, he rose to his feet to make his way to his present home. Maybe he'd met the love of his life. Beautiful Faylena. He was seeing her in the morning! *And as late as it's getting, it won't be long 'til noon.*

TRAVELING THE BROKEN ROAD

POE

Poe the crow was hatched nearly a dozen years before. He was the last chick remaining, safe in his nest, until one early June morning a windstorm raged through the neighborhood. It blew down most of what had been Poe's home up to this point, a lovely Linden tree, along with the nest with him in it. The new hatchling landed hard on the ground far below; his left wing was shattered and bloody. The nest rolled away like a tumbleweed.

Poe found himself in a world of hurt and all alone. It's tough to begin life like that, barely cognizant of anything. At first, he was unaware that there were others in the world, or that he ever had parents. There was nothing but pain from his head injury and his damaged wing.

It was surprising that he survived, but as soon as he was able, he dragged himself into nearby bushes. Rain began to pour down, leaving him cold and shaking, but also created puddles of water that aided his survival.

LILY

Miraculously, a small girl named Lily found him, scooped him into her cupped hands, and rushed inside to her parents, excited to have a pet of her own. They immediately dashed her hopes. "Lily, this bird is hurt very badly. See, its wing is broken, and he'll never be able to fly. In fact, he'll most likely die in the next day or two. Put him back where you found him, sweetie. It's just nature's way. We'll buy you a bird from the pet store if you really want one."

Lily tightened her hold on the half-conscious fledgling, startling him and pulling him away from memories that were calling him back to the nest. For the first time since the girl had rescued him, the small crow became acutely aware of his surroundings. He looked up into a pair of intense blue eyes and saw nothing but kindness there.

"I'm naming him Birdie, and I don't care what you say. He's going to live! Just wait and see. Can you help me? I don't know how to take care of a bird." She looked at her father intently. "How do we fix him?"

Her father seemed to melt on the spot. Here stood Lily with rare excitement in her voice and a new light in her eyes. "How could I possibly say no to you?" her father said.

BIRDIE

My name is Birdie. Birdie is my name. Birdie. That's my name. Birdie. The tiny crow smiled up at his rescuer, she smiled back, and from that moment he was in love.

Soon Lily's bed was covered with bandages, all types of gauze, ointments, and a half dozen popsicle sticks. She held him gently while her father placed a small hand-made splint on his broken wing. *Oh! That feels better!* He felt himself relax a bit as the pain lessened.

Then Lily made a nest in a shoebox for him with mismatched socks and an old T-shirt. At first, she used an eyedropper to give him a drink. When he was better, she brought him choice worms and grubs and fixed an empty tuna fish can for his water. By now, her parents seemed just as enamored as she and delighted with his steady return to health.

Lily sang to him and carried him everywhere she went. Some days she propped him up on her bed and then surrounded him to the left and right with her dollies and favorite stuffed animals. Birdie felt honored to be placed in the center and made over and coddled. None of Lily's toys received much more than a word or two most days.

But good things must come to an end, Birdie at last realized. Nurse Betty, Lily's favorite dolly, was his undoing. She ruined everything for him. Everything. Little by little, Lily's attention became divided more equally between the two of them.

Birdie hated the large doll for it, but he feared her too, and he believed she knew it. For certain, she always had her eyes on him. Terrible eyes, one with its unmovable lid stuck half open, never closing. The other eyelid would shut when Nurse Betty was lying down. But not the monster eye. Not even at night.

What an ugly, ugly dolly, the baby crow thought. Hair missing in patches. Her white uniform was no longer white, an old-fashioned nurse's cap riding on her massive head.

But it was that monster's half-open eye that terrified him day and night. Night and day. Did it actually glow? Maybe.

This fear and obsession started one otherwise wonderful, sunny day. Birdie was propped up on a pillow, and he, Lily's small prince, dressed in his princely attire, was attended to by his princess, Lily, as she fed him small pieces of a blueberry scone with sprinkles of sugar on top.

"You're my little prince, Birdie. Forever you will reign over us all. Your word alone will command armies and establish the final rule in the land.

"We'll all bow to you," she said as she brushed the crumbs from his small face and attempted to clear the bed covers of them, too. In the process, she knocked Nurse Betty to the floor. The oversized doll landed with a clunk. Lily rushed to pick her up, upset and remorseful. "Oh! Nurse Betty, you are my favorite. I'm so sorry. And I've been ignoring you for Birdie. He's just a bird. I'll never not need you! Why, I've had you forever, and he's brand new. I'm so sorry," she said as she rocked her dolly in her arms.

The small crow crumpled; a whimper escaped, and Lily rushed back to his side, pale-faced and tearful. In that instant, he once more became her little prince. He softly whimpered again, and she held him closer. Nurse Betty was forgotten. Maybe for good. Birdie smiled.

But in the dark of night, moonbeams from the window brought a new feverish light into Nurse Betty's singular half-open eye. The small crow tried his best to stay alert until the sunlight erased the shadows and Lily came awake to fuss over him. Then and only then was he safe, as the ugly doll, presently relegated to the top of the nightstand, watched on.

EDITH

The next thing Edith and her husband noticed was that their little girl was sleeping through the night and seemed to laugh and skip through the days. Often one or both of them quietly listened just beyond the door as she played in her room. Their only child could be heard talking up a storm to all her dollies lined up on her bed—but most especially to one small, helpless crow. Was Birdie an unwilling audience of one or did he love her fiercely as they did?

One afternoon, Edith tapped softly on her daughter's door before walking into the bedroom. She was on a special mission and her heart was dancing. She was bringing her precious child an antique brooch, one that had once belonged to her own mother. It was time.

She placed it into Lily's outstretched palm, then let her, after Lily's insistence, pin it onto the miniature dark-purple doll blanket wrapped around her charge, thus securing the soft wool snuggly around his small frame. Lily said it for sure made her Birdie look like a prince or a king with his jewels, and her new friend would never be cold again.

Edith attempted her most-serious look though she was beaming on the inside. "You'll have to be careful with this. You'll be responsible for a precious family heirloom. It was a priceless antique *even before* your great-grandmother was given it as a gift so long ago. You'll be *so careful*, right?"

Lily shook her head emphatically Yes, and smiled, quickly turning back to her Birdie.

Edith felt herself slipping from the room. Carried along in the currents of a river of memories, as she, herself, felt the age-old tradition of something passing from mother to daughter, to daughter, and on. The legacy of it. Deeply she soaked it all in, deep into her bones. She had lost her mother at a very young age, and these special times she now spent with Lily were diamonds in her heart. None of it did she take for granted. What was the value of the diamonds on the brooch? What was monetary value anyway?

A memory came rushing unbidden to Edith of her mother's words when the jewelry was placed into *her* hands. "See the red stone in the middle? That's a ruby, Eddie. Think of it as my heart—and all those magnificent diamonds surrounding it—that's my love flowing out of my heart for you.

"It's showing its age—you'll have to take good care of it, but I think you're ready. You can keep it in its special box.

"I'm so proud of you and I'll be with you always," Edith's mother had said. Yet, a scant ten days later, Edith's mother was dead. *Could a person depend on anything?* Edith thought to herself before forcing her tumbled thoughts back to the present and to her husband standing just outside the room, motioning her to join him.

"Robert, this had to be a gift from above, what we've been praying for, what the doctors and therapists could never do. Our baby is going to be okay. She's sleeping. Her nightmares have stopped—she hasn't had one—not one—since we brought that broken-winged bird into our home. Did you ever think you'd see the day?"

"That bird and our Lily weren't the only ones broken. I've noticed the lines on your forehead start to disappear. I think you've come back to me, too." He placed a soft kiss on her lips. "Our little darlin' has stepped back into the light. I don't think she's afraid anymore."

Tension dropped from both of them as they acknowledged the path their family had trod and how they had healed. Months earlier, the safety of their home had been breached and Lily had taken the brunt of it. She alone had seen the intruder, an innocent on a late-night trip to the kitchen to sneak one last cookie, when she came face to face with a burglar. Each surprised the other. The would-be thief made a quick exit as Lily began to scream. And she screamed and screamed, long after her parents enveloped her in their arms.

Not until she received a sedative in the ER did the yelling cease. But that wasn't the end of it. From that point forward, the little girl could not sleep until the early morning light came into her bedroom. This was repeated night after night after night.

Snuggled up between them in their own bed made no difference. Medications made no difference. Therapists were useless. Naps throughout the day were a must, but Lily grew pale, lost weight, and the light nearly disappeared from her turquoise eyes. Until now. Birdie had brought a miracle!

BIRDIE

Birdie recovered daily, and his initial headache and confusion slowly dissipated. He began gradually to remember an earlier time in a nest crowded with five siblings. He remembered his mother and father bringing food to hungry mouths and making sure their babies were safe and warm. He remembered his mother humming a certain tune every time a squabble broke out, another daily with the rising sun. His father liked to laugh. He remembered that. Oh! And Nurse Betty remained on the bedside table, untouched. Unloved. Life was good and not only did he feel safe, he, a prince, would soon rule the world. No "maybe" about it—he would rule the world. He was destined for it.

Birdie was growing too big for his shoe box, so Lily found a large red plastic egg crate for him. One sunny day, she talked her father into carrying it outside into their large backyard "so my Birdie can get some fresh air and a change of scenery." Robert removed the wrapping from his left wing and placed the pile of gauze beside him. "I think it might feel good to have that off for a bit. Lily, you can help me put it back on when it's time to bring him back in.

"Take your little robe off him for now—he'll be too warm in the sun. Oh. And we'll take the brooch back inside and put it into your jewelry box so you won't lose it."

"Please, Daddy, he loves to wear it. Let's just push his royal robes back and leave them and his jewels."

Birdie looked up. Lily's father pretended to look thoughtful, then chuckled. "I don't suppose I can take the little prince's sparklies away and for sure I can never seem to say no to you."

Birdie immediately felt himself relax in the heat of the afternoon. His injured wing didn't hurt one bit! He was on his way to recovery, and he was elated. He stretched out both wings and was satisfied that soon he would be well and could fly. He saw several birds up in the air, gliding easily on the warm breezes. His precious Lily smiled down at him.

"We'll leave him out here a little while, it's a beautiful day," Lily's father said, as he placed a large, slatted box top over the sides of the egg crate. "This will keep him safe from cats," her father explained.

As Birdie watched Lily and her father walk back across the expansive lawn and then into the house, he felt a strange shudder move through him. *Why am I suddenly afraid?* he wondered. He liked his new family and his new home. Lily was really good to him. Maybe it was true love he felt for her. Maybe he'd stay here forever. No, he wanted to find his folks. He could fly back often and visit her so she wouldn't worry and miss him so much.

Oh! Maybe his injured wing felt a little weak, that was all. Still, it felt good to stretch it out a bit.

The sun shone down, and the sky was cloudless and blue-sky blue. So why was he somehow feeling afraid? Something bad was coming—that is what he thought.

A SHADOW FELL OVER THE CAGE, AND LOOKING UP, HE SAW TWO BOYS leaning over the egg crate. Birdie knew instinctively he was in for a world of trouble.

One of the boys removed the slatted covering and reached down to grab him. "Don't touch him!" the other shouted, as he roughly pushed the shorter boy away. "Charlie, he's crippled and he's filthy. Probably has fleas."

Crippled. Huh? Who's crippled? thought the young crow, eyes wide. *What's that even mean?* Instinctively he shrank back away from them, causing the larger of the two boys to sneer.

CHARLIE

Something seemed to wink and twinkle in the sunlight. Charlie Dunbee, the younger of the two, noticed it, and made a slow-motion grab for it, careful to shield his movements, and —with sleight of hand—pulled what looked like some sort of jewelry from the crow's neck and into his pocket. He'd take a look at it later when he was alone. This shiny thing was his! His alone. It was about time something special belonged to him. And nobody needed to know about it either.

Carl, his seven-year-old brother, tucked his unruly coal-black hair behind his ears, momentarily exposing a pair of life-less eyes before it fell back over his face. Carl began to laugh, and Charlie watched as the small crow trembled.

Carl spoke in a sly and calculating voice. "Go ahead and take him if you want cuz I'm starting to think about this in a whole different way. Cuz maybe this is our lucky day, and we were meant to find this fine fellow.

"Grab him—Band-aid stuff, too—you'll need it if you're hoping he can ever fly. See, here's my brand-new brainstorm—this could be a money-maker! Tie a string to one of his skinny legs and charge kids to see him take off flying, then down to the dirt when he hits the end of it. I'd almost pay for a ticket myself! What do ya think, Spaz?"

"My name's not Spaz! Don't call me that. I'll tell Ma and you won't get supper. Just cuz you don't have to wear this stupid brace doesn't make you better than me." Charlie reached down, rubbed his leg, and grimaced. "You're gonna go hungry tonight cuz I'm tellin'.

"And you know what," Charlie hissed, "you're just jealous cuz Ma pays more attention to me. I'm tellin' and you'll go to bed without supper."

"Who cares?" Carl spat out the words. "It's just soup. I'm sick of soup! Someday I'm gonna be somebody. I'll have anything I want to eat. Sky's the limit." Carl squinted up into the sun before looking back at his brother. "You know I was serious. You might make some money off this ugly excuse for a bird. Hey! Got an idea. He's a spaz just like you, a cripple. A crippled crow for a cripple like you." His older brother's laugh felt more like a sinister sneer to Charlie, but he wiped his eyes, turned his face up to him, and forced a smile.

"That's more like it. You don't want to be a crybaby. Nobody likes a crybaby. I'm trying to help you and all you want to do is run home and tell Ma made-up stories to get me in trouble. Now hear me out. I think there could be real potential here. Let me think a minute. We need some kind of hook. Hmm... we could spin it as a trained crow. A talking bird. A crazy one. No – this poor crippled crow—we'll call him Poe—the World-Famous Crow. Poe the Crow!"

BIRDIE

Birdie let out a tortured cry, a loud sort of whimper, expecting at the very least sympathy and maybe for his world to righten, but instead, Charlie grabbed him roughly by the neck and squeezed. Birdie cried out in earnest, his royal robes falling off him, he, a prince no more.

"Hop in the wagon and I'll get us out of here. Yep, grab Poe tight. Poe the crow! He might just be our ticket outta here. Come on Spaz, I think I hear someone comin'."

My name is Poe. Poe is my name. My name is Poe?

POE

Poe's nightmares were filled with strange and twisted memories of this, the most terrible time of his life. Carl and his brother, Charlie, had run off, leaving Poe trapped within a rickety, rust-colored bird cage, a junkyard find haphazardly held together with a piece of frayed clothesline. Before they left, they abandoned the contraption along with him held captive in an alley close by.

Poe had survived three long and terrible days by this time without a thing to eat or drink. It was nothing but blind luck that finally saved him.

He was burrowed down amongst the crumpled-up newspapers at the bottom of his small jail, when a young boy spied it and ran to set the cage at the curb, along with a heaping pile of trash growing bigger by the minute.

The annual neighborhood cleanup had brought out a crowd of all ages. There was a festive feeling to the event, and Poe could smell the cookies some were handing out. He caught a whiff of hot chocolate, too. He knew those heavenly smells, but from where?

Lily. For a nanosecond, he remembered her. Chocolate chip cookies and cocoa were her favorites. And she always made sure to share with Poe.

Not seeing the small bird inside, the cage was carried to nearby dumpsters, only to be knocked over the next morning by a passing garbage truck. The worn-out birdcage was in ruins, and incapable of holding anything. Not one soul noticed the little bird; there was no one to witness his slow escape.

EDITH

Lily's mother's face wore the haggard expression of a survivor of war. "What can we do? Should we put out fliers? Lily is wrong. He didn't fly off on his own. He didn't leave her! Someone or somebodies took that bird. His bandages are gone, and Grammie's brooch. He didn't just fly off. He didn't leave her. He didn't, he couldn't!

"Someone took him... maybe if we offer a reward." Her eyes hardened. "Whoever did this—I never would have believed I could have such hate in my heart toward another."

"I thoroughly dislike bringing this up now, but... " Robert said to her, his voice dropping low. "We need to contact the insurance company about the brooch. They'll need to know right away, too. I'm sorry for my part in it. I should have insisted we bring it back into the house. That part's on me; those diamonds alone are worth a fortune, let alone the ruby. It's one of a kind."

"That's the least of what we've lost," Edith said, as her

angry face dissolved into tears; and she pushed him away as he reached out to hold her.

Travel-Weary, Travel-Worn—Twelve Years Have Passed

LILY

Despondent beyond belief, Lily had thrown Nurse Betty into the closet all those years ago, and buried her under piles of discarded dollies, stuffed animals, and more. Her friend had left her. Only his royal robes remained in their rightful place of honor on her bed to this day.

Never again did she effortlessly drift into sleep. Not then and not now. The nagging wondering of what she had done wrong was with her always. Why Birdie had left her... flown away without even a goodbye.

She found pleasure in playing with her puppet theater, in creating characters and mimicking voices. All this was encouraging to her parents—they told her so time and time again. Still, Lily's hair fell out in patches (or did she herself pull it from her head?) and deep and blessed sleep never came.

Doctors were called in. Specialists were enlisted and a lifetime of therapy was initiated. She herself at last acknowledged she had grown into a beautiful and talented young woman. Hers was quickly becoming a household name—actress Lilian Tuttle; huge fame was building. But true peace, that elusive thing, always seemed to be out of her reach, no matter how diligently she sought it. And nothing else really mattered.

CARL

Carl Dunbee was himself a dissatisfied, unhappy human being. Small-time burglary with its limited returns was at best an unreliable profession. Ever since his first arrest, jobs were hard to come by. Charlie was a well stone around his neck, but surprisingly even to himself, Carl found he loved his younger brother fiercely.

POE

Poe the crow oftentimes found his thoughts unfocused, sometimes to the point of wondering where he was and how he had gotten there. Memories, though, danced through both nighttime dreams and daydreams, unrelenting, taunting him, calling him. If only he could sift and sort them out. Gnats. Nothing but gnats.

Almost without fail, one image pervaded his sleep. A singular glow-in-the-dark, half-lidded eye watched him. Never looked away. Followed him everywhere. Poe unable to pull *his own* eyes away.

DID YOU KNOW?
SOME FUN (AND SERIOUS!) FACTS
ABOUT THE MOON

1. The moon is Earth's one and only permanent natural satellite.

2. There is no air on the moon, but there *is* water! Scientists found water in the moon's soil, which gives us hope that living there one day might be possible.

3. Moondust smells like gunpowder and has been known to make astronauts sneeze and become stuffed up like they had a cold!

4. The surface temperature on the moon can reach roughly 253.4 degrees Fahrenheit (123 degrees Celsius) during the day and -243.4 degrees Fahrenheit (-153 degrees Celsius) at night.

5. ON EARTH, WE *ALWAYS* SEE THE SAME SIDE OF THE MOON. THERE are many myths about what the back of the moon looks like (most of us call it "the dark side of the moon"), but none of us on Earth have ever seen it with our own eyes staring at the sky! In 1959, a Soviet satellite took the first photographs. In 1968, on the Apollo 8 mission, human eyes saw the other side of the moon for the first time. We know few facts about that side of the moon, but we do know it looks *completely* different from what we see each night.

6. THE MOON CONTROLS THE OCEAN'S TIDES HERE ON EARTH.

7. THE MOON IS THE ONLY PLACE WHERE HUMANS HAVE SET FOOT beyond Earth.

8. THE MOON CYCLES THROUGH EIGHT TOTAL PHASES EACH MONTH: New moon, waxing crescent, first quarter, waxing gibbous, full moon, waning gibbous, third quarter, and waning crescent.

9. THE MOON IS MOVING FURTHER AWAY FROM THE EARTH EACH YEAR. Scientists discovered that the moon started much closer to Earth. Each year, it moves about 38cm further into space. It is said that it is moving at about the same rate as your fingernails grow.

10. THE MOON *ISN'T* MADE OF CHEESE! IT'S ACTUALLY MADE OF oxygen, silicon, magnesium, iron, calcium, and aluminum.

WHAT DO YOU THINK?
DISCUSSION QUESTIONS

1. How did Sophie feel when she first heard Justice talking? Why do you think she felt that way?

2. How do you think Sophie's relationship with Justice will change throughout the book?

3. How does Justice's desire for revenge affect his son, Preying Mantis?

4. What is the symbolism behind Murfee's scarlet cape, and how does it reflect her desire to change her life?

5. If you were in Sophie's position, what would you do to help Justice and his son?

6. WHAT CONNECTIONS CAN BE MADE BETWEEN THE COMIC BOOKS Murfee discovers and the science of flight and aerodynamics that Father teaches in school?

7. WHAT SIMILARITIES CAN BE DRAWN BETWEEN MURFEE AND THE superheroes she discovers in the comics, and what lessons can she learn from their adventures?

8. IF YOU WERE IN MURFEE'S SHOES, WHAT DECISION WOULD YOU make about making a deal with Poe or hiding in the crevice? What factors would you consider in that decision?

9. WHY DOES MURFEE CLIMB THE TOWER OF HAY BALES, AND WHAT does she realize while she's up there?

10. HOW DOES JUSTICE TRY TO HELP SOPHIE AFTER DISCOVERING what happened in the attic?

11. HOW DOES MURFEE REACT WHEN SHE SEES THE GREAT horned owl?

12. WHAT DOES THE BANNER MADE BY PIP AND SQUEAK SAY, AND what do they do with it?

13. WHAT DO MADDY AND MINREE PACK FOR THE RESCUE MISSION?

14. WHAT DO MILO, MOE, AND DAHSON DO AFTER THE ROCKET SHIP explodes?

15. HOW DO PIP AND SQUEAK FEEL ABOUT THEIR PART IN THE PLAN, and what do they do after sliding down the spoon?

16. WHAT WAS MANTIS THINKING ABOUT WHEN POE WAS TELLING HIS story?

17. DO YOU THINK MANTIS WAS RIGHT TO WANT TO HELP POE AND THE mice? Why or why not?

18. HOW DOES JUSTICE'S SUGGESTION TO FIGHT FOR THEIR FATHERS relate to Sophie's fear and overall situation?

19. WHAT PLAN DOES MANNY PROPOSE TO MURFEE TO SAVE HER family? Do you think it is a good plan? Why or why not?

20. HOW DOES SOPHIE'S ATTITUDE TOWARDS ADVENTURE DIFFER from Justice's?

ACKNOWLEDGMENTS

"Catch a Falling Star," written by Paul Vance and Lee Pockriss, is a song made famous by Perry Como's hit version, released in 1957. Its melody is based on a theme from Brahms' Academic Festival Overture.

"Dream a Little Dream of Me," a 1931 song composed by Fabian Andre and Wilbur Schwandt with lyrics by Gus Kahn, was recorded by Cass Elliot and The Mamas and The Papas in 1968 and sold nearly seven million copies.

"Fly Me to the Moon," originally titled "In Other Words," was written in 1954 by Bart Howard. Frank Sinatra recorded his version in 1964 which was closely associated with the Apollo missions to the moon.

"It's a Lovely Day Tomorrow," written in 1938 by composer Irving Berlin, expressed feelings of both hope and despair during the American Great Depression, and went on to lift spirits during the dark days of World War Two.

ABOUT THE AUTHOR

Kate Holmgren writes children's stories. To her, this is a bit of a wonder, for her father, a tough old bird of a cowboy, had long been known as the storyteller in the family.

But on the journey of motherhood, traveling down roads of blacktop or clay gumbo in an old green club-cab pickup with three very active little boys, she chanced upon her own storyteller's heart. Her sons listened in wonder; Kate sensed her father's mantle of the teller of tales coming to settle upon her own shoulders.

Kate's stories continue to interweave humor, risk, faith, and courage. They ask questions about what it means to be a hero, a part of a family, and a friend. Currently, she is at work on a trilogy, *A Hidden World*, woven of travels filled with amazement all their own.